TOP OF THE MOUNTAIN

REBEL VIPERS MC BOOK 5

JESSA AARONS

TOP OF THE MOUNTAIN

This book is a work of fiction. The names, characters, places, and incidents are all products of the author's imagination and are not to be construed as real. Any similarities are entirely coincidental.

Top of the Mountain Copyright ©2023 by Jessa Aarons. All rights are reserved. No part of this book may be used or reproduced in any manner without written permission from the author, except in the case of brief quotations used in articles or reviews. For information, contact Jessa Aarons.

Cover Designer: Charli Childs, Cosmic Letterz Design

Editor: Rebecca Vazquez, Dark Syde Books

TABLE OF CONTENTS

WARNING & DISCLAIMER	VI
DEDICATION	VII
PLAYLIST	IX
PROLOGUE	1
CHAPTER ONE	6
CHAPTER TWO	16
CHAPTER THREE	28
CHAPTER FOUR	35
CHAPTER FIVE	43
CHAPTER SIX	55
CHAPTER SEVEN	61
CHAPTER EIGHT	67
CHAPTER NINE	72
CHAPTER TEN	80
CHAPTER ELEVEN	89
CHAPTER TWELVE	96

CHAPTER THIRTEEN	105
CHAPTER FOURTEEN	110
CHAPTER FIFTEEN	119
CHAPTER SIXTEEN	127
CHAPTER SEVENTEEN	130
CHAPTER EIGHTEEN	131
CHAPTER NINETEEN	140
CHAPTER TWENTY	147
CHAPTER TWENTY-ONE	162
CHAPTER TWENTY-TWO	173
CHAPTER TWENTY-THREE	181
CHAPTER TWENTY-FOUR	190
CHAPTER TWENTY-FIVE	204
CHAPTER TWENTY-SIX	215
CHAPTER TWENTY-SEVEN	222
CHAPTER TWENTY-EIGHT	228
CHAPTER TWENTY-NINE	240
CHAPTER THIRTY	248
CHAPTER THIRTY-ONE	263
CHAPTER THIRTY-TWO	273
CHAPTER THIRTY-THREE	281

CHAPTER THIRTY-FOUR	289
CHAPTER THIRTY-FIVE	297
EPILOGUE	302
ACKNOWLEDGMENTS	304
ABOUT THE AUTHOR	306
OTHER WORKS	309

WARNING & DISCLAIMER

This content is intended for mature audiences only. It may contain material that could be viewed as offensive to some readers, including graphic language, dangerous and sexual situations, murder, abuse, and extreme violence.
The book you're about to read may not be what you're used to in the Rebel Vipers MC universe, but it is filled with the one thing that makes this club so special - family.
This is a story of reconnecting, rebuilding, and revisiting your favorite characters so far.
There is no suspense or danger in this story, but it does contain an abundance of heartache, mixed in with even more romance, and a whole lot of love.
<u>Author advisory: Due to some emotional moments ahead, a tissue or two (or a few dozen) are advised to have on hand as you read this book. Hold on tight and enjoy the ride. The bikers may have gone emotionally rogue a few times, so brace yourselves as we begin this journey together.</u>

This book is for anyone who has ever been in love . . . whether it lasted many, many years, is still going strong, or only lasted one day. Platonic or romantic, we all crave love, and this book is my love note to all of you.
Stay strong and shine on, you crazy diamonds!

PLAYLIST

CLICK HERE TO LISTEN ON SPOTIFY
When We're 80 – Thomas Rhett
Take My Name – Parmalee
If You Love Her – Forest Blakk
Blue Eyes Crying In The Rain – Willie Nelson
Forever To Go – Chase Rice
All Night – Brothers Osborne
On My Way to You – Cody Johnson
Cum On Feel the Noize – Quiet Riot
Baby Got Back – Sir Mix-a-Lot
Speechless – Dan + Shay
My Person – Spencer Crandall
Another – Adam Doleac
Gimme All Your Lovin' – ZZ Top

PROLOGUE

MOUNTAIN

TWENTY-ONE YEARS AGO
Knock knock.
Well, who the fuck could that be?
I spent all morning doing grunt work at the salvage yard the club opened last year, and just got done eating a late lunch, so I could use a damn break. There's a club girl on her knees between mine and she's got her greedy fingers on my even greedier zipper. My dick is hard and weeping, and he really wants to come out and play.

But looking around the main room, I see no one appear to get the door, so it looks like it's up to me and my hard-on.

"Sorry, but this is gonna hafta wait," I tell her as I try and gently push her out of the way so I can stand up.

Like the good club girl she is, Cherry walks away and climbs on an empty barstool to wait for me. Heading for the door, I think about her round backside and have to adjust myself in my jeans. Damn, she's got some junk in her trunk. Okay, that's not helping.

Left hand giving one last press against the denim and my right hand on the doorknob, I swing the door open and freeze.

If I wasn't so damn pissed off that the woman at the door decided now was the time to arrive and cockblock me, I might find her even prettier than she is. But saying that isn't even right. This woman is beautiful. And if I were an easy man to convince, I'd think she was sent here just for me.

Hold the fuck on, Mountain. We have no clue who this woman is. We don't do women other than one-night stands and club girls. Stand down, sailor.

Locking my face into an expression I use quite often to intimidate and show people I mean fucking business, I start to really take her in as she looks me over in return, like I'm a prize stallion. I don't know if I should feel appreciated or like a piece of meat.

She has the bluest eyes I've ever seen, aside from my son's. Her long, deep brown hair is pulled back into a low ponytail, and as she shifts her feet, it moves in the sunlight to reveal lighter strands mixed in. There are a few wavy and wild loose pieces around her face, and if I didn't see her car across the parking lot, I'd say she looks a little windblown, almost like she rode here on the back of my Harley.

Whoa! Watch where your mind's going there, buddy.

She looks like she drove here with the windows down. At least, that's what I tell myself to talk my barely contained dick down inside my jeans.

I cross my arms and widen my stance as I continue taking her in.

Tight dark blue jeans, check. Light blue t-shirt, check. Black tennis shoes, check.

Fuck me, she really is beautiful.

When her eyes finally raise high enough to meet mine, I've reached the point of being half amused but still a little pissed off, so I can't help but bark out, "Are you done undressing me with your eyes?"

"I guess so, but would you mind taking your shirt off so I can see what's hiding underneath?" The words are barely past her pretty pink lips when she slaps a hand over her mouth, hiding it from me. She then closes her eyes like she's trying to hide in plain sight.

Sorry, little lady, I can still see you.

I try to let out a chuckle, but my tongue is tied by her boldness and I end up having to hide a cough behind my fist. "Alright then. So other than removing my clothes, is there a reason you're here?"

Her eyes fly open and she starts talking fast. "I'm so sorry about that. Apparently, my brain-to- mouth filter is broken." Then, like she's starting over, she shakes out her hands, crosses her arms in front of her chest, and continues. "I'm looking for my sister. Last I heard from her, she said she lives here."

A sister? Our club's not one to have random women hanging around, so other than a couple club girls and Old Ladies, the choices are limited. And since I know every chick here pretty damn well, and don't think any of them have a sister I haven't met, I'm starting to wonder if this woman is lost. "And who's your sister?"

"Her name's Roxy."

And my life instantly flashes before my eyes. I haven't heard that name in eight years, and I could've gone the rest of my life never hearing it again.

My dick goes flaccid in a millisecond. Fucking bitch of a mother I gave my son.

Honestly, knocking her up was a complete accident but convincing her to actually carry the baby to term was a damn miracle. Just thinking about the three years I spent with that woman makes my teeth hurt from clenching my jaw so hard.

What happens next is one hundred percent pure instinct. My body takes control and I have no power over myself.

Reaching my right hand out, I grab hold of the edge of the door and swing it shut in this bitch's face. I need to separate us and close out whatever bad mojo she's trying to bring back into my life. But I'm the one who's shocked when the door stops mid-swing.

"What the hell is wrong with you, you brute?" the little pixie shouts as I step back and the door slams against the inside wall.

Everything happened so fast, in maybe five seconds. I know I fucked up and need to fix it, because the instant I see the anger on her face, I know I never want to make her look at me like that ever again. If she ever does anything but smile around me, I'll spend every day of the rest of my life making up for whatever I did wrong.

What the hell is wrong with me today? One minute, I want her gone for messing up my afternoon delight, and the next, I'm saying I want her here forever. Fuck.

I need to fix this, now.

Pulling the door shut behind me, I step out on the porch to join her and try to pull my head out of my own ass. "I'm sorry about that. Hearing that name causes a gut reaction."

"Oh," she says as her face drops into a look of confusion.

I need to get to the bottom of who this woman is and what she's doing here looking for Roxy. And why she doesn't know the sister she's looking for is dead.

So, I start with the easiest question I can think of. "So, you're Roxy's younger sister?"

She kicks the toe of her shoe against the porch floor and tucks her hands in her back pockets. Looking up at me, she takes a big breath. "Yea. I had a little situation with our parents and wanted to talk to her. They disowned me and kicked me out of my condo. I needed to get away, so here I am. She sent me a letter about ten years ago and this is where she said she was. Is she here?"

Wow. That's fucked up. I don't know much about Roxy's background, but from what little I managed to coax out of her, these women have some awful parents.

Leaning back against the porch railing, I cross one boot over the other and prepare to throw her world off its axis. But I start simple. "Ummm, let me start by introducing myself. I'm Jethro, but everyone calls me Mountain. Roxy was my ex-girlfriend, and I'm the father of Connor, her now ten-year-old son."

Her arms fall to her sides as she stares straight at me. "Was? What does that mean?"

Well, here goes nothing. "I hate to be the one to tell you this, but Roxy left us eight years ago."

"Where'd she go?" The expression on her face drops. She looks crushed.

CHAPTER ONE

MOUNTAIN

PRESENT DAY

"All right! That looks good right about there," I say into the radio in my hand.

There's a loud hiss as the brakes engage on the semi being driven by Wrecker.

"Ten-four" comes through the speaker as the rig shuts off. "Last load of the day."

"Get your ass out here and help these nincompoops we call Brothers," I say with a chuckle into the radio. "I swear, they'd drop it on their heads if we weren't here."

"Damn, Pops." Whiskey appears at my side and slaps his glove on my arm, leaving behind a smear of dirt and dust and who knows what else. "Nincompoops, huh? That's a nice thing to call those of us who've been setting things up, working all morning in the dirt."

"Was that working you were doing?" I slap him back upside the head and start walking away, laughing. "Looked like playing in the dirt to me."

"Oh, fuck you," he calls out, chuckling back. "Make sure the trailer is positioned properly over the blocks so we can drop this house on the foundation."

"What do you think I'm doin', son? Pickin' my ass? Go kiss mine," I sass back at my boy. He may be thirty-one years old, and I may only have one of my legs still attached to my body, but I swear, one of these days I'm going to kick his grown ass just like I did when he was a kid.

Thank heavens he has an Old Lady now, and she knows how to put him in his place, because my days of raising that pain in the ass are over. I love him more than life itself, but sometimes I wonder who I pissed off in another life to give me a child like him.

"I'm just kiddin', Pops." Whiskey chases after me and wraps me in a giant bear hug, almost lifting me off my feet. "You know I love ya."

"Put me down, you brute." I can't help but reply with a full belly laugh. "You're gonna knock a crippled man over if you don't quit messin' around."

As much as I complain about him, and probably call him a dumbass every other day, I wouldn't trade my boy for all the gold on this planet. To be quite honest, the day he was born was the day I was saved from myself.

His birth mom was a piece of work, and I had no idea what I was going to do with a baby. I was just a few years into running the Rebel Vipers MC and didn't know if a baby was going to fit into my lifestyle. The moment Roxy threatened to have an abortion, everything changed. I knew I had to have him. I hadn't even met him yet, but just knowing he was coming turned my life around.

I knew I had to make this club a success. Everything I've done every day since is for my son. I may not have been able to keep his mother from leaving us, but I did somehow manage to find another woman to help me raise him. My Blue is more of a momma to Whiskey than her older sister ever could have been.

Fuck, even when I think that to myself it sounds messed up. Long story short, the woman I married, Lana Renee Hill, my wife of just over twenty years, is the younger sister of my son's mother, Roxy.

Eight years after Roxy left us and got herself killed in a car accident, her sister showed up at the clubhouse front door and knocked me off my feet. I made her my Old Lady three days later, put my momma's diamond ring on her finger that same night, and wifed her up six months later. She has been by my side in this crazy life ever since, making me the luckiest man ever.

Twenty years later, with one grandbaby and two more on the way from my daughter, Sunshine, here I stand in the backyard of the club's compound, watching my Brothers set up a double-wide modular home for another generation of members.

Just last week, the day after our yearly rowdy Halloween party, our club added a new Prospect. Ray, a friend of Steel's who he met while in prison, was given his Prospect cut. He, his wife, Sara, and their seven-year-old son, Jamie, are going to be living in this new home.

While it's definitely not the normal thing for a Prospect to be getting his own place, Ray's situation is different than any of us have dealt with before.

Firstly, Ray is the only Prospect we've had who is married and has a family. We can't just have his wife and kid crash in the bunkroom with all the other Prospects. Second, the three of them are currently living in a 1970s motorhome in the parking lot of the compound. The thing is rusting on every edge, all four tires go flat at least once a week, and the damn thing doesn't have any heat. It's early November here in Wisconsin, and we can't have anyone sleeping outside unprotected in winter.

After some talking with the club officers, it was decided to bring in a modular home for them to live in. Several dead trees were cleared out, a foundation was poured, and blocks were brought in preparation for the two semi-trailers that showed up this morning carrying the pieces of the home.

Now that they are backed on the concrete slab, the workers from the home building company, along with members of the club, are starting all the finish work. By the end of this week, everything will be complete and the Ledger family will be moving in for good.

Since my prosthetic leg and I are bupkis for helping with crawling around on the ground and connecting the pieces of this giant jigsaw puzzle, I pass my clipboard and radio off to Diego and head inside. My stump is starting to itch like a motherfucker and if I don't get it off soon, I'll be in a world of hurt.

Skirting around the cabins, I head for the clubhouse's back door, which opens to the hallway where my and Blue's apartment is. I make a pit stop to put on a clean t-shirt and flannel, then slide my cut back on and make my way to the main room.

As I come down the hall, the first thing I see is my Old Lady. Blue is sitting at one of the large dining tables with several other ladies, including my son's fiancée, Duchess, and my daughter, Sunshine.

Before I can say anything, Blue turns my way. "Mountain," she looks shocked to see me, "what are you doing in here already?"

I head straight for her, and she stands just as I get to her side. "There's not much me and my one leg can do, so I came in to check on you ladies. Gotta make sure you're staying out of trouble when all the Brothers are out of sight."

"Oh goodness." Blue grabs my arm. Even though it's been a little over two years since my accident and amputation, she sometimes still worries about me standing too long. "Do you need to sit?"

"I'm good, love, but thanks." I drop a kiss on her forehead before she sits back down. "What are y'all up to in here? It looks like someone robbed the magazine aisle at the grocery store."

And it does. There are numerous magazines and notebooks and different colored pens littered all over the table, and each woman has something open in front of them.

"What would you say if I told you we wanna have a wedding?" Duchess pipes up first.

That gets my attention. "I'd say it's about time someone around here gets hitched. Duchess, Angel, who's going first?" They're the only two Old Ladies with engagement rings, so I'd think it has to be one of them.

"How about all of us, Pops?" Sunshine drops a bomb I didn't see coming.

My daughter, who I didn't know about until this past spring, is in a relationship with Steel and Ring, two of my club Brothers. While it's not a common thing for three people to be in a relationship, it works for them. Both men love her very much, and Steel's daughter, Opal, calls her 'Momma'. The biggest shock I got, even more than her being my daughter, was when she announced that she's pregnant . . . with twins.

"What do you mean all of you? You're all getting married?"

"Duchess and Angel brought out all these wedding magazines and it got the rest of us thinking," Sunshine says, spinning her chair to face me. I can feel the happiness radiating off her in waves.

"All four of us are ready to get married, so why not do it all at once? It'll save us time and money."

"And we'd all invite most of the same people anyway," Star adds, "so why not make it one big shindig?"

"And two of the four of us are pregnant." Sunshine gushes as she says those words. "So, one party, split the work between all of us, and it'll be planned in a flash."

"I love the idea!" I'm totally shocked, but I really shouldn't be. Knowing the women in this club, as soon as they get an idea and are given the green light, they charge ahead and take no prisoners. Give them a few days and they'll have the details on lock. "What do your Old Men say about this?"

My question makes everyone at the table laugh.

"You know as well as I do, Whiskey will do whatever he's told," Duchess says with a smirk. "He's been buggin' me about a wedding since the day he gave me this ring."

"Hammer too." Angel is giddy with excitement. "Now that we have two growing boys, he wants my last name to be the same as theirs."

"As soon as Buzz hears everyone is getting hitched, I have no doubt he'll wanna be first in line," Star replies with a giggle.

Star, who until a few weeks ago went by the name Stiletto, is the newest Old Lady of the bunch. She was a club girl who was claimed by Buzz, and the day they announced to everyone that he was claiming her, they also shared the news of a baby of their own.

"That man may have just put his name on your back, but the smile on his face every time he sees you doesn't fool anyone," Raven gushes as she squeezes Star's hand. "He's crazy about you and your baby."

Raven is another new Old Lady in our family. She, much like Sunshine, is in a relationship with two Brothers. But unlike her fellow Old Lady, Raven's men are also in a relationship with each other. Not long ago, Smoke and Haze were just Prospects, but once they both earned their patches, they let their feelings for each other be known. And not long after, they found Raven, and they've all been together for a few months now.

It was also recently discovered that Haze is the son of my deceased brother. Brick was my brother by blood and a couple years younger than me. After he passed, we learned that he had a son with a woman who didn't want him to take part in raising the boy.

I still can't believe Brick knew he had a son but never told me. Long story short, Haze discovered the secret by chance, and now I have a nephew—a missing piece of my departed brother.

"I know my men will be all for it." Sunshine kicks back in her chair and crosses her arms, drawing me out of my reverie. "Ring and Steel would've married me yesterday if they could've."

Sunshine's crazy confidence definitely comes from her Hill family genes. I may not have helped raise her, but she has my spunk for sure.

"I remember that feeling," I say as I step closer to Blue and duck down to steal a kiss. Tangling my hand in the loose bun she's got her hair twisted into, essentially untangling the tresses, I hold the back of her neck and draw her close. My tongue duels with hers until we both need to break for air.

I rest my forehead against Blue's as her cheeks blush, and all the ladies start crooning around her.

"Ooooo, Blue," Duchess calls out.

Standing tall, I tuck a loose strand of hair behind her ear and run my finger down her cheek. "Remember the day I married you?"

"How could I forget?" Blue sits back, out of my reach, and her smile drops just a bit. I don't think anyone else notices, but I can see even the slightest shift in my wife's expression. "You pestered me for months before I finally agreed. Then you swept me to the courthouse without telling anyone," she says with a chuckle, and I can tell something's wrong.

"Yea," Belle, Skynyrd's Old Lady, calls out from the head of the table, "we didn't know you were gettin' hitched 'til you showed up back here with the rings already on your fingers."

"How have I never heard this story?" Duchess asks, elbow on the table, fist propping her chin up.

My eyes slowly leave Blue to answer. "Whiskey never told you?"

"Nope." Duchess's chin nudges side to side. "Scoundrel of an Old Man I've got never said a thing."

Just as I'm about to grab my Old Lady and whisk her away to get some answers on why she pulled away from me, the room fills with sounds of laughter, roughhousing, and the usual ruckus of the Brothers. Staying at Blue's side, I turn to see every single one of them walk in, sweaty and dirty . . . and they smell disgusting.

Every man whose woman is at the table approaches the group but quickly gets themselves pushed away.

"Eww, you smell worse than Krew's diapers," Duchess utters in a nasally voice, her nose pinched between two fingers.

"And you look like you rolled in a diaper. Gross," Star calls out as she skirts around the table, away from the wiggly fingers of her chasing beau, Buzz.

"You need to go take a shower before you come anywhere near me with those lips, mister." Angel puts her hand over Hammer's mouth and nudges him away. "I swear, you regressed and relearned manners from our three-year-old."

"Taren has better manners than all of us," Butch, Hammer's dad and Taren's grandpa, comments.

"Dinner will be done in fifteen minutes. Off to the showers, the whole lot of you." Blue gets up and tells everyone what's what. As she skirts around me, she slaps me on the butt. "That means you, too."

"I already changed my shirt," I reply with a laugh. Thinking her laughter and flirtation is a good sign, I try to make a move. Stepping in front of her, I press my chest to hers, look down into her blue eyes, and lay it on thick. "But I'll shower if you join me." I throw in a wink for good measure.

"Um, I don't know." She drops her chin and looks everywhere but at me. "I have to help with putting food out."

Not understanding what's wrong but knowing this isn't the time or place to push for answers, I back off and let her have her space. "Maybe another time then." I drop a kiss on her cheek, hoping to ease even just the tiniest bit of the tension between us.

"Yea." Blue finally meets my eyes again, but there are tears barely holding back. "Maybe later." And with that, she ducks out of my reach and beelines straight for the kitchen.

I've been a little worried since I walked in and saw her shock at my unannounced presence. The worry bumped to concern when she lost the sparkle in her smile. But now, my nerves are wrecked as I watch her walk away.

Did I do something wrong? I know things haven't been easy lately, but I attributed it to the unrest that's been floating around the club for the last year. I thought it was just adding up on her and she didn't know how to react. I always planned to talk to her privately to see if there's anything I could do for her, but the timing never felt right. Now, I'm beginning to regret brushing things under the rug.

We may have fought occasionally over the years, but she's never run away from me before. What if it's me who's the problem?

Does she not love me anymore? Halloween may be over, but I'm a little spooked.

CHAPTER TWO

BLUE

Rolling over, I reach out to snuggle up to my husband, but the only thing my hand finds is a cold bedsheet. Reaching back to turn on the lamp, my eyes finally focus as I sit up and take in his empty half of our bed.

I look at the alarm clock and see it's just after two in the morning. I've been asleep for three hours. The top sheet and comforter on Mountain's side of the bed are turned down a little from when I crawled in, but the fitted sheet is smooth and unwrinkled. Mountain never came to bed. Where is he?

Tossing back the covers, I swing my legs over the side of the bed and slide on my slippers. Standing up and stretching, I grab my plush fleece robe from the clothes tree by my dresser and head for our little living room.

After Mountain's motorcycle accident two and a half years ago, we gave up our private cabin and moved into a space inside the clubhouse that the Brothers had converted into an apartment of sorts. We have our own bathroom, bedroom, closets, and an open area that serves as a kitchen, eat-in dining, and living room. For the two of us, it's perfect.

With Mountain being in a wheelchair a lot or using crutches when he doesn't like wearing his prosthesis, it's easier being inside and on one level, so he doesn't have to traverse any stairs or roll across the grass to enter the clubhouse.

After Whiskey claimed Duchess, he moved back into the cabin he grew up in and brought his lovely lady with him. They're now engaged and have a three-month-old son, my grandson, Krew.

That little boy is honestly the light of my life. Seeing as I entered the picture when Whiskey was ten, he was way past his infant and toddler years. I'd like to think I helped shape the amazing man he grew up to be, but I missed out on so much.

I also lost a baby of my own a couple years after Mountain and I married. Due to a blood clot and excessive bleeding, a hysterectomy was needed to save my life, so my one and only chance to have a child of my own disappeared in an instant.

That was the worst day of my life. I woke up that morning thinking I had everything I'd ever wanted. But as I started to bleed in that bank parking lot, I saw my life flash before my eyes.

I was losing the one thing my Old Man wanted more than anything—another child.

Mountain has always said he doesn't blame me for what happened, but sometimes, the smallest nugget of doubt creeps out of the shadows and rears its ugly head.

So now, anytime I hold Krew, I try not to reminisce too much about the past, but it's hard. I've decided to remain focused on soaking up as much time as I can with all the kids being raised here and always let them know their BeeGee loves them.

As I step out into the hallway and head for the main room, I hear voices and instantly recognize Mountain's deep timbre. But's it's not until he's fully in sight that I see something I never thought I'd see—another woman in his arms.

Mountain and Raquel, one of the club girls, are sitting side by side on one of the couches, and she has her arms wrapped around his neck. From behind them, I can't see where his arms are, but his head is turned to her as she plants a kiss on his whisker-covered cheek.

I'm the only woman who's supposed to be that close to him. His salt and pepper coloring is something only I have the right to admire. He's *my* husband. *My* Old Man. *Mine*. It's time I make my presence known and figure out what I walked in on.

"What the hell is goin' on out here?"

Both of their heads swivel at the sound of my voice, and as soon as they see it's me, they're both on their feet and talking at once.

"It's not what it looks like," Mountain persists, his hands up in the air.

"We were just talking." Raquel's voice has a slight wobble as she takes a few slow steps back.

"Shit, Blue, I swear nothing happened."

"I was just asking for his advice." She looks like she's about to cry, or maybe already had been.

All their fast responses are like a double-edged sword and I don't know what to think.

Are they just spitting out whatever responses they think they need to say to cover up whatever they want to keep hidden? Or is what they're saying actually the truth, so it comes out easy and I should believe it?

I've never in my twenty-one years here ever doubted my husband's faithfulness, but right now, I can barely tell which way is up. This has to be a bad dream—no, a nightmare.

"Raquel," Mountain points toward the far side of the room, "why don't you head back to bed? It's probably best if I straighten all this out."

"I'm sorry, Blue," Raquel whispers as she backs away. "I'm sorry." And she's gone.

I turn to Mountain and stare at him like I'm just seeing him for the very first time. He may have many more gray hairs than he did the day we met, but he's still the handsome, strong sailor he was back then. I think that's why my heart hurts so much.

His dirty blonde hair has a mix of salt and pepper at his temples, and his beard is a smidgen longer than it had been, but the edges are still trimmed clean as usual. Mountain is wearing his leather cut, like he does every day, and it does nothing but accentuate the muscles he has hiding under his tight black t-shirt. Those are still as hard as ever.

It's like I'm looking at the man I married and gave my life to, except the person I'm seeing is someone I don't know.

"Blue, I swear, whatever you think you just saw is not really what was goin' on." Mountain slowly approaches me as he talks, until his boots are just inches from my slippers. "She just needed someone to talk to and I was here."

"Why does that sound like something a cheater would say?" I thought I was going to stay strong, but as soon as the word 'cheater' passes my lips, I break. The emotions crash over me and my chest heaves in sobs I can't seem to control. "How could you do this to us?" I cry out through the tears running down my cheeks.

I'm so numb, I don't even try to wipe them away. I just let them fall.

"No, no, no, no, no, love." Mountain closes the last distance between us and wraps himself around me, his arms banding me to him like a constrictor. "I have never, nor will I ever, cheat on you. I couldn't. I love you too much to even think of that."

The words he's pleading with me to hear are registering in my mind, but my heart is still trying to start beating again after its perceived betrayal. My ear pressed to his chest, I can hear his heart beating wildly, but I'm not caught up with him yet. I knew something was wrong with us, but I never imagined this.

"What did I do to make you do this?" I cry through my hiccups, trying to make him understand how much this hurts.

Letting me free, Mountain places his hands on my shoulders, lowers his face to right in front of mine, and locks me into his deep brown gaze. "You listen to me right now, Blue. I was not and have not ever been unfaithful to you. You're my wife, my partner, and my Old Lady. From the day we met, you have been all I think about."

"But—"

"No buts," he growls, eyes squinted. "I couldn't sleep, so I came out here to watch some television. Raquel was having a rough night and needed someone to talk to. All we did was sit on the couch, and she was asking for advice about her younger sister."

Something in his gentle words melts my heart just a bit, but I try to stay strong and wait for him to say something that sounds wrong. I don't know why I want to catch him in a lie, but it's almost like if he does lie, I'll feel vindicated for my harsh reaction. Because if this all really turns out to be a big misunderstanding, I'm going to feel like such an idiot.

Not able to continue standing under his strong gaze, I back myself away and start pacing back and forth. I need to move to let my thoughts out.

"What about her sister?" I ask.

Mountain points at the hall and asks, "Can we go to our room and talk?"

I turn to face him, hands on my hips. "No, I wanna know what was so important, it had to be discussed at two in the goddamned morning."

"Raquel's sister, Victoria, wants to come to the clubhouse to see what being a club girl is like, but she doesn't want her to." Mountain lets out a huge sigh and rubs his eyes with his thumb and pointer finger. When he finally looks at me again, I see the sadness in his eyes. But before I can think of what to say, he keeps talking. "I just told her that if her sister wants to come, maybe it's best to invite her. Otherwise, if she just shows up unannounced, we'll have no control over who she sees first. By knowing when she'll be here, maybe the rowdy Brothers can be warned to stay away from her and she'll think the place is boring and not come back."

Feeling a little snarky, I can't help but lash out. "Since when did you get involved with other people's family problems?"

"Apparently since members of my own family won't talk to me about their problems, I need someone to talk to." The dig he throws back hits deep. "I have a feeling whatever this is going on between us has been building for a while, but I seem to have missed the memo. I have never, ever, in our twenty-some years, done a single thing to hurt you like this. I don't know what you want me to say, Lana. What do you want from me?"

Now, I'm the one who's crushed. He said my legal name like it was nothing. Mountain occasionally calls me by that name, but it's usually in an intimate situation. He'd called me Blue even before I knew what the name meant, so hearing him not say it now hurts deep.

My left hand flat across my heart, I gasp for air. "You didn't call me Blue."

I think I'm out of air. And if it weren't for Mountain rushing toward me, pulling me back into his embrace, one hand at the back of my head and the other around my waist, I probably would've fallen to the floor.

"Shhhh, my love." He rocks us back and forth. "I'm so, so, so sorry I did that. You are my Blue. You will be 'til the day I die. I swear on my mother's grave. Please, don't hate me . . . please."

Clutching the front of his t-shirt, I sob into his chest. I don't think until this very moment I realized I was hurting this much on the inside. The years of self-imposed regret and wondering whether I'm not good enough, not perfect enough for this man, come rushing out of my heart, and I hold onto Mountain for dear life.

It feels like forever before my heart starts beating again, but I'm finally able to take a breath and look up at him. The sadness I saw before is tenfold now, and the anguish I feel is written all over his face.

"Tell me what you need, Blue. Tell me."

"I need to know why, if you couldn't sleep, why didn't you wake me. Why did you come out here?"

"I know it's not an excuse, but I need to sit down and get this leg off. Let's go to our room and I'll try to explain."

Knowing how much he tries to hide his bouts of pain, I let him off the hook, for now, and lead him down the hall. Once we're in our private space, Mountain takes off his cut, hangs it on the back of the door, and turns the lock. He pulls me under his arm and leans on me just a bit as we make our way into our bedroom.

Once I have him sitting on his side of the bed, I let him go and crawl into my side.

Many times, I have offered to help him with his prosthesis when he's in pain, but he always insists on dealing with it himself. Seeing his stump is unavoidable, but there are times I think he likes to pretend his leg is still the way it was.

So, when he pushes away my attempts at helping, I back off. Maybe I need to be pushier and make him see that my help isn't out of pity, but instead because of my love for him. But like many other things I know I'm guilty of dodging, I let him do his nighttime routine on his own.

Maybe he was right about our lack of communication.

As Mountain scoots into his spot and pulls the covers over his legs, he doesn't say a word to explain his earlier absence. If I don't get some kind of answer, even a half-assed one, I'll never be able to get back to sleep.

When he goes to turn the nightstand lamp off, I pull on his right arm to stop him. "Can you tell me now why didn't you come to bed?"

Letting out another sigh, I have a feeling he only said he'd answer me just to get me out of the main room and in bed. He hems and haws to give an answer, so I snap.

"Speak to me, *Jethro*." I throw his real name back at him in a bit of revenge. His angry look lets me know I hit the spot. "Tell me now."

"Fuck, fine." He runs a hand over his hair, messing it up. "It's only been recently that I've been feeling a wedge between us. But it wasn't until earlier when I asked you to shower with me, and you practically ran away from me, that it really hit me. You've never turned down shower time with me before. That really hurt.

"I tried to come to bed earlier, but when I walked in here, I just stared at you sleeping and couldn't risk waking you. I needed some space to think, and in here, in our room, it was too much.

I went to the main room to try and let the quiet drown my thoughts out, but it didn't work. Talking to Raquel was just a distraction. Hearing someone else's problems let me not think about my own."

It's like he's taking every thought inside my head, pulling it out, and saying it out loud. It's scary and a little bit too much of the truth smacking me in the face.

Not knowing the root of the problem, combined with the apprehension to say what he's feeling, is exactly what I'm feeling. It's eerie that we know each other so well. It really shows how our connection has grown over the years.

But our mutual issues still don't fix things.

Picking at the edge of the sheet, I ask, "Do you not want to talk to me anymore?" If he can't share his deepest fears with me, how can he expect me to share mine?

"I'd talk to you all day if I could, Blue." He reaches out and links our hands together. "I just need to know what to do to make things better for you. Tell me what's wrong. What did I do to hurt you?"

How do I answer that when I'm still trying to figure it out myself?

One step at a time.

"I pulled away from you earlier because all the talk about wedding stuff really overwhelmed me. All the other Old Ladies were talking flowers and cake and songs, and I locked down. I didn't get that. I had no advice to give them when they started asking questions."

"Then I came in and started talking about our wedding and dug a little deeper into your pain, didn't I?"

"Yea, a little," I reply as I stare off. "In a way, you saved me from answering their questions. But when you talked about our wedding day, and Belle made a joke about how you just swept me off, I started to shut down. Then I bolted as soon as I could."

"Lay with me, Blue." Mountain slides down so his head is on his pillow. "Please, let me hold you. We can keep talking if you want."

Not being able to refuse the gentle, soft, loving side of him, I let Mountain pull me down and roll toward him. He pulls me close, and I lay my right arm over his chest.

Looking up at him, I ask probably the hardest question I've ever asked him. I don't know if I'm ready for what he might say, but a bridge can't be built unless you start on one side. "Are we gonna make it?"

Using his left hand, Mountain lifts my chin and drops a soft kiss on my lips, barely touching but still so powerful. "We will. I swear to you, I'll never leave your side." With his eyes still closed, he professes, "Even if you decide you don't love me anymore, I'll never love another."

"I don't want that."

Opening his eyes, he traces my cheek with his finger. "Do you ever wonder what your life would be like had you not come here all those years ago?"

"No," I whisper. No matter the rough road we've battled, I've never thought that.

"Why not?"

Tapping a finger on his chest, right over his heart, I give him the truth I've been holding back. "Because I know this is where I'm meant to be."

"But what about . . ." he starts, but his words fade as he looks away.

"But what? How do we fix this? I don't know."

"Me neither." His words come out so soft, like he doesn't want them to be real.

"I'm scared, Mountain. Really scared. What do we do?"

"I don't think there's anything we can do right now," he starts, and his eyes are finally back on mine. "But listen to me good, Blue. We'll figure it out somehow. We will."

Not knowing how to process everything that's happened in the last hour—or even the last few months, it seems—I feel myself starting to shut down again. But I need him to know I'm hearing what he's saying too. "I love you more than the air I breathe, Mountain. Please bear with me. I don't know what I need yet, and it may take some time, but please don't think that I don't love you."

"Our love has never been a question for me. I'm just afraid of everything else."

I try to hold back a yawn, but I can't. Plus, I just want this talk to be over and done with, because I have nothing more to give right now. "I hate leaving things unsettled, but can we finish this another time? There's so much going on around here, I'm having a hard time finding which way's up."

Mountain's eyes scrunch in confusion. "Are you sure? I feel like we need to get to the bottom of this. I don't wanna let things be left unsaid."

"If I knew what to say to make everything better, I'd say it, but I don't." I rest my hand on his cheek this time and hope he feels me. "I know this isn't over, but I just want you to hold me and keep me safe and let me fall asleep dreaming of you."

Linking my hand with his, he kisses the back of my knuckles and rests our joined digits to his chest. "Anything for you, Blue. Whatever you need."

"Good night, Mountain."

"Good night, my blue-eyed goddess."

Thinking about what Mountain said about us drifting apart, I can't help but feel the same. And even though he's right, and we should be discussing it before things get too bad, I know I'm not ready for what that all might mean.

So, until that time comes, I'll put on a happy face in front of everyone and figure out what to do another day.

My marriage, my life, my happiness, it all rides on what happens next. But if I can't feel the ground under me, how do I get there?

CHAPTER THREE

MOUNTAIN

All morning I've been worrying about Blue. As soon as we woke up, I tried to get her to talk more about what happened last night, but she shut me down with an excuse about watching Krew so Duchess could go into the bakery for a few hours.

I had every intention to start by apologizing for how bad things looked, for being so close to Raquel when there was no reason for us to be in that position, but she never even gave me the chance. I know I shouldn't have done that, but she just brushed me off every time I tried to say something. Then, when I tried to pull her in for a hug, she ducked out of my reach and skirted away.

I didn't even get a 'good morning' kiss. *Fuck*, I sound like a damn pussy.

Blue booked it out the door so fast, her shoes weren't even tied. She just shoved the laces in, slid her feet in on top of them, grabbed her keys and phone, and walked out.

When I finally made it to the main room, after sulking in private for an hour, Raquel apologized for her inappropriate behavior.

She begged me to let her do the same to Blue, and while I said it was okay, Blue won't even give her the time of day.

When she came back into the clubhouse with Krew earlier, she saw Raquel was sitting at the bar and turned right around and went into the kitchen. Had I not seen it with my own eyes, I never would've believed it had someone said it happened.

It's now just past noon as I walk out of our room, unsuccessful again at getting her to talk while Krew naps in the baby swing.

Hearing voices in Whiskey's office, I backtrack my steps to peek in at who's all inside. I see my son, Ring, Steel, Hammer, and Buzz talking, and I step back out of sight. It looks and sounds like a soon-to-be-grooms meeting. And even though that definitely does not include me, I can't help but listen in.

They're talking about what to do to spoil the women they're lucky enough to have snagged and somehow convinced to marry them. They all got that part right. Every man in this club who has a woman at his side is downright unworthy of that woman, me included.

I guess I missed it whenever the women had dropped the news of a joint wedding to the men, but it sounds like all the Brothers are on board. Wanting to know more, I keep listening.

Buzz suggests they send all the women on a spa day in preparation for the big day, but since no date has been set yet, they can't make any plans. That leads to the question of where to send the ladies. The group consensus is they need to ask someone for help. That makes me chuckle to myself, because as smart as they all are, none of them have a clue about hair or nails or massages.

Steel then suggests asking Blue, and I have a moment of panic. Last night, Blue did everything she could to avoid talking to me about our wedding. I hope them asking her for help won't be too much for her.

Knowing what I do now, I regret not having the patience to let Blue plan a big wedding and spoiling her like my Brothers want to do for their ladies. To be honest, I rushed her to get hitched. I was too scared back then that she would see through all my bullshit and realize she was worth so much more.

At the time, it had been hard enough that Blue made me wait six months to get married, so as soon as the time passed, I was right back at pestering her. She was so sick of my begging by then, much like when I proposed, she caved to my demands. I arranged all the paperwork we needed and we got married a week later.

I wasn't letting her have any more time to rethink her love for me. I slid the five-diamond, burst pattern, wedding band on her finger, right next to the engagement band, and made her mine forever.

Then, one year later, I gave her the matching anniversary band I had made, completing the full set. And here we are, twenty years later, and I'm scared out of my wits.

Needing some air, I head out the back door. As soon as I step onto the patio, I smell the distinct aroma of cigars and know Bear is in his usual spot.

Slumping into my chair next to him, I reach for the stogie he's holding out for me and light it up.

A few puffs in, Bear finally speaks. "What's got your berries in a bunch?"

Sighing, I take another puff, then unload. "Blue and I are having some issues due to all this wedding talk that suddenly popped up. But I've got a feeling there's more to it. I've got no fuckin' idea which end is up and I'm lost about what to do next."

"Whoa, that's a lot to hold in." He kicks a leg up and props it on the bench of the picnic table in front of us.

"You have no idea," I reply with a groan. "Not only that, I'm still trying to process this whole Haze being my nephew thing."

"That's a tough one. I never saw that coming."

"I just don't get it. How did Brick and I both end up having kids we didn't know about? Why did their mothers hide them from us?" I tug on my beard with one hand while taking a smoke with the other. Once I have my breath back, I continue. "Were we really that bad back then? Is the club life really horrible for moms? I mean, first, Roxy left me and Connor when he was a baby. Then, come to find out Sandy kept Sunshine away until she was dead and didn't have to answer for herself. Now, this craziness about Erin writing Brick but not telling him Haze was here in town the whole time. Like, was it the club, or just us Hills? What did we do wrong?"

Both feet back on the concrete, Bear turns his chair toward me. "Well, let me start by saying I'm sorry, Mountain. Had I known you were thinking things like that, I woulda kicked your ass years ago. You should've come talk to me earlier."

While his lighthearted banter gets laughter from us both, his sincerity mixed with humor is what I like most about Bear. But as much as it helped ease me a bit, I'm still torn-up inside.

I tap my cigar on the ashtray before answering. "I would've had I known what to say, or even that there was a problem. Everything just seems to have gone upside down, building up one day at a time, and I've finally hit the point where I can't pretend there's nothing wrong."

"I'm not really sure what to say about you and Blue, because I can't say I knew there was a problem."

"Well, thank God for that," I mutter as I stare out across the backyard. "I'd rather our problems not be thrown around the club like the latest gossip. Blue doesn't deserve that."

"So, onto the other thing," Bear drawls out.

"It's okay. You can say it. Apparently, the Hill men are shitty-ass fathers and being involved with a Rebel Viper isn't worth it."

"Hey now, I'm sure if you ask Peanut and Belle, they'll tell you club life wasn't all that bad. I've been with Peanut for fifteen years and she brought Wrench here when he was a youngin'. And look at him now—he's all grown up and doing really well."

"I know." I know I'm sighing like a bitch, but I can't help that he's got a good point. "He and Steel are running Rebel Repairs like a well-oiled machine."

"Exactly." Bear takes a long puff of his cigar and proceeds to blow the smoke out in a swirly pattern.

"Show off," I call out as I lounge back even more.

"And what about Belle and Skynyrd? They've been together since the dawn of time, longer than we've all been a club. Hell, Belle was with us from day one. She even helped with some construction of this place. Buzz is practically at the point where he's running BIT, whether Skynyrd wants to admit it or not."

"Yea yea, keep rubbing it in. I get your point."

"Can't help it that I'm right."

"Just don't let Skynyrd hear you say that about the shop. Even though business is better than ever, he grumbles every month that things should be run like they were thirty-five years ago when he opened the place."

"See! It's not all bad. You have to find the good in things, otherwise, you'll never survive."

"You're right."

"And I'm sorry about you and Blue. I promise not to say anything to anyone, not even my Old Lady."

"I appreciate that, Brother." I hold out my fist, and we bump knuckles.

"And yea, there may've been a few women who passed through here and didn't stick around, but a lot still have. Look at the women here now. Duchess practically knocked your son off his feet with her fire. And Sunshine managed to snag two Brothers."

"That's my little girl you're talkin' about," I grumble.

Bear smiles and shakes his head. "As much as you hate it, she's not a little girl anymore."

"Ain't that the damn truth. I wish I had seen her grow up."

"But now she's got a little girl of her own for you to spoil."

That does make me smile. "Opal is a cutie for sure."

"And if we know those men she hogtied, they'll give you lots more grandbabies to love. Shit, you've got two on the way," he says, followed by a whistle. "And Whiskey too. I give that boy one year to have Duchess knocked up again."

"I hope so. Krew needs a sibling. Maybe a sister or two."

"No matter what happens, every child in this club is part of our family."

"I couldn't have said it better myself."

One more drag and Bear's cigar is down to the end, and he drops the butt into a bucket of water we have out here for that very reason. "Our club will be in good hands when we're gone and buried, I have no doubts."

Feeling a lot of nostalgia since I stumbled out here, I give my friend my thanks. "Thank you for being my friend all these years, Bear. I wouldn't have any of this if it wasn't for you."

"Oh, fuck off." He flips me off as he stands. "I just came when you called."

"I'm serious, Brother. I wouldn't have known the first thing about starting a club had it not been for you." I flip him off in return with two hands. "So, fuck off your fuck off and take my thank you, asshole."

"Fuck you very much, Hill." With that, he slaps me on the shoulder and shimmies to the side when I try and punch his leg. "I'm gonna go find my Old Lady and show her my appreciation for her stickin' with me. Maybe you should go do the same."

I watch Bear head inside as I again lean back in my chair. Flicking the cherry off my half-smoked cigar, I set it in the ashtray to burn out. Knowing Blue doesn't like the smell, I need it to go out and the smoke to dissipate some before I head back inside.

I'm not sure where she is right now, or if she'll even talk to me, but she couldn't have gone far. She's got to be around here somewhere.

CHAPTER FOUR

BLUE

It's been a couple days since my confrontation with Mountain, and I'm still doing everything I can to avoid talking about it more. Luckily, today is the day before Thanksgiving, so it's a big meal prep day and I have a reason to stay busy and out of the way of any man.

I'm in the kitchen with most of the women, and currently in the walk-in pantry with my arms full of giant cans of vegetables, when the door swings open behind me. *Shit.* Raquel walks in and stands where there's no way out but through her.

I've been avoiding her, walking the other way any time I see her enter the same space as me, and while I know it's childish, I can't help it. Deep down inside, I know what I walked in on wasn't what I initially thought it looked like, but the emotions and logic in my head weren't seeing eye to eye. And to be honest, they still aren't one hundred percent.

"Look," Raquel starts as I try to skirt around her, her continued words stopping me in my tracks. "I know what I did was wrong and I'm sorry."

I slowly turn around. "Sorry?" Why is she sorry? It's me who has the problem.

"I know I shouldn't have been that close to Mountain. I apologize for kissing him on the cheek. That was way outside of my limits and I know that. I know you probably hate me now and that's why you won't even look at me. If you want me to leave, you have every right to tell me to do so, but please, just let me stay through the dinner tomorrow. My sister is coming to visit, and I want to have one last good memory before I pack my things. I know it's a lot to ask, but I'm begging you, please, one more day."

Setting the cans on the closest shelf, I approach Raquel and wrap her in a hug. She stands there, stiff as a board as I start to cry. Pulling back, I can tell she's in shock. Her eyes are round as saucers and her hands are plastered to her sides.

"Raquel, I'm not mad at you." I set one hand on her shoulder as I quickly wipe my tears. I feel her deflate, the tension flows from her whole body. I feel a little relief too now that we're talking. "I'm mad at myself, and at Mountain, but not you."

"But what I did—"

I cut her off. "Yes, what you did wasn't right, but that has nothing to do with why I've been shunning you. And for that, I apologize."

Both of us have our hands tucked in our pockets. She looks a little unsure, but I nod at her, hoping she'll be open too and share what's on her mind. "I'm still sorry. Are you and Mountain okay?"

"Honestly? Not really." I shake my head. "But please don't tell anyone else this. This is something I need to figure out for myself."

"I still would understand if you'd want me to leave. I just ask for one more day. I don't need my sister asking even more questions."

"I don't want you to leave, Raquel, I promise. I've just been keeping my distance so I don't explode on you when what I'm dealing with isn't your problem. I don't want to dump that on anyone."

"Really?" Her eyes get bright for the first time since she practically ran away from me that night. "I can stay?"

"Yes, of course, you can stay."

"But what about what I did? I know I shouldn't have been that close to Mountain. It's just that I came out into the main room, expecting it to be empty 'cause everyone should've been sleeping. Then he was there, just staring off into space."

"Can I be honest and say I'm still a little mad and curious about how you two ended up like that on the couch?"

"Please do," she insists. "When I came out, he was just leaning against one of the dining chairs, staring out the window. I called his name, and he almost fell over when he snapped out of his trance. I was worried his leg was bothering him, so I said he should sit."

"Stubborn man doesn't like to admit he should be off that leg more often."

"I know you tell him that all the time, so I was trying to get him to sit. He asked me why I was up so late, and we got talking about my sister."

"He mentioned that after we went back to our room. She wants to come here and be a club girl?"

"She keeps asking me about it, and I always tell her no, but she insists."

"Can I play devil's advocate and ask why you don't want her here? You're here, after all."

"She deserves more than this. Not saying we aren't treated well here, because we are. Like, you could've beat my ass and thrown me to the curb two days ago just for sitting next to your man, but you didn't. And I'll never forget it. I owe you so big and swear to be your personal servant for as long as you need me to. I just don't want Vicki here, to be like me. She's better than me, and I want her to stay that way."

"Do you want me to beat you up?" I raise my fists, playfully throwing tiny jabs with a smile on my face, trying to lighten the mood with a joke. "I can, ya know."

And just like that, with our combined laughter, the animosity between us is gone. Raquel's giggles at my attempt at being Rocky make any issue I had with her disappear.

"I probably deserve at least one black eye for pushing the boundaries, but if you could wait a couple more days, I'd appreciate it," she says as she wipes the tears of laughter from under her eyes.

Leaning against the shelving unit to my left, I cross my arms and hook my left foot over my right. "I know Mountain is a great listener, so whatever advice he was giving you probably deserved that kiss on the cheek."

"He is really great," Raquel replies with a now sad smile. "Again, I know it's none of my business, but if he's so easy to talk to, why won't you tell him your problems? I can't lie and say I haven't noticed things between you two haven't been off for a little while now. It's not normal for you guys to be so distant."

Hearing her say she noticed how off things have been makes me wonder who else has picked up on it.

"Do you think anyone else has noticed us being off? Like any of our family?"

"I don't think so." Raquel shakes her head. "One of the perks of being a club girl is being treated like we're not there sometimes. We sit back in the shadows while everyone and everything just goes on around us like we're invisible. I try not to, but sometimes I notice things people probably would like kept unknown."

"Speaking for myself, I appreciate that very much. I know I need to talk with Mountain, and I will, I just need to get my own ducks in a row before I do."

"I totally understand." She holds a hand out to me, and I can't refuse her need for acceptance. "Thank you for not kung pow-ing me out on my ass. I love this place too much to lose you all."

"Maybe you need to think about what you just said a little more." Pulling her in for a hug, I then take a step back but keep her hand in mine. "If this place has been so good to you, maybe you should let your sister see it and decide for herself. Maybe she has something going on that she needs the support."

"I never thought of it like that."

"Maybe after she comes to visit tomorrow, sit her down and see what she's got going on. If you open up to her, maybe she'll do the same in return."

"Blue," Raquel expresses with a bright smile, "I wish our mom was as amazing as you."

"Home life not so good?" I wrap her in one more quick hug.

"You have no idea." If she rolled her eyes any harder, they'd be staring out the back of her head.

"Oh, honey, I didn't leave Florida with only a duffel bag full of clothes and the cash I stole out of my father's desk for no reason." I hand her two giant cans of green beans, pick up the corn and carrots, and lead her back into the kitchen. "The stories I could tell you about my parents would knock your socks off."

"Really? Wanna exchange stories, then you be my mom from now on?"

Her easygoing from being scared of me to wanting me to be her mom is quick, making both of us laugh. "Let me tell you about my father's plan to marry me off to his forty-five-year-old business partner. I was twenty-nine and wanted nothing to do with that slimeball, so I left. Packed one bag and hit the road."

"Is that how you ended up here?"

"Sure is." I set the cans on the stainless-steel island and take the ones from her. "Drove straight to Tellison with only a letter from my sister and a name—Mountain. Roxy wrote that he was her son's father, so I thought finding him would help me find her."

"But you were too late."

"Eight years too late."

"Sorry to butt in, but are you talking about how you came here?" Duchess is sitting on the far end of the island, measuring and dumping ingredients into an electric mixer she has spinning away. It must be cupcake time.

"Yup. Raquel here was explaining about her sister coming to visit tomorrow to see what club life is like. Then we got to discussing who had the worst parents growing up, so I told her about my parents' attempt at an arranged marriage."

"That's messed up on so many levels," Sunshine says as she chops a bunch of celery for the homemade stuffing. "My mom may have kept who my dad was a secret, but at least she didn't try and marry me off to make money."

"Your mom did what she thought was right." I hug Sunshine as I walk behind her. "I'm just glad you're here with us now."

"Me too," she gushes, her face glowing with a smile.

"And those babies of yours, they're gonna be the cutest little buttons."

"Are you gonna find out what they are? Boys or girls?" Angel asks as she empties the dishwasher.

"I've thought about it, but wanna wait 'til our next appointment." Sunshine lifts her cutting board and dumps the celery chunks into a giant bowl of seasonings and tiny pieces of cut-up bread. "I want Ring and Steel to see the babies first and then let them decide."

"Do you have a preference either way?" I'm a nosy nelly, so I can't help but ask. "Those are my grandbabies in there, and BeeGee needs to know what color stuff to start buying."

"Can I tell y'all a secret?" Sunshine looks around the room like she's trying to see if anyone is hiding in the corners. "I know something I haven't told the guys yet."

"Oooh, tell me," Raven demands as she drops into a stool next to Sunshine. Her hands are coated in flour from mixing the ingredients to make pie crusts. "You know I can keep a secret."

All the Old Ladies, and Raquel, Cinnamon, and Meredith, circle around the island and wait for the news.

With one last look around to check if the coast is clear, Sunshine leans in and whispers, "Whatever gender one baby is, the other is exactly the same."

"What does that mean?" Meredith asks as she looks around the circle. Her confusion is adorable, and it's clear that she loves Sunshine so much. Being Steel's younger sister has brought Meredith into our fold, and I have no doubt that one day her Prince Charming in leather will see her for the beautiful flower she is.

I wrap my arm around Meredith's shoulders and squeeze her tight. "What your soon-to-be sister-in-law is saying is that the babies are identical twins."

The gasps and chatter kick in right away but are brought to abrupt silence as the kitchen doors swing open and Steel, Hammer, and Whiskey walk in, crashing our party.

"What's going on in here?" Steel asks as he rounds the group, heading for his woman.

"We can hear your chatter all the way from the main room." Whiskey nuzzles Duchess from behind, hands on her hips.

"None of your business," Duchess replies as she turns and smacks her Old Man with a towel. "Just lady talk."

The number of women within the club circle has grown like crazy over the last year, and they already have the Brothers trained fairly well. It didn't take them long to pick up on when to stay out of the way. The men may think they run this clubhouse, but if it weren't for us women, it probably would've fallen down years ago.

We all laugh as the men just roll their eyes at us and head back out to wherever they came from. And much like when the Brothers talk about Church or "club business", when "lady talk" is happening, the men disappear like thieves into the night.

CHAPTER FIVE

MOUNTAIN

For someone who just the other night complained about me not coming to bed, my wife sure is taking her sweet ass time finding our bedroom tonight. I hear her puttering around with something in the kitchen of our apartment, but I have no clue what she's doing.

Avoiding me as usual, Blue spent all day in the main clubhouse kitchen with the other ladies, prepping and organizing things for tomorrow's Thanksgiving lunch. At least, I think that's what she was doing in there.

I tried to stop in at one point in the afternoon but was stopped as Whiskey, Hammer, and Steel were pushed back through the swinging doors by a laughing Blue. The second she saw me, her smile disappeared . . . and so did she. Back into the kitchen she went without even one word.

When I asked the guys what they were doing in there, they all laughed and said they went in with the intention of sneaking something to snack on, but the women quickly banished them from the kitchen and told them they weren't allowed to be part of "lady talk".

Blue magically appears in our room but makes a beeline straight for the bathroom. Before I can say anything, the door shuts and I hear the lock engage.

Well, that's never happened before. In twenty-some years, she has never locked me out of any room. Especially the bathroom. I remember in the early days, sometimes that was the only place we could find privacy from our nosy teenager to sneak in some adult activities.

I've lost count of the number of times I ambushed her after she was finished brushing her teeth or washing her face. There were many mornings where I'd spin her around, hike up her nightshirt, and grab her up by her ass cheeks to wrap her legs around my waist, then fuck her against the wall. My favorite times were when I'd sneak into the house in the middle of the day and pull her down the hall by her hand. I'd shut the door behind us, bend her over the vanity, and take her from behind without even taking our clothes off.

What happened to those days?

Finally, she appears a half-hour later, and I pounce.

I'm so sick and tired of the cold shoulder I've been getting, I can't take it anymore. I straight as fuck ambush her ass as soon as she's clear of the bathroom door.

After her hairdryer shut off, I hopped my one-legged ass over to the wall and leaned against it, knowing she'd be out any minute.

With my hands on her hips, I push Blue forward, forcing her down face first onto our bed. The bed isn't far from the door—there's just enough space from mattress to wall that you can stand sideways and touch both at once—so she doesn't fall very far or hard.

"What the hell, Mountain," she exclaims as she tries to roll over to look at me. But too bad for her, I move faster.

Pushing myself up so all my weight is on my right leg, I hop once to get between her spread legs and kneel on the edge of the bed. I lucked the fuck out with my amputation being from the shin down because I still have both knees, so I'm able to kneel and put pressure on both legs without causing any pain.

Bracketing her shoulders with my hands, I lay overtop of Blue, pushing her down to the mattress under me. "I'm doing something you and I haven't done in way too damn long."

Blue turns her head and pushes the loose hair out of her face so she can look up at me. "And what's that? I don't remember you ever scaring me like that. Or attacking me unprovoked."

"No," I growl as I grind my hips into the crease of her ass. "You don't remember the times I'd pull you into a room and ravage you in the middle of the day?" She tries to interrupt me, but I lower my head to kiss her neck and continue. "What about all those times you'd send me dirty looks across the room, and I'd walk away from my Brothers mid-conversation to eat you out whenever you wanted? You don't remember any of that?"

With every word, I feel Blue's body shiver and squirm under me. I know damn well that behind her closed eyelids, she's replaying some dirty memories in her mind.

"That was so long ago," she replies, panting as she presses her cheek to the comforter below.

"Then let's make some new memories." I lean back to let her have some room to breathe. "Roll over so I can see those clear sky eyes of yours."

Surprisingly, she does what I ask. Maneuvering herself within the confines of my hands and knees, Blue manages to twist herself around so now we're face to face. Chest to chest. My rock-hard bulge is the closest it's been to her soft, warm center in way too long. Months too long.

Now, if only the look in those pretty blue eyes was one of happiness and assurance.

"What are you doing? I just wanna go to bed. I'm tired."

I'm not going to lie, hearing those words is a punch straight to the gut. No man, or woman, wants to hear 'I'm tired' from their partner. I sure as hell don't. I just need to show her, prove to her, that this is what we both need. I'd never force myself on Blue, that's not the type of relationship we've ever had, but I can't say I've never pushed the boundaries on fun a time or two. And this just happens to be one of those times where I *need* her.

"I know you don't really like me very much right now," I lower myself to her again, kissing across her cheeks and over her nose, "and you probably don't wanna talk," onto her other cheek, down to her lips, "but I need you too much to care." I slam my lips down on hers and kiss her like I damn well mean every word.

I take her mouth aggressively, and shockingly enough, she kisses me right back.

Her hands wiggle at my sides before she continues lifting them up and over my back. Her short nails lightly scratch my skin as she continues her journey to my shoulders. Once her arms are pinned beneath mine, she slides them between us and sets her hands on the front of my shoulders.

Our kisses continue the entire time, our tongues dueling for control, teeth nipping whenever one or the other has the upper hand. It's not until Blue has her hands pressed against my chest, one on each pectoral, that I feel her pushing me away.

Imagining the worst, that she really doesn't want this, I straighten my arms and force my lips to separate from hers.

Looking down into her much happier eyes, I can't help but let out a deep breath. "What's the matter? I didn't hurt you, did I?"

"Oh no, that's not it."

"Then what's wrong?" I brush a strand of chestnut hair off her forehead before tracing my finger down her cheek. "Please don't push me away. I need to feel us again. I need you, Blue. Only you."

"I need you too. I just needed to take a breath before you continue to smother me."

Blue's smile grows like the brightest sunrise I've ever seen. Her lips curl up, her cheeks flush bright, and she gets these tiny creases at the outside edges of her almost clear eyes. She's never been more beautiful to me, though I probably think that every day.

Tracing her hands around the back of my neck, Blue's fingers thread into my hair as she pulls me back down to her. We're kissing again, but this time, instead of me pressing her, it's her kissing me full force.

Hurting . . . no, needing . . . to see and touch more of my wife, I take back control of our kisses and start moving south. Going lower with each press of my lips to her skin, I eventually hit the neckline of her t-shirt. Running out of bed below my knees, I realize if things are going to continue, the two of us will need to rearrange.

I get my foot back on the floor and lean against the edge of the bed. "I think you need to scoot your tiny ass up, so I have room to get between these legs properly."

"Well, all you had to do was say so, mister," Blue sasses back with a wink.

In a move I haven't seen in way too long, Blue rolls onto her hands and knees and crawls away from me, flaunting that fine ass in my face as she heads for the pillows. Once she's in the middle of the bed, she flips back over to lay herself out for me like a goddamn feast.

"Fuck, you look delicious." And with that, I'm crawling up the bed again, positioning myself between her spread legs.

Picking up where I left off, I kiss down the front of her body, overtop of the too large, too long t-shirt she's wearing. I get to the bottom edge and bite the hem with my teeth. Giving it a tug, I look up at Blue from my crouched position. Whatever she sees in my eyes, she must get my silent message.

Sitting up, Blue whips her shirt off and it goes flying the second it's over her head.

What I see shocks me to my core. Naked . . . skin. My wife was naked underneath that ratty old t-shirt, not even wearing any of the pretty panties she normally likes to traipse around in. I can't tell you how many of those damn lacy and silky things I've had to replace after ripping them away from her body.

"Well, well, well," I croon as I use my right hand to trace down the middle of her chest. "What do we have here?"

As my fingers circle her bellybutton, the sensation must get to be too much for her, because Blue falls onto her back and grabs hold of the comforter with both hands. "Shit."

"Looks like someone may have wanted me more than she originally hinted at, huh?" Arranging myself over her, I pepper kisses across her chest and torso. "Is this what you wanted, Blue?"

"Maybe." Her one-word reply comes out with a sigh. "Maybe I was trying to show you what you've been missing."

Oh, the little vixen wants to play, does she?

I've been craving the touch of my woman's skin for way too long. If playtime is what she wants, I am more than happy to dish it out.

"I've sure missed this." Moving my fingers down to the tiny patch of short dark curls at her pussy, I slide one into her damp, glistening folds and find her hard bud.

Blue bends her knees, spreading her hips even wider open for me, so I drop my hips flat to the bed and get my face as close to her center as I can.

Licking from asshole to clit, I open her to me, and Blue explodes on my tongue. Her flavor is the same as it's always been, like ice-cold lemonade on a hot summer day. She's tart and sweet and just what a man needs to quench his thirst.

Burying my shoulders beneath her thighs, I get to fucking work. I lick and bite and twirl her clit while holding her folds open with two fingers. Blue begins chanting gibberish as I swallow down every bit of the juices she's releasing for me. Suddenly, she grabs hold of the back of my head and brings me down even harder into her.

I take the opportunity to press my tongue into her channel and taste right from the source. Moving my weight to my forearms, I fill my hands with the fine ass she's got and go to fucking town. Rubbing my short beard back and forth, all over her, I soak in her arousal. I need to get her scent on me, and mine on her. It's addictive.

My dick is pressing hard against the bed, and if I were a weaker man, I'd rut myself into this pillowtop and flood my flannel pants. But no, this is all about Blue and what she needs. And what she needs right now is for me to make her come, so I double down.

It doesn't take long for her inner muscles to begin to spasm. Blue pulls my hair even harder, and my scalp starts to sting. That's how I know I've hit the spot. Then, just as fast as I start counting down, Blue comes like a rocket blasting off at zero.

While she may taste sweet, the words coming from Blue's mouth are anything but. "Fuck. Fuck. Dammit. More," she loudly cries out. Her thighs press tight against my ears as her whole body trembles. It's a feeling I've experienced many times in my life with this woman, so I keep my hands on her hips and hold on until she relaxes in exhaustion.

As Blue's legs fall open, I'm able to get back up on my hands and knees and crawl up her sweaty, sated body, dropping kisses on every inch of skin.

Starting at her left hip, my lips skim to her bellybutton, up her stomach, across her ribs, and over her sternum, finally settling themselves on her left breast. Letting my tongue twist around her nipple, she shivers as goosebumps appear across her body.

Lightly biting the tight bud with my teeth, I tug just a bit. But even the little bit of pain causes Blue to arch her back, bringing the twin beauties up to me, like she's offering them as a sacrifice.

I let her nipple go and keep kissing higher. Across her chest to her other shoulder, up the right side and underneath the curve of her neck, and onto Blue's round cheek, until finally, my lips meet hers.

Blue sighs as our mouths meet, and I take it all.

Every breath. Every moan. Every gasp. I steal them from her and love her right back.

"Mountain," she says when she turns her head for a breath, "let me."

"Let you what, love?"

I feel her fingers press against my cheeks, so I open my eyes for her.

"Let me love you," Blue whispers while tracing the line of my chin.

The glint in her eyes has me struck down. Whatever my Old Lady wants right now is hers, because the smile that spreads across her face makes me happier than I've been in months.

I probably look like a demented clown right now, but I can't hold my happiness back any longer. "Whatever you need."

Blue's hands glide down to my shoulders, and I feel her tiny push. "Roll over. I need to be on top."

"You ain't gotta ask me twice." Arms banded around her hips, I flip us over, causing Blue to squeak as she lands her ass on my lap. "You wanna ride me, hop on, cowgirl." And with that, I buck my hips.

"Hold on there, stud," Blue orders, letting a little of her accent drop. It's not often I hear the slight twang she had when she first moved here, but when Blue is relaxed and happy, she lets it slip. "We gotta get you outta your britches."

That makes me laugh. As Blue slides her butt down my legs, I lose hold of her hips and intertwine my fingers behind my head. If she's going to put on this show, I'll just lay back and watch her tits bounce and sway as she moves.

Her tiny fingers find the elastic band of my pajama pants and she pulls them down as I lift my ass to accommodate. The next thing I know, I'm naked as the day I was born.

Blue rests back on her haunches for a bit and peruses my body with her eyes. I'd like to think I haven't let myself go too much since we met, and I know I've got muscles for days, so I puff out my chest and let her get her fill.

But just as fast as my pants disappeared, Blue is on top of me, taking me for a ride.

Her right hand strokes my dick from root to leaking head, then her folds blossom around my tip and she lowers her weight on me.

I feel Blue's pussy open as my dick goes deeper with each rock of her hips.

Two. Three. Four. And her plump backside is flush with my hips.

Unable to hold back any longer, my hands untangle and find Blue's waist. I hold on tight as her hands slap down on my chest and she really starts to move.

"Fuuuuck, yes," I groan as my eyes roll to the back of my head.

"You're . . . so . . . deep . . ." Blue pants as her entire body shakes.

In this position, I can't even pretend to think I have any control of what is happening right now. My brain has decided to take a vacation, and the woman riding me is one hundred percent leading the show.

If I could get any deeper inside of Blue, I would, but with how she's moving and bouncing and handling me, I have no power. While I ambushed her, intent on getting what I wanted from her, Blue has taken the reins and is leading me across the finish line.

"Oh, shit. Oh, shit," Blue calls out. "Right there. Oh, shit."

Something I'm doing must be right. Blue's head falls back, and her hair billows out behind her back, bouncing with every rise and fall of her pussy on my cock. The long, deep brown waves are flowing like she's on the back of my Harley.

Fuck, I'd give anything to feel that again—Blue's arms around my waist, her legs spread around my ass, her chin resting on my shoulder. We'd ride around for hours, no destination in mind, just to get away.

I really need to consider what it'd take to ride again. But the time for that isn't now. Right now, the only one doing the riding is my wife.

Letting one hip go, I twist my wrist and find her center with my thumb. Pressing against her clit, I zero in on the hard nub sticking out and tap just once before Blue sets off again at my touch.

Tingles run down my spine, I feel my balls draw up tight, and I know I'm a goner.

I come so fucking hard, and every bit of anything that was inside my body is now inside of Blue's still spasming channel. From the top of my head to the tips of my toes, every ounce of energy, power, and cum is shooting out of my dick and into my woman.

How I'm still in one piece, I don't think I'll ever know. But that's what Blue does to me. She rips me to shreds, and I love every minute of it.

One hand on my chest, Blue slides off me and falls to my right. "Holy shit," she says, letting out a quick breath. Her chest rises and falls as she lays there, eyes open and staring at the ceiling. Turning her head my way, her eyes squint a little as she chuckles. "Good thing we have a big bed. I thought we'd bounce off the side there at the end."

"I'll take that as a compliment," I reply with a smirk and a wink.

Now that she mentions it, we did move during our rodeo. We started out in the middle of the bed, but now, I'm lying more to the left, which is my side, closest to the bathroom door, where the whole show began.

Swinging my knees over the side of the bed, I hop up and grab my crutches to assist my trip into the bathroom. Not wanting to turn the light on and blind myself, I feel for the countertop and grab a couple washcloths from the drawer below.

I run them under warm water and wring out the excess. Using one to wipe off my dick, I head back to the bed to clean the mess I made on my lady.

Once we're both clean, under the covers, and Blue is tucked into my side, I feel like there's something I need to say. She hasn't said a word since we finished making love, and my mind is running a mile a minute.

Turning to my right, I lift her chin and hope she can see me in the dark. "I know we've been pulling away from each other lately, and I'm sorry for my part in that."

Blue's eyes go wide, and I catch her shock in the dim light shining through the door leading into the living area. "Mountain, I'm—"

"No, listen, please." Kissing her lips to silence any protests, I hold her cheek in my hand. "I have some things in my head I need to sort through myself, but whenever you're ready, when *we're* ready to talk, just know I'm here. No matter what, everything will be okay."

"How can you be so sure?" she asks with a sniffle.

A tear drops from the corner of her eye, and I quickly wipe it away with my thumb. "I know we'll get through whatever this is. I know it."

"I love you, Jethro." Blue presses up to me and kisses me. Her lips are a little puffy from our rough love, but her words are soft and gentle.

Lying back down in our bed, I hold my wife in my arms until she falls asleep.

It may be foolish, but I hope this is the start of us rebuilding whatever we seem to have let get broken. Here's to hoping, anyway.

Now to get my own shit figured out, so when Blue is ready to talk, I am too. Because right now, I don't know if anything I have to say would help us or just hurt us even more.

CHAPTER SIX

BLUE

As great as I should feel after a night like I had, I'm really not feeling the joy or happiness I'm accustomed to. Normally, after a round of lovemaking, or really hot, dirty sex with my Old Man, we take a breather and go for another round or two. But that didn't happen.

For some reason—one I'll probably realize was a good thing later, but right now am sad about—Mountain decided that after-sex talk was going to entail a mood-killing truth about how crappy our personal relationship has been lately. He acknowledged we had a problem, even said he knew he was part of the problem, but then laid the rest of it all on me.

When *I'm* ready, *he's* ready. What does that even mean? Why does it have to be me who needs to be ready to talk first? Why can't he man the fuck up and tell me how to fix us?

But who am I to complain? I've got a really nice life here. I'm fifty years old, and for the last twenty-one years, things have been almost too easy. We fell in love so quick, maybe we both need this time to figure out what we want from this life.

So, for the time being, until one of us pulls our head out of our respective backsides, I need to focus on today and what I'm thankful for. Because I have a lot.

It's Thanksgiving Day and the clubhouse is full of the people I love and who love me in return . . . including one stubborn husband of mine.

As the other Old Ladies, club girls, a couple family friends, and I finish prepping the sides for our meal, Skynyrd and Mountain have commandeered the large center island to carve the two dozen turkeys they grilled. While that may seem like a lot of bird to the average household, when you have one hundred and fifty people waiting to eat together, the food goes fast.

Also, it leaves us with a fair amount of leftovers, whether the men know about it or not. When the Brothers start grumbling in a few days about being hungry and nothing is as good as last week's turkey, they're always surprised when a big pot of turkey noodle soup appears for dinner that night. Sometimes we women have to keep things a secret just to see them smile.

Once everything is set out on the passthrough counter, and all the serving dishes are filled to the brim, I kick everyone out of the kitchen. With a few curious looks, and one attempt by Duchess to question why, I shoo them all out the door, telling them I'm fine and I'll be right out to call everyone up for lunch.

I just need a minute. I need a minute to take a breath, to reset my mind to the thankful and gracious place it should be today, then I can face the crowd out in the main room.

Pushing my way out the swinging doors, I faceplant into the chest of my nephew, and he wraps me in his arms. "Thank you for today, Blue," Haze says.

I don't know why he's standing here, or what inspired him to choose this time to love on me, but I soak it in. Wrapping my arms around him, as much as I can with his bulk and muscles, I hug him back. "Anything for my boys."

As we separate, I catch Bear's eye and nod for him to start.

"All right, you hooligans," our club Wise Man calls out, "let's pray!"

His bark is met by a few mumbles of being 'sooo hungry', but we all listen as Bear tells us to love our friends. He thanks whatever higher power is out there for our family, calls out for our continued safety and growth of the club, and lastly, blesses the food we're about to eat.

Somehow, the stampede of big boots doesn't overwhelm the pitter-patter of the much smaller feet mixed amongst them, and everyone gets through the line in one piece. There are a few breaks to swap out empty dishes for full ones, and even one broken spoon, but based on the happy chatter and clatter of silverware, I'd say today is a success.

I trail the end of the line, filling my plate with turkey, gravy, mashed potatoes, green bean casserole, and a dinner roll before I head to find somewhere to sit amongst the chaos.

In addition to the two long cafeteria-style tables that fill what we call our dining room, the Brothers spent most of the morning assembling the spare tables we keep in the storage room and setting them up all over the main room. There are people eating at the bar, some have plopped their butts right on the hardwood floor, and a few even pulled chairs up to the pool tables.

Just as I'm about to join Hammer, Angel, and their boys' pow wow on the floor, a hand appears at my waist, and I'm pulled back into a rock-hard chest. Knowing exactly who's behind me, I rest my head on his shoulder, and allow myself to soak in a few seconds of Mountain's attention.

"I saved you a seat on the couch by me, love." With a kiss to the top of my head, he threads his fingers in mine and leads me deeper into the room. "Just the two of us."

When I get settled in my spot, Mountain disappears but quickly reappears with a soda in each hand, then takes his seat beside me. As we eat, we chat with everyone around us.

It's not long before I hear Angel call out from behind us as Taren makes a break for it. He runs away from his mother but stops dead in his tracks as he rounds the corner of the couch and ends up at my feet. With his adorable caramel eyes, I can't help but swoon as he holds his arms up. Like the big 'ol softie I am, I scoop him up into my lap. Holding him tight, I sink back into my cushion and enjoy the tiny toddler snuggles, t-shirt stained with spilled gravy and all.

Mountain pulls me and my bundle into his arms and starts talking to Taren about motorcycles. For a few minutes, I listen to him explain that one day he'll teach Taren how to change the oil in his Harley. It's adorable . . . and makes my heart cry out at never being able to experience moments like this with a child of my own.

As the room grows louder, and after everyone has gone back for seconds, or thirds for some of the men, Whiskey and Steel get up and call for everyone's attention. "Listen up, assholes!" Steel whistles.

"Shut up!" Whiskey claps twice, sounding like a crack of thunder. "We've got an announcement to make!"

"Are you two finally gonna admit you secretly love each other and are riding off into the sunset together?" Brewer calls out, bringing a chuckle from around the room.

From the couch in front of us, Ring taunts back, "That'll happen the same day you let a woman tie you up with those kinky ropes you like to hide but everyone knows you have."

From the other side of Ring, Opal kneels up and squishes his face between her tiny hands. "Papa, what's kinky?"

The laughter from before erupts even louder, and even I can't hold back.

"Nothing, munchkin," Ring replies when he can speak. He pulls Opal into his lap and tries to give her a stern warning, but his chuckles are making him hard to believe. "It's a naughty word and you should never say it again."

Sunshine leans into his side and whispers something in his ear, and I swear the grown man, even with all his broody darkness, blushes.

"Alright, enough outta you fuc-fudgers." Whiskey hides his own bad word with a cough. "The news is that we're gonna be havin' a wedding here in one month's time." With one finger pointing around the room, he practically shoots mean-mug lasers out his eyes. "And I expect everyone to be on their best behavior and to pitch in to do whatever the brides tell you to."

"Brides? As in more than one?" Kraken questions from a recliner to my left.

"You heard right. Brides, as in more than one," Steel answers. "Sunshine, Duchess, Angel, and Star are all tying the knot on the same day."

Not that I would expect anything less from this crowd, the cheers, applause, and whistles kick in from all around.

"When's the big day?" I hear someone ask.

Whiskey takes Krew from Duchess's arms, then pulls her up from her spot at one of the tables to stand beside him. He wraps his arm around her and tucks her into his side, one arm for each of his people. "These ladies are either crazy or doing this out of pity, but none of us are gonna question it. The nine of us are saying 'I do' here, in this clubhouse, on Christmas Eve."

Mountain untangles himself from around me, drops a kiss on my temple, then gets up to hug his son. Angel appears to take Taren back and get him ready for his nap, and I watch my husband congratulate Whiskey and Duchess. And there goes my heart again.

Not wanting to look like a party pooper, sitting all alone on the couch as the party moves from eating food to being loud and rambunctious, I join the celebration. I make it a good half-hour before it all gets to be a little too much. Stealing my grandson from a busy, chattering Duchess, I tuck us into a recliner and rock the sleeping baby as I take in the room.

Watching the happiness around me, I do the only thing I can. I make a wish.

I wish that my much-needed talk with Mountain is a good talk, whenever it happens, because I don't think I can keep going like this. Even after last night, and feeling his love for me, I don't know what to do with all this uncertainty.

I wish I was stronger. I've never felt this weak before. Hell, it only took the man three days to convince me to marry him, so why am I being so indecisive now?

I wish that until the time comes to face my demons, I don't make an even bigger mess than I'm in right now. Uncertainty has never been my best friend.

But until then, I'll keep to myself as much as possible and think about what's best for me.

I just hope I end up on the right path.

CHAPTER SEVEN

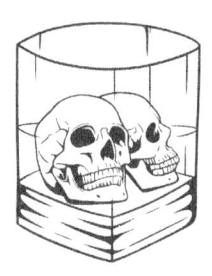

WHISKEY

Who needs a damn alarm clock when you have a three-month-old baby in the house? Not me, that's for damn sure. Especially when this one's momma was up two times last night, refusing to let me help take care of said crying baby.

In my eyes, my boy may be the most perfect baby in the world, but until he learns how to tell time, even I will grumble and groan when he wakes up before the sun rises. At least now he seems to understand the difference between night and day.

Until a couple weeks ago, he'd be awake all night and want to sleep all day. Somehow, his mother managed to do something called sleep-training to get him on a schedule we could handle. And just in time too, because I was about to start taking naps in my office just to get away from our cabin.

Sliding Duchess off my chest, thankfully not waking her, I creep out of bed, slide on a pair of clean boxer briefs, and head for the room across the hall.

The room that Krew sleeps in now is the room I used when I was growing up. When I was two, my Pops and Uncle Brick, along with Hammer's dad, Butch, bought the first three cabins we have on the compound. Today, there are five cabins total, in addition to the new factory-built home we just brought in for Ray and his family.

I push the door open and head straight for the crib where my son lays. As soon as Krew sees me, his crying comes to a halt. Looking back at me are two bright blue eyes, ones I say are identical to his momma's, even though she says the same about mine, and I lose my breath for a second.

Every time I look at my son, it's like seeing him again for the first time. The day he was born was the day my life really began. Until then, it was all about me, my motorcycle, my Brothers, my club, and my woman. But that day, at the very moment he was born, everything got brighter and clearer, and I knew I would be a better man.

My club may still be number one in most aspects, because that's how it is in this life, but the moments I can carve out where it's just me and my boy, it's all about him. And if anyone tries to come for him or his momma, I wouldn't think twice about killing them with my bare hands.

I saved my Old Lady once, and I'd do it all over again, minus her being hurt, if it got me to where we are today.

After a particularly nasty diaper change, I dress Krew in a long-sleeve onesie with colorful turkey feathers sewn on the butt, warm up a bottle, and start a pot of coffee before settling us in the living room.

My ass isn't on the couch cushion for more than a minute when I hear footsteps coming down the hall. I look up in time to see my Duchess yawn and look around the room. When she finds us, a little spark flickers in her eyes and she smiles. "There's my boys."

"Good mornin', momma," I call out as I look down to burp Krew, halfway through his formula. "Coffee's started, come sit with us for a minute."

Folding her legs beneath her as she sits, Duchess snuggles into my right side as I switch the baby back around to finish his breakfast.

Duchess plays with the itty-bitty sock-covered toes sticking out under my arm and lays her head on my shoulder. "When'd you two wake up?"

"Not too long ago," I reply with a kiss to her forehead. "We just sat down when you came out."

"Let me finish feeding him, and you go get the coffee." Duchess holds out her arms, and I swiftly hand him over without dropping the bottle.

As I pour coffee into two mugs, mixing creamer in with my lady's, I think about how great a baby's life must be. Babies really have it made. Hungry? Cry and someone will make you a bottle. Poop your pants? Cry and someone will clean up after you. Are you tired at two in the afternoon? Just yawn, close your eyes, and sleep whenever and wherever you want.

Turning around with a mug in each hand, I almost trip over my own bare feet. And who would blame me when what I see is Duchess's ass sticking up at me?

Laying Krew in his baby swing, she stands straight, turns around, and sets her hands on her hips. "I could feel your eyes on my butt just then, you perv."

"I'm not a perv," I reply with a laugh. "I can stare at your booty any time I want. I put a ring on it, remember?"

I hand over her coffee and get a few sips into mine when she knocks me off my axis again.

"Are you sure you wanna get married?"

Turning to face her, I give her the business. "Of course, I am, Duchess. I wouldn't have put that ring on your finger had I not."

She looks down, twisting said ring around, causing the diamond to sparkle under the overhead lights. "Are you sure?" When her eyes meet mine again, she looks a little sad. "We can back out if you want. I'm happy how we are."

Taking a giant sip of my much-needed morning caffeine boost, I prepare myself for a battle. Setting my mug on the end table, I give her my undivided attention. "Do *you* wanna back out?"

"No," with that, she sits up quick, "I just sometimes wonder if this all happened too fast for you. I mean, it was just barely a year ago when we met. Now, we've got one baby and are thinking of trying for another one, and I'm just scared is all."

"Kiana Marie." I take her mug away and put it on the coffee table. Taking her face in my hands, I lower my forehead to hers. "When you wake up on Christmas morning, you'll be waking up with my last name, come hell or high water. Do I make myself perfectly clear?"

"Yes," she whispers as she nods.

Pulling her in for a kiss—a deep, powerful, tongue included kind of kiss where hopefully she feels my love and understands how serious I am about this—I don't let her up until we both need a breath. "I love you, Duchess. I told you that months ago and nothing's changed." And again, I draw her lips to mine. "We'll get married and work on making a dozen more babies. Maybe I'll knock you up again on New Year's."

With that, Duchess laughs and pushes me back. She collapses to the middle cushion and crosses her arms. "That was a fluke and you know it. We'll have another baby when my body is ready."

She may think she wants to be mad at me, but she's not. My Duchess loves having my baby inside of her. "The doctor gave us the all-clear a few weeks ago, so we can practice every day 'til your belly takes another one of my babies. And we'll do it over and over again 'til we have enough to make the starting lineup for a football team."

And that earns me a fluffy pillow to the face. "You're insane. Maybe we'll have three or four, but that's it."

"We'll have as many as I give you, woman." Tossing the offending decorative pillow onto the floor, something I don't see as necessary but my woman says we must have many of, I pull Duchess onto my lap.

"Whatever you say, hotshot," Duchess sasses as she wraps her arms around my neck. "Are you busy this afternoon? The other Old Ladies and I want to hit up the bridal store in Henderson to see if we can find our dresses. And that's not a place I can take the baby."

"You go do your dress thing, and Krew and I will hang out with all the other dads and kiddos."

"Thank you for being such a good dad." Duchess pulls my face to hers and kisses me damn silly.

I use my lips and tongue to stop her from saying any more crazy things about limiting the number of children we will or won't have. I stop her from thanking me for the millionth time for doing what I was put on this planet to do, which is to be the father to her children, and settle in to distract her for as long as I can.

Moving my kisses down her neck, I imagine what our life will look like one month from now. "I can't wait to see you in your wedding dress. And then help you take it off."

Duchess pushes on my chest a little, then finagles herself around to straddle my lap. "Wanna practice now?" she asks as she tugs at the edge of my way too big t-shirt she's wearing.

Looking over her shoulder at Krew, I find him still staring at the animals twirling around above him. His eyes are slowly blinking and will soon be closed as he dozes off into a milk coma. "How long 'til the monster is awake again?"

"We've got about a half-hour." Duchess whips the shirt off and throws it somewhere behind me. "Make it count, Old Man."

And boy, do I ever. Several times.

CHAPTER EIGHT

MOUNTAIN

"Alright, who pissed off the weatherman? This storm is fuckin' bullshit. I mean, have you seen how fast it's pilin' up out there?"

Turning in my chair, I glare at Kraken, who's sitting down to my left. "Would you shut up? We all know what it looks like outside. Most of us woke up to the sight of pure white when we looked out our windows." One smack on the back of his giant bald head and he's whining again.

"Yea, but . . . it wasn't supposed to happen this early." Kraken slumps back in his chair and crosses his arms. "It looks like the end of the world out there. A real biker's worst nightmare."

If it weren't for the fact that the man is over six feet tall, has a beard bushier than an overgrown forest full of grizzly bears, and has skin covered in various nautical-themed tattoos, you'd think Kraken was a five-year-old boy whining that someone took away his favorite toy.

But I have to give it to him, even though I won't say it out loud, this weather does really suck. When I woke up this morning, the first thing I saw out the giant picture window was a blur of white. A blizzard on a Monday, what a crap-tastic way to start a new week.

I just sat there and stared at the falling flakes, and probably would've fallen back to sleep had it not been for Blue calling out my name.

For the first time since I got married, I slept on the couch. I swear it wasn't intentional, but when I came in last night to go to bed and found Blue already sleeping, I felt a little dejected. I didn't want to wake her, so as quietly as I could, I pulled the door almost closed and stayed in the living room. After grabbing a spare pillow from the closet and the blanket off my recliner, I laid down on the couch. Next thing I knew, it was morning, and I was waking up alone.

The look I received from my wife when she came out of our room and saw me sitting there was gut punching. When she realized I hadn't come to bed, I watched her get a little teary-eyed before she put on the fakest smile I've ever seen and pretended like nothing was wrong. Though we both know everything is wrong, but neither of us know how to fix it.

Let's face it, we're both fucking chickens and don't want to be the one to speak first.

More grumbling from my Brothers snaps me out of my self-pity party and back into the real-world problems we're facing. We have no power, which means everyone who lives on the compound is crashing in the clubhouse until further notice.

Luckily enough, we knew some inclement weather was coming, so last night everyone moved their Harleys into the bays at Rebel Repairs, just so they didn't get snowed on. But none of us expected to see almost three feet of the fluffy shit when we woke up, or that there'd be a forecast that more is coming, without an end in sight.

"Oh, grow up, ya big cry baby," Whiskey groans from his spot at the head of the table. "This happens every year and you always complain."

"None of us like snow, but for some reason we all chose to live here," Tiny complains, joining the pouty man party.

"I didn't choose to live here," Wrench vocalizes his grievance. "My dad apparently thought it was a good idea to move to BFE instead of staying in sunny California."

Bear pulls a pen from the pocket of his flannel and throws it at his son. "I never woulda met your mother and had you had I not moved here, so quit your bitchin'."

Whiskey bangs his gavel, quieting all the mumbles. "All right, that's enough outta all of you. Yea, it sucks none of the cabins have power. And yes, the clubhouse is only running on half power, but 'til it's come back on, the generator is all we've got."

Steel chimes in. "All families in the cabins will be moving into the clubhouse 'til further notice. They're all waitin' out in the main room for an update, so let's just hash out the problems now."

Cypher raises his hand from his perch in the front right corner of the room. "Only half the lights are on, and I've got all my computers shut off, but is there any chance I can reboot at least one to make sure my system didn't crash when the power went out?"

Poor guy has been sweating bullets since everyone trudged downstairs and the severity of what's going on was realized. That boy lives in his room for days at a time, only coming out when he needs to eat or when he's forced to socialize at club-related events. We really need to get him out more often.

"You can plug in one computer in the kitchen. It's the only room that's fully powered up," Whiskey starts but raises a finger to everyone else. "But everyone else is on electronic shutdown. No charging your phones, no turning on the televisions, no lights on unless absolutely necessary."

"We have half the main room lights on, but don't be flipping any more switches," Hammer adds. "Now that the generator is all we've got, we can't be wasteful. Dad and I are in charge of making sure it stays gassed up, but that also means don't be touching cords or moving things around. If you didn't put it there, don't fuckin' touch it."

"Is everybody clear on that?" Steel questions the room.

Everyone replies with halfhearted agreements.

"Next bit of info before we go break the news to the Old Ladies." I watch as my son pinches the bridge of his nose and groans. "Since all the families will be in the clubhouse, sleeping arrangements may need to be altered a little bit. We currently have two empty rooms upstairs, which Hammer and I will be taking, but that leaves one family left without a place to go. While Butch has volunteered to crash in the Prospect bunkroom, we still need to find a room for Ring, Steel, Sunshine, and Opal."

"They can have one of our rooms," Haze offers as he points across the table to Smoke. "We're living in what used to be their rooms, so it kinda makes sense."

"I'm good with it," Smoke agrees. "It may be a little cramped for everyone, but we can make do."

"Thanks, guys. We appreciate it." Ring reaches over and slaps Smoke on the shoulder. "Plus, it'll be nice to be back in our old space. Opal will think it's like a sleepover."

That's one thing I love about our club. While we all may have our kickass, take no prisoners, killing bad guys side to us, when it comes to each other and our family, everyone pitches in.

When I found out I had a daughter, I didn't know how things were going to turn out. Luckily, she found her new home here, and I get to see her every day. Then, when Brick passed and the secret about Haze being his son was blasted into the open, I was wrecked. I still am in many ways, but if it weren't for this group of crazies, I probably would've sunken into a hole and not come back out.

"Anyone got anything else?" Whiskey asks the room.

"I got one thing, if y'all don't mind," Butch speaks up. "As the guy who's in charge of yardwork and makin' sure all the Prospects do their shit on time, can everybody give them a break every once in a while and help out with shovelin' the porches and such? I'd rather none of them fall asleep out there, end up in a snowbank, and die of hypothermia. I don't wanna be diggin' frozen bodies out when this shit storm is over."

"We can work out a rotation for all of us to head out every so often and keep the doorways clear," Whiskey starts, "even if the farthest we can go to escape the madhouse this place is gonna turn into is the porch railing."

That gives everyone a reason to chuckle.

"I don't know if this is gonna be fun or a giant shitshow," Whiskey says as he bangs his gavel to end Church, "but we're about to find out. Club meeting in ten."

Isn't it just our luck? The worst blizzard in years hits the week right after Thanksgiving and traps all of us inside, and just when the ladies decide to start planning the biggest wedding any of us have ever seen. Yea, we're all in for a shitshow for sure.

CHAPTER NINE

BLUE

"BeeGee." I look to my right and find Opal standing next to me, hands tucked in her tiny pockets. She's rocking back and forth on her heels, a timid smile on her face.

"What's up, pumpkin?" She just turned five a week before Halloween, so I gave her the special nickname that only I call her.

Opal looks back at Sunshine, who gives her a smile and a thumbs up. Looking back at me, she rests her hands on my arm and asks, "Can I sit wiff you durin' the meeting?"

"Of course, you can." I lift the edge of the giant, blue-checkered fleece blanket I'm huddled under. "This chair is the perfect size for just the two of us."

As she climbs up into my lap, I think about what a crazy morning this has been. When I opened my eyes and realized how fricking cold I was, this wasn't what I imagined. I thought maybe the pilot light had gone out on the furnace, so when I rolled over to wake Mountain to ask him to go check it out, an even bigger shock greeted me . . . Mountain wasn't in bed.

I reluctantly tossed back the blanket, put on two pairs of socks, sweatpants, one of Mountain's insulated hoodies over my t-shirt, and trudged my sleepy self into the living room. And that's when I knew something was wrong. Seeing the pillow and blanket beside him, I realized my husband slept on the couch, and I didn't tell him to go there.

A few times over the years, I've threatened to make him sleep on the couch, but whether by his sweettalking to get out of whatever mess made me mad in the first place, or me loving his kisses too much and folding like a house of cards in a hurricane, we've always slept in the same bed. Unless he was gone on a run or multi-day ride, I haven't slept alone since I moved here.

Hell, even though Mountain gave me my own room when I arrived, the first two nights I was here he refused to let me sleep in it. Insisting that his bed was ours, I always knew where he was when I closed my eyes. All we did those two nights was lay there and talk to each other, learning anything and everything there was about the other.

There was no hanky panky until that third day.

Not until Mountain slid this ring on my finger, threw me over his shoulder, and we had our way with each other for the first time in the cabin I called home for many years.

Still to this day, I can't forget the way he looked at me when I laid in that bed ... our bed ... naked in front of him for the first time. I was nervous as all get out, shaking like a leaf, but he was staring at me like no one ever had before. Even though I'd been with a few guys before him, Mountain was the first *man* who made me feel beautiful. Like I was more than enough, worth more than just a good time.

I wish I found him in that awestruck trance more often. Especially now.

Two tiny hands frame my cheeks, bringing me back to the present. "Are you okay, BeeGee? You look sad," Opals whispers.

Oh, from the mouths of babes. If she only knew, not that I'd ever want her to feel like this. I wish on the brightest star that she never feels an ounce of my sadness. This tiny sprite in my lap is too precious for the troubles we adults face.

"I'm okay, pumpkin." I tug her hands down and kiss her cheek. "I was just daydreaming is all. No worries."

"Okay, good." Opal snuggles into my chest and pulls the blanket up to her chin. "It's too dang cold in here to be sad. If you cry, your tears will be ice-tickles."

"Do you mean icicles?" I look over at Sunshine and Duchess, who are on the couch to our right. Both of them laugh at Opal's mispronunciation.

"That's what I said." Opal nods as she stares up at me like I'm crazy. "Ice-tickles. My daddy said ice-tickles can be very dangerous so we should never touch them. They can fall'd down and hurt you. I don't want your tears to hurt you, BeeGee."

"Thank you so much for thinking of me, but I promise, I'm fine." Kicking the recliner back to put my feet up, I cocoon us tighter to keep the chill at bay. "Just waiting for your daddy and Papa and all the others to be done with Church so we can figure out the plans for what to do until the power comes back on."

"And Grandpops too, right? He's in Church."

"Yes, he is."

But before she can ask any more questions, the double doors open and a sea of leather cuts, denim jeans, and grumpy bikers come pouring out.

For the last hour, all my fellow Old Ladies, the menagerie of kids, Prospects, and club girls have been huddled up in the main room. Everyone is dressed in layers, wrapped in blankets, and willing the clock to move faster.

Before she crawled in my lap, Opal was playing go fish with Jamie, Sara, and Diego. When the kids got super whiny after hearing they couldn't watch cartoons, the Prospect offered to play with them. They surprisingly made it through four rounds before Jamie got bored and ran off to color with some of the older boys who have camped out at one of the dining tables.

"Listen up," Whiskey calls for everyone's attention, so I put the leg rest down and swivel our chair a little to the right so we can see everyone.

"I know this isn't what we all expected when we heard 'snowstorm', but we just gotta deal with the hand we were dealt. Until further notice, everyone is to stay inside the clubhouse. That means no one's allowed outside, not even to the cabins. If you're someone who lives in an outside cabin, you have temporary room assignments 'til the power is back up and running. Ladies, make your men a list of what you need for a couple of days, and we'll be making a bundled-up trek out there shortly to bring back whatever we can. But only necessary things, please."

Whispers kick up between Angel, Sunshine, and Duchess, but they quiet back down when Whiskey holds up his hand.

"I know it's not ideal, especially with all the little ones, but we can't have anyone out there, especially with the power lines down. It's just not safe. We've got a generator running out back to power limited things such as the kitchen, furnace, hot water heater, and about half the lights, but that's it.

"That means no electronics, no phones, no tablets, no televisions, and no radios other than the one behind the bar we have set to the local station. We have several gallons of gas, but the less we plug in, the longer the generator will last. So please, if anyone has any questions or needs something they don't have, ask around. No trying to be brave by trekking outside. You'll never make it past the edge of the porch because we're not plowing 'til we get word the storm is lightening up. Any questions?"

"Any idea how long the storm is set to last?" Angel questions.

"Last I looked, it'll be well into tomorrow night before we see any break," Whiskey replies as he runs a hand through his hair. "Cypher has been given permission to use one laptop to keep our security systems online, so he'll be in charge of keeping an eye on any reports. But, please, don't be bugging him every five minutes, or asking to check your emails—he's not your personal Jeeves. You can't be asking him questions just 'cause you're bored."

"Then what the hell are we supposed to do for two days? Pick our noses?" Trooper bends his knuckle and pretends to dig for gold.

Whiskey flips him off. "Read a book, do a puzzle, fuck your Old Lady, I don't care as long as everyone stays inside and out of trouble."

That causes several Brothers to whine and grumble.

"But I don't have an Old Lady," Saddle, the club Road Captain, hollers. "What am I supposed to do with all my free time? Play with myself?"

"Excuse me." From the far end of the room, Cinnamon, one of the club girls, calls out. She's got her arms crossed and right eyebrow crooked up. "What are we, chopped liver?"

Raquel and Jazz are on either side of her, snickering along with the rest of us as Saddle stumbles over his words to try and come up with something to say to defend himself. "I . . . umm . . . I think . . ."

"Cinn," Jazz playfully nudges her with her elbow, "be nice to the poor guy. He's getting old, ya know."

The number of club girls has dwindled down to three over the last year, and it's starting to affect the Brothers. While I've never been a fan of the idea of a club girl, most of the women who've come through our doors have been good to the members. With a few exceptions of bitches out to get more than they deserve, or ones who have ended up betraying us, overall, club girls are good to have around. They keep the single Brothers happy and help around the clubhouse with whatever is needed.

With the mood in the room back to fun and laughter, Whiskey draws the meeting to a close. "I know this isn't what any of us expected when we woke up, but as long we're all together, we'll be just fine. Any more questions, find an officer and we'll try to sort it out."

"What's for lunch?" Jamie tugs on Ray's pant leg. "I'm starvin'."

"Boy, hush." Ray rubs a noogie on his son's head. "If you keep eatin' like you do, you'll be bigger than me sooner than later."

"God, help me," Sara says as she rolls her eyes.

"Meeting adjourned," Whiskey bellows, and the room grows way too loud all in one second.

Feeling a tug on my sleeve, I look down to the bundle in my lap. "Yes, pumpkin?"

Opal's eyes are open wide and she looks shocked. "Is Jamie really gonna be bigger than his dad?"

I can't help but laugh. "I don't know. I guess we'll have to wait ten years or so and see what he looks like when he's older."

"Ten years?" Opal gasps, turning to face me. "He'll be so old by then."

"But you'll be ten years older too, ya know?"

Opal taps her chin with her finger, purses her lips, and stares up to the ceiling. When she finally looks back at me, her face has turned sour. "He'll have boy cooties if he's older. That's gross."

"Oh honey," I flip the blanket over her head, making her giggle, "you'll like boys one day, I promise."

Once Opal has the blanket back down, static has a bunch of strands of her hair sticking straight up. "My daddy and Papa say boys are bad."

"Shhh . . . it'll be our secret." I bring my finger to my lips.

Mirroring me, Opal does the same. "Okay, BeeGee." Wiggling down, she takes off running.

"Opal! Slow down or no dessert for you later," Sunshine scolds before rolling her eyes. "What am I gonna do when I have two more of that running around?"

"Whiskey told me he wants a whole football team," Duchess says with a groan of her own, "and I'm not even pregnant yet."

"Be thankful you two had time to prepare for your babies," Angel sasses as she stands up, baby Ace strapped to her chest. "I woke up one morning without a care in the world except me and my man. Next thing I knew, I had a toddler and newborn, just like that." She ends her rant with a snap, then walks away.

Looking around the room, I try to find Mountain, but all I see of him is his back as he heads down the left hallway. He disappears from sight, assumingly into Whiskey's office with all the other officers. They're walking single file, almost like they're ants marching to a picnic, or soldiers off to war on a dangerous mission.

But one thing I notice about the Brothers with him, every one of them looked back at least once to find their Old Lady before they disappeared from sight. Every one of them did . . . except one. And I don't know how to feel anything but hurt about that.

Now that I have the chair back to myself, I spin around to face the tall, skinny windows lining the length of the wall by the dining tables. Through the mass of people sitting around the tables, I can see the snow swirling around outside. As cliché as it sounds, it really does look like a life-size snow globe out there.

Here, I can pretend I'm in my own snow globe, in a bubble away from any problems or questions or worries that I'm not enough. It's just me, my blanket, and the snow falling around me.

What now?

CHAPTER TEN

SUNSHINE

Twenty weeks pregnant and not sleeping in my own bed isn't a good combination. Add in two grumpy men, two growing babies the size of artichokes, and a constantly whining kiddo, and I'm ready to lose my damn mind. And this is only day two of snowmaggedon.

"Opal Marie James! If you don't sit on your tushie and leave Teddy alone, I'm gonna make you take a nap with all the babies."

"But Momma—"

"Don't 'but Momma' me, little lady. I told you to quit buggin' him. He's napping on his bed, so leave him alone."

"But I'm booooored. When's the snow gonna stop? I wanna play outside."

"You and me both, sister, but there's nothing I can do to fix the weather."

That gets her attention. Hands on her hips and head at an angle, she looks at me like I just stole her candy. "You're not my sister. You're my momma."

Every time I hear her call me 'momma' I almost cry. The first time she said it, I pulled her into the biggest hug and tried to hide my tears from her. Too bad her Papa Ring walked in at just that moment and squawked about why I was crying and how he hated seeing my tears. When I told him about Opal calling me 'momma', he called Steel in from the garage and the four of us sat down to have a family talk.

Opal apologized for making me cry, but I quickly told her she did nothing wrong and that I loved her.

When Steel asked her why she called me 'momma', she looked at him like he had three heads and told him straight out, "'Cause she's you guys' Old Lady, so that makes her my momma. Duh!" The ease of her response stunned us all into silence, then made us laugh.

She then ran off to her room like it wasn't the second-best day of my life, the first being the day I agreed to be Ring and Steel's Old Lady.

"Yes, Opal, I am your momma, but that also means you need to listen to me, please. We can make a snowman when your daddy and Papa say so, okay?"

"Okay."

Her sad face makes me want to cry and give in to her request to go outside, but it's not safe, so I have to be the mean mom and not let her have her way. "But until then, I need you to listen and be a good big sister."

Opal sits on the couch next to me and puts her tiny hand on my stomach. "So, I don't wake up the babies in your belly."

"Yes, that's right. We can't wake up the babies." Whatever it takes to make her cool her overactive jets, I'm all for it. "They're sleeping right now."

I don't know if they are or not, but I'm not going to tell Opal that. Until these two start moving enough for people on the outside to feel them, I can say whatever I want.

"HEY! Watch it!" Someone shouts, causing everyone in the room to stop in their tracks and turn to find the source.

Tucking my right leg under my left, I rotate to see the ruckus going on behind me. Not surprisingly, Gunner has gotten himself worked up about something, and he's face to face with Ray in front of the bar.

While Gunner may be a big man at just over six feet tall, no one in this club is taller or wider than Ray. He's easily over seven feet and wider than the average door. Poor guy has to walk into most rooms at an angle just to fit through the door frame.

"I told you to keep your kid away from my shit," Gunner scoffs up at Ray. "He broke my pencil."

"It's just a pencil, man." Ray reaches down to Jamie, who's been hiding behind his dad's legs, and holds out his mitt of a hand. Jamie hands the broken pencil to Ray, who then tries to give it back to Gunner. "Just resharpen it and it'll be fine."

"My pencil sharpener is electric, and I can't use it 'cause of the damn snowstorm. How the fuck am I supposed to sharpen it, huh? With my fuckin' teeth?" Gunner gets louder with each word.

The room grows quieter as Gunner gets louder.

Opal crawls into my lap and hugs me tight. I wrap my arms around her, trying to shield my cub from the big bad wolf.

I see all the women around the room get more uncomfortable as the conversation goes on.

The two men continue to hurl insults at each other until Ring tries to step in. "Guys, this isn't the time or place for this. If you're gonna go at it, take it outside to a damn snowbank."

"Oh, shut the fuck up, Ring. Your pseudo kid was whining earlier too. Why don't you go tell her to be quiet?"

And that's when all hell breaks loose. Heck, if I didn't have said child in my lap, I'd be the one moving right now.

Ray pulls his arm back, takes one swing, and Gunner goes down like a lead balloon. He then uses Gunner's shock to his advantage and pounces. One elbow up, Ray flops down on Gunner in a move I've only seen in a wrestling match on television and in seconds has him flat on the ground. Ray is straddling Gunner's waist, wailing on him, and Gunner tries to hit back but only manages to get a few punches in before Hammer, Steel, and Kraken intervene to split up the duo.

It takes Steel and Kraken to keep Ray from charging again, while Ring and Hammer haul Gunner down the hall to Whiskey's office, where several of the officers had been until the noise out here obviously alerted them to a problem.

"All right, show's over," Steel calls out after passing a pissed-off Ray to Sara. He makes his way to us, but as soon as he sees Opal wrapped around me, he realizes something more is wrong. Settling himself next to us on the couch, Steel envelopes both of us in a hug. He gives me a quick kiss before reaching for Opal's chin. Drawing her face to look at him, he softly asks, "What's wrong, munchkin?"

"I don't like that guy," she says with a sniffle. "He's loud and mean to us."

"Oh, I know." Steel scoops her from my arms. "He's a mean bully, isn't he?"

"Yea," she says a little louder.

"And what do we say about bullies?"

"That we should ignore thems 'cause they need to go in time out."

"Not exactly," Steel chuckles as he pulls on one of her braids, "but it's close enough for now."

"Are you okay, Opal?" I ask. "Do you wanna go play with Jamie now? He looks a little sad over there." I point to where Jamie is standing, wrapped around his dad's leg.

She must hear me talking because Sara looks our way and waves Opal over.

Opal is running away in a flash, worries forgotten, to play with her best friend like nothing was ever wrong.

"You're the best mother in the world," Steel whispers in my ear as he hugs me from behind, before turning me to face him and lifting my feet into his lap. "Seeing you grow our babies is the best thing ever. I can't wait to keep knocking you up for the next twenty years."

That makes me laugh. "Are you crazy? The way these two are growing already," I rub my small but still swollen belly, "I'm never gonna let you near me again. Ring either."

"Hey now," Ring grumps as he squeezes in beside me. "What'd I do this time?"

"You two made me like this," I point two fingers at my belly, "and your Brother over here wants me like this for years! Years!"

"I could get on board with that," Ring says with a nod.

"You two have lost your minds." I shake my head and lean back, listening to these two knuckleheads discuss my reproductive schedule for the next decade or two. If they think they're going to get five more kids out of me, they've got another thing coming.

"Ahem. Excuse me, Sunshine."

My daydream of locking myself in my room to get away from my crazy horny men is interrupted by a cough. A chastised Gunner stands behind the couch we're seated on, with Whiskey to his left and Hammer on the right. His face looks a little worse for wear, and no doubt both his eyes will be black and blue by morning.

I get to my feet, with help from Ring since he has to do so anytime he's around, and I face off with Gunner. The two men standing at my back may be crazy, but I love them more than anything. And unlike Gunner's bodyguards, mine are here to support me, not be watchdogs.

"What do you want?" I cross my arms, glaring up at his ugly mug.

His eyes drop to the floor as he scuffs his boot, pouting like my five-year-old. "I'm sorry for being loud around the kids. It won't happen again."

Gunner jumps a little as Hammer puts a hand on his shoulder and squeezes. "And if it does happen again?"

"If I make one more kid cry before the lockdown is over, I lose my club privileges and pay for three months and will only be allowed back if all the moms agree to it."

"He's already been stripped of his Enforcer title," Hammer adds. "That's now going to Wrecker."

Honestly quite shocked, I look to Whiskey. "Is this for real? Is the title strip really necessary?" I never expected that to happen. Titles mean everything to these men. I can't even imagine what Gunner is feeling. But maybe this is the kick in the pants he needs to straighten his shit out, whatever it is that makes him dislike kids so much.

"It's for real. No bullshit," Whiskey replies as he knocks Gunner upside the head. "Someone's on very thin ice. Either the bullshit stops or he's out on probation and back to Prospect duties. I've had enough of the constant complaining, and he's already had too many chances."

"We're taking him around the room and making him apologize to all the moms one by one," Hammer says with a snarl. "And the punishment starts now, but only if y'all agree that he gets to stay."

"What do you think, love?" Steel wraps his arm around my shoulders. "Are you okay with him staying?"

Looking between Ring and Steel, then over to the bar where Duchess and Angel are huddled together, a baby in each of their arms, I wonder what to do. Both sisters nod at me, seeming to give me their stamp of approval to do what I see is best, and I decide then to give a little bit of my own justice before letting this jerk off the hook for now.

Marching around the couch, I get all up in Gunner's space. I poke him in the chest with my pointer finger, then sock him in the gut for good measure. He coughs once as I stare up at his shocked face. "If my baby girl, or any child here, sheds one more tear because of you, what your Brothers do to you will be circus peanuts for what I have in mind."

"But I—"

"But nothing, Gunner. You made my daughter cry," I snap. "And you called Ring her pseudo dad. That was rude and uncalled for. He stepped up when Steel was gone and took care of her like she's his own. I never heard one peep of you doing anything of the sort. You deserve any punishment they give you."

"He called Ring what?" Steel begins to growl at my side. "Her pseudo dad. Are you fuckin' kiddin' me? I oughta kick your ass for that bullshit, you fucker."

"It's okay, babe. I got this." My eyes are still locked on Gunner. "I'm good with you staying for now, but this is the last warning.

After this, no matter what everyone else decides, I'm done with you. Any more bullshit and you'll no longer be my family."

I turn away, done with him and his bullshit, and immediately see Ring with a very defeated look on his face. Knowing I have one more thing to fix before we can move on from this mess, I grab hold of Ring's hand and pull him away from everyone's prying eyes.

Not worried about Steel, because I know that he knows the two of us need some time alone, I close Ring and myself into the ladies' bathroom . . . the same bathroom where our journey began not so long ago. I lock the door behind us, and as soon as it clicks, I'm wrapped in two muscular arms covered in black cotton and my face is pressed into the leather of his cut.

"Don't listen to a word he said." Sliding my arms around his waist, I hug Ring back as tight as I can. "You are just as much Opal's dad as Steel is. She loves her Papa so much, and so do I. And so do these babies inside me."

Ring's arms are banded around me, his hands gripping my sides. "I love you so much. Please don't ever leave me."

I hear the uncertainty in Ring's voice, and even though I tell him all the time that I'll never leave him, he still has his days of doubt. I can't imagine what it's like to be abandoned like he was, so I decided very early on to show him how much he means to me every day.

Nuzzling deeper into him, all I can do is show my love. "You'll never be alone again, Ryan." I kiss his chest.

Ring's whole body relaxes with a huge sigh. He steps back and places his gentle hands on either side of my face, cupping my cheeks in his palms. "How'd I get so lucky to find you?"

I stretch up on my tiptoes to gently kiss him. "I drove up to the gate and *I* found *you*."

His smile is beautiful and heartbreaking at the same time. "Hold me tight and I'll never let you go again."

"Kiss me like you own me, Ring."

And he does.

CHAPTER ELEVEN

MOUNTAIN

After the earlier excitement, and the stress I'm putting myself under with this mess with Blue, I needed a few minutes to myself. But with a clubhouse bursting at its seams, there's nowhere to go but out.

So here I stand, freezing my nutsack off, hiding out on the front porch, smoking a cigar.

To be honest, I'm out here wallowing in my own self-pity. For the first time in my sixty-one years on this planet, I've lost control of myself. It's no wonder my wife looks at me the way she does. All I've seen in her eyes the last few days is sadness. Maybe that's my sign to rethink where I stand in this family.

Am I too broken?

Now that I only have one leg and can't ride anymore, should I even be in the club?

Do the other members want me gone?

Is my son ashamed of me?

Is Blue ashamed of me?

While she says she still loves me, am I worthy of her love?

Should I make it easier on everyone and just move out?

Would Blue want that?

Do *I* want that?

I'd never force her to leave the life and home she's built here, so if anyone were to go, it'd be me.

Turning my back to the wind, I take one last puff, then smother the butt in the pile of snow covering what I know is a bench. I flick it out into the parking lot, then turn to head inside. But before I take a step, I hear a small mewing sound coming from somewhere behind me.

Turning my old ass around, I look for the source of the noise. And there it goes again.

With just enough light from inside coming through the front windows, I can see a shadow of movement below the snow-covered bench. I take a step closer to investigate, and this time, a loud meow calls out to me.

It's a cat. It looks like the damn thing found a place to hide from the weather, and I came out at just the right time to find it.

Crouching down as much as my titanium leg will allow, I call out to try and coax the feline from its hiding place. "Here, kitty, kitty. I won't hurt ya. How 'bout we get you inside and warmed up?"

I don't know if this thing understands a word I say, but no more than five seconds later, a tiny dark head pops out from under the bench, followed by two paws. Not wanting it to run away, I reach down as quick as I can and lift it up by its scruff.

Meowing in my face like I'm trying to murder it instead of save its life, the tiny furball cries out even louder.

"I got ya little," not sure if it a boy or girl, I stop and reconsider my words, "little one. It's time we go inside."

Not wanting to drop the kitten, I fumble to unzip my Carhartt a few inches and set my new wet best friend inside. Zippering it enough so it can't escape, or scratch my chest to smithereens, I call it a win and head for the front door again. This time, I'm able to open it and feel the heat blast my face before something outside interrupts me again.

Stomping my boots to get the snow off, I call out, "I need a towel, maybe a blanket, and someone find Doc for me."

"What's goin' on, Pops?" Whiskey is standing in the alcove to my left, pool stick in one hand, beer bottle in the other.

"I found us a trespasser." I yank my gloves off with my teeth, shove them in my coat pockets, then pull my zipper open. The kitten's head pops right out, and it lets out a tiny meow as I scratch the back of its neck.

"Oh my gosh, it's a kitten," Duchess exclaims as she rushes to my side.

"Looks like a tiny little thing." Whiskey steps in for a closer look. "Where'd you find it?"

"Under one of the benches," I reply as I see Blue heading my way. She's got a couple large towels in her hands.

"What do we have here?" Blue unzips my coat the rest of the way, and using one of the towels, scoops the kitten into her grasp. Using both of her hands, she surrounds the kitten in the gray cotton, rubbing it dry. When its head reemerges from the fabric, all of the slicked down hair I saw before is poofed straight up. It looks like a whole new animal.

"Someone rang for me?" I turn to see Doc walking over.

"Mountain found this baby outside." Blue hands the kitten, towel and all, to Doc. "I know you're not an animal doctor, but can you just give it a onceover? Maybe tell us if it's a he or she so we can stop calling it an *it*?"

My wife's wit makes me and several others laugh.

"I'll see what I can do," Doc replies with a chuckle. Kicking Buzz and Cypher off one of the couches, Doc sits and unwraps the bundle. "Let's see here." He lifts the gray fur monster to eye level and peeks between its legs. "Alright, Mountain, your new admirer is a girl."

Hanging my coat on a hook by the door, I make my way over and plop my tired ass on the couch next to him. "Is she gonna be alright?"

Doc sets her on his lap and runs his hands along her body, feeling her legs, lifting to look at her paws, then lifting her tail to check who knows what. "I don't see anything physically wrong with her, but I guess only time will tell. We've got no clue where she came from or how long she was out in the cold."

"What can we do to help her?" Duchess asks. She's camped herself on the arm of the couch beside me.

"I suggest giving her some food to try. Oh, and some water too. Who knows when she last ate or drank anything."

"Like what? We don't have any cat food here?" I ask, reaching out a hand to pet the kitten who's now walking in circles on Doc's lap.

"Take some of the shredded chicken and venison we have left over from last night and mix in some scrambled eggs." Doc hands the kitten to me, then gets up to follow Duchess into the kitchen. "But make sure to mash everything into really small pieces. And rinse all the seasonings off. Too much salt is bad for their digestion."

Lifting its two front paws onto my chest, the kitten attempts to climb. Placing one hand under its backside, I give her a boost. I lean back against the couch cushion, and she comes to rest with her head between her paws, looking straight up at me.

Listening to her soft meows, I can't help but like her already.

"What's that, Grandpops?" Opal climbs up next to me and sees what I have. "It's a kitty cat. Oh my gosh, can I play with her?"

"You can pet her, but be gentle." Opal reaches over and strokes the kitten's back, causing it to purr. I even feel the rumble on my chest. "She likes you, munchkin."

"I like her too. Can we keep her?"

"Oh, I don't know about that." It's barely been fifteen minutes since I found her, and keeping her hasn't even crossed my mind.

"But please, Grandpops," Opal begs, pouty lip and all. "I'll help you take good cares of her."

"How about we let the kitten eat some dinner first before we decide what to do next?" Blue reappears in front of me, saving me from giving my granddaughter anything she wants.

"Okay," Opal draws out with a whine.

Doc lays a new clean towel out on the coffee table, and Blue sets a small plate of food and a bowl of water on it. I recognize the bowl as the water dish Teddy used when he was a puppy. That white furball grew so fast, and now is a barking cloud, but it's good to know his puppy things are good for something.

Scooting forward, I place the kitten on the towel, and she goes straight for the water. It doesn't take her long to dive into the food, then she's right back finishing all the water.

"Looks like someone was hungry, huh?" I scratch the side of her neck as she burrows into my hand.

"I'll go dig through the pantry to find a box of some sort so she can use the bathroom," Doc suggests as he stands watch. "While we're all stuck here, we might as well make her feel at home too." And he walks off.

The little daredevil crouches down, then leaps into my lap. She spins herself in a circle a few times, then curls into a gray-colored ball on my lap. Her eyes blink up at me a few times, then she meows one time.

"Oh, sorry." I chuckle as I start petting her. "You're a little diva, aren't you?"

"Looks like you found yourself a new partner in crime, Pops." Whiskey claps me on the shoulder, then rubs her head with a finger.

Her tiny purrs sure know how to hit a guy right in the feels. Damn, this isn't how I saw my day ending. What a turn of events.

I went outside hoping to sort through some of my troubles, and I came back in with a four-legged friend. Things could be worse. It could've been a skunk hiding under that bench. Now, that would've made my whole fucking week.

As the spectators grow bored of the sleeping kitten, I look around the room for Blue. I find her right away, camped out in a chair at the end of one of the dining tables. She has Taren in her lap, and he's paging through a book, pointing to whatever is on the pages. Every so often, he looks up at her as if he's making sure she's still there watching him.

I totally understand his being enamored with her. Blue is beautiful. She's everything. And just like that, the burned-out lightbulb that's been floating over my head for days pops back on.

Blue is my everything. I could never leave her. I could never leave this place and try to live a life without her. She's my rock, and I need to get my shit straight . . . and fast.

As if she feels my gaze on her, Blue lifts her head and looks right at me.

Needing her to know I'm thinking of her, I toss her a wink and nod my head her way.

And like a schoolgirl caught sneaking glances at her crush, Blue's cheeks grow a rosy shade of red as she blushes. She ducks her head back down when Taren calls for her attention, but with one last peek, her eyes meet mine before returning her attention to the boy.

What a lucky little man.

CHAPTER TWELVE

BUZZ

I have to be quite honest, when I heard snowstorm lockdown, I got excited. The majority of my Brothers and their families are going bat shit crazy being stuck inside the clubhouse, with nowhere to go and no real end in sight, but I like it.

Growing up in the Rebel Vipers MC was the best. I got my first dirt bike at the age of ten, I kissed my first girl at twelve, got my driver's license the day I turned sixteen, and slept with my first club girl at seventeen. And as it turns out, I met the love of my life at the age of twenty-nine.

Regardless of the fact that my parents and I didn't live on the compound like most of the other families, I never felt excluded. I got to see my friends every day, and even though I was an only child, I never felt alone a day in my life.

Like right now, for instance.

The clubhouse is full of activity and everyone is looking for something to do to fill their time, but what I'm doing right now beats anything I could ever come up with. I'm lounging back on a couch in the main room, holding my pregnant Old Lady in my arms. If I don't have to move, this couch is going to have an imprint of my ass on it here soon.

Star is engrossed in a book about what to expect when you're expecting, oblivious of the ruckus around her, and I'm trying like hell not to make it too obvious that I'm reading right along with her. If my Brothers knew how scared I was to become a dad, they'd probably call me a pansy-ass . . . then kick my ass.

While I've seen lots of my Brothers become dads, several of them in very recent times, I'm still scared shitless. I've never changed a baby's diaper. I've never heated up a bottle. I don't know what it means when a woman leaks milk out of her knockers.

I'm clueless.

Tucking her shoulder-length, almost white, blonde hair over one shoulder, Star turns her emerald-green eyes back at me. The smirk on her lips and the sparkle in her eyes tell me I've been caught red-handed.

Shifting in my arms, her back rubs against my chest and she lifts her lips to kiss my stubbled cheek. "Are you done pretending you're not reading this book too?"

"I have no idea what you're talkin' about," I reply before dropping a kiss on her temple. But I know I'm not fooling her. She reads me way too well sometimes.

"Okay, whatever you say, mister tough guy." Snuggling back into my chest, Star's nose is back in the book in seconds. But this time, she pulls my left hand into hers and sprawls it across the front of her belly.

At four months along, her bump is tiny but noticeable, and I can't help but fall a little more in love with her every day it grows. Just thinking about the day she told me she was carrying my baby, makes me wish I could experience it all over again.

MIDDLE OF OCTOBER – TWO MONTHS AGO

Flipping through a tattoo magazine, I'm drawn away from a killer black and gray image of a pin-up girl on some dude's bicep when there's a knock on my bedroom door. Tossing down the magazine, I get out of bed and check to see who's knocking.

When I came up about an hour ago, most of the club was in the main room, hanging out and having a relaxing evening. While it may be the weekend, with the craziness that's been happening around here lately, things have been calming down earlier than usual. No wild and crazy parties here tonight.

Opening the door, I'm met by the prettiest thing on two very long, very inappropriately dressed for the hallway legs. Grabbing Stiletto's hand, I yank her into my room, shut the door, and back her up against it.

Stepping forward so there's not a centimeter between us, I press my lips to hers and flick my tongue against her still closed lips.

Her hands find my chest, and I feel a little pressure as she tries to push me back, but I don't let her. I frame her face with my hands and hold her head in place as I coax her to open to me. And the second she does, I dive in for more.

For who knows how long, I stand there, holding this woman to me, breathing in every breath she lets out. I consume each and every moan and gasp, locking them into my memory so I have them for days and months and years to come.

After countless minutes, I slow down my attack. My kisses move from her lips to her cheek, then finally to the spot on the side of her neck that I know drives her wild.

"Buzz," she moans, pressing on my chest again. "I need . . . we need . . . to talk."

Getting one last nip in, I finally let her have some space. Not much space, just a few inches, but enough to where I can see her face. That's when I notice, in addition to the plump lips and flushed cheeks I just gave her, Stiletto's eyes are bloodshot. It looks like she's been crying.

Instinct of never wanting to see a sad woman, I pull her over to my bed and sit her next to me. I hold her hands in mine. "What's wrong?"

"Umm . . . I'm not exactly sure how to say this," she replies after a few seconds. She's looking down at our hands, fiddling my fingers with hers.

Now, while I may have not yet claimed this woman yet, the two of us have had a few conversations about making her mine permanently, so I'm not sure why she's so unsure of telling me anything. Whatever she has to say, I'm all ears. I may still be working out a plan in my head of how to go about announcing our relationship to the club the right way, but once I have all my ducks in a row, she'll be mine for real.

I'm sick of this pretending we're not a couple business. I'm over the sneaking around and watching her talking to my Brothers just to hold off any suspicion that things are different. It's been a few months since we agreed to give this thing between us a real try, and I'm ready for more.

"Whatever it is, I'm sure it's not worth these tears." Using my thumb, I swipe one lone tear rolling down her cheek.

Her eyes finally meet mine, and my world changes in an instant. "I'm two months late."

"Two months?" It takes a second to sink in, but when it does, I snap to attention. "You're pregnant?"

Stiletto wipes the back of her long sleeve t-shirt cuff-covered hand under her nose, and along with a sniffle, she nods. "Yes."

Her one word sounds so small and so worried, I can't help but pull her into me. I slide my hands under her butt cheeks and lift her whole body into my lap. When I have her sitting on my right thigh, with her long legs draped over my left, I place my right hand on her lower back and slide my left under the cotton of her shirt to lay it flat on her stomach.

"So, you're tellin' me," using my thumb, I rub up and down, "that my baby is right here? Right inside your belly?"

"Yes."

Still with the one-word answers, I need to get more information out of her. "Holy shit, that's amazing." I press a quick kiss to her lips, then start asking questions. "When? How? I thought we were always careful. Not that I'm not happy, because I am, I'm just a little surprised is all."

The shock that blossoms across her face is instant. "You're happy?"

"Of course, I am!" I exclaim, holding this precious life, both precious lives, in my hands is a bit astonishing but still a very good thing. "Why wouldn't I be?"

"Because we didn't plan this," she begins to explain. "We just started whatever this is between us. No one knows about us yet. And craziest of all, I'm only twenty-three, for Pete's sake. Am I ready to become a mother? I barely have *my* life figured out. How can I do this? I don't know if I *should* be doing this."

"Hey, now, none of that." I try not to sound like I'm scolding her, but her words are just plain wrong. "It doesn't matter how old you are. Shit, it doesn't matter that I'm ten years older than you. None of that stuff matters. All that matters is that it's gonna be me and you and this baby, and we're gonna be a family. That's all that's important. The rest we can figure out as time goes on."

"But what about my going to school? I still need to graduate next spring." Now, her questions aren't really aimed toward me. They're more her shooting out whatever is jumbled up in her mind, needing a safe space to get it all out. "And what about me getting a job? No one is gonna hire a pregnant woman."

"Love, it's okay," I softly reply, trying to pull her down to Earth. "One day at a time, okay? But first, can you tell me when this happened? Then we can look at a calendar and see how your schooling fits in."

"I think it happened when we were in Sturgis."

Oh! Oh yeah. That was a good trip . . . until all hell broke loose and we had to build a plan of attack to rescue Angel from that psycho Cartel reject. But the couple of nights I was able to pretend Stiletto was all mine were the best.

"So, you're sayin' I made you mine right about the same time I *really* made you mine?"

Chuckling at my wiggly eyebrows, the happiness I'm used to seeing on her face comes back full force. "I guess you could say that."

Lifting her by her hips, I set Stiletto back on the bed and hop to my feet. Resting my hands on my boxer-covered hips, I stand tall and tell her what's what. "That's it. You're mine. I'm makin' you my Old Lady right damn now."

"But—" She tries to interrupt, but I keep going.

"I don't care what anyone says. You've been mine for a couple months now, and I'm done pretending."

"No, Buzz," she protests as she gets to her feet in front of me. "We don't have to do that. I'll leave and we can figure out a plan to co-parent. We don't have to rock the boat if you don't want to."

"I'll rock the damn boat and sink it if I have to." Setting my hands on her shoulders, we lock eyes. "I told you two months ago when we agreed to be exclusive that I wanted to find a way to make us work. It's been workin', right? Us being together?"

Panic kicks in for the first time. What if this really isn't what she wants? What if she wants to leave? Then what do I do?

"It's been working, kinda."

Needing more, I ask, "Do you want us to be together?"

"But what about—"

"No buts, Amber." Up until now, I have never said her real name out loud, but I can't use her club girl name anymore. It's not right. She's more than that. She's more than club property. Amber is mine.

"You said my name." And here come the tears again.

Cradling her face in my palms, I kiss her forehead, then press mine to hers. Eyes closed, I give her my truth. "Tell me what you really want. I need to know, because I need you. Only you."

"I want to raise this baby with you more than anything." Her words are softer than a whisper. "I never planned on being an Old Lady, but if that's what you want, I want it too."

Closing in that last breath, I kiss my woman. No tongue. No aggression. Just the meeting of lips. The joining of wandering souls. The beginning of something new.

After we came back up for air, I loaned Amber a pair of my too large for her sweatpants to cover her exposed legs—because she's mine now and no one else gets to see that much of her skin—and practically dragged her downstairs. Asking Whiskey for a few moments of his time in privacy, the three of us sat in his office as I finally spilled the beans to him.

I told my childhood friend I was going to be a father in a few months. I informed my President that I was claiming this woman. And I let the woman sitting beside me know she no longer was going to belong to anyone but me.

Whiskey was very surprised at first, but I think it was more due to the fact that he hadn't seen this coming. He's usually a very intuitive man, and we caught him totally unaware.

He told us he was very happy for us, and if this is where life has brought us in our journey, he would be right there to support us.

I asked that he put in an order for an Old Lady cut, and while I sent her to her room under the guise of packing all her stuff to move into my room, I told Whiskey the new name I was giving her.

Inquiring about getting her a skeleton key necklace like the other Old Ladies have, Whiskey gave me a business card with the jeweler's information and sent me on my way.

Two days later, I draped said necklace around her neck as she cried happy tears.

The following weekend was when we shared our big news with the club.

When Sunshine announced that morning that she was having twins and was going to be surprising Ring and Steel with the bombshell, I was a little worried our news was going to come across like we were trying to steal their spotlight. But that's the exact opposite of what happened.

I told everyone I had an announcement, shocked everyone saying I was claiming an Old Lady, then pulled said lady in for a kiss that made me dizzy.

Cuddled into my arms, Star said the best words I've ever heard in front of our family for the first time. "And we're having a baby."

We were immediately bombarded with congratulations. Duchess practically threw Krew into Gunner's arms just to be the first to get to us. "Oh my gosh! This day just keeps getting better!" She pulled us in for one of her infamous hugs, and I knew from that moment on, everything was going to be okay.

Leaning my shoulders back into the cushions, I tug Star even closer to me. Sprawled out on the couch like this is the most relaxed I've been in months, maybe even ever. Add in that my woman is practically in my lap, and I'm in heaven.

I may not have planned on claiming a club girl as my Old Lady, but when the universe decides its plan for you, sometimes you just need to find your star, grab on tight, and never let go.

CHAPTER THIRTEEN

BLUE

What a way to kick off the first day of December. Here we are on day three of what the Brothers have dubbed 'Snowmageddon' and we're all still stuck inside. Luckily, the storm seems to be lessening, according to the weather report, but the wind is still nasty and blowing like crazy. The snowdrifts across the parking lot make the normally flat surface look like a mountain range.

After helping cook everyone a huge breakfast, I'm sitting with a lot of the other women, hunkered down around the two large dining tables.

There's actually an imaginary line dividing the main room in two. The Brothers have congregated on the east half. They're playing pool, have a couple games of poker going, and have every bar stool claimed. Us women have taken over the west side for wedding detail organization.

I'm currently camped out at the end of the table, feet propped up on the seat next to me, and I have the kitten on my chest. I seem to have found a new friend who won't leave my side.

Despite the kitten only wanting Mountain yesterday after he found her, since we woke up this morning, I've had a tiny four-pawed shadow. In fact, I woke up with a face full of gray fur because the tiny thing somehow managed to get out of her box, up onto our bed, and then snuggled herself beside my head on the pillow.

When Mountain rolled over and tried to coax her toward him with promises of scratches and attention, I swear she rolled her eyes as she meowed at him before nuzzling deeper into my shoulder. She then proceeded to follow me into the bathroom, into the closet while I got dressed, then chased me out the door when I tried to slip out without her.

After almost getting herself stepped on because she was under my feet every time I turned around in the kitchen, I plopped her tiny self in a box with a roll of paper towels to keep her occupied. By the time she had the whole thing shredded to smithereens, it was time to eat.

So now, here we sit, and I have the kitten inside my sweatshirt, her head poking out the zipper mid chest.

When Opal had finished her pancakes, she climbed on my lap and asked what we were going to name the kitty. I then had to break her heart and tell her that Mountain said we weren't keeping her. We can't give her a name because he says once the storm is clear, we need to take her to the humane society. Mountain is worried that the cat may belong to somebody, and he doesn't want to steal it.

Opal was sad at the news, but she seemed to be okay when I told her we're just taking care of the kitten until she can go back to her home. I told her that if Teddy were to get lost, and someone found him and took care of him, we'd want them to bring him back home. She understood that, saying that Teddy better not get lost because she'd get tired if she had to search for him forever, then she ran off to play with him.

If I have to say one good thing about the kitten on my chest, it's that the women around me aren't asking me to 'come look at this' or 'what do you think of that' or my least favorite 'what would you have picked if this was your wedding'.

I'm so happy and excited for every one of the four brides here, because God knows I love all of them to pieces, but if I have to look at one more flower, or one more napkin color, or one more shade of white or ivory or cream, I'm going to snap and scream at everyone in this room.

I'm happy they're all in love.

I'm happy they're all getting married.

I'm happy they're all getting everything they want . . . but I'm anything but happy myself.

It's none of their faults. Quite honestly, it's mine. But that still doesn't tell my heart to not hurt when I look back and wish I had everything they do. That's not to say any of them wouldn't throw it all in the trash and rush to the courthouse to marry their soon-to-be husbands, because they would, it's just I'm being petty and jealous, yet can't and wouldn't ever show it.

So, while I'd rather be in my room, hiding under the covers in my bed, crying and eating a pint of chocolate chip cookie dough ice cream, instead I'm trying to stay strong, at least on the outside, and be supportive of the women around me.

Angel, thanks to her amazing organizational skills, has a binder in front of her with all the final wedding details that she, Duchess, Sunshine, and Star have all agreed on. In that binder is a list for each of them, so once they can go out and finally shop for stuff, everyone can get what they need. The decisions have all been made, are unanimous all around, and just need the weather to clear to get the wheels of this wedding train rolling.

If there is one thing to be extremely thankful for, it's Black Friday sales. Once the announcement was made to the club on Thanksgiving, they had the all-clear to start planning. The ladies were so excited to have a date set, they went out together and were lucky enough to find something they each loved at one store, and all for a really great deal.

Zoning out all the goings on around me, I let the sounds fade off to a distant hum. The clubhouse is loud, but not annoyingly so, so I again stare out the windows at my snow globe.

I'm snapped out of my reverie when someone lifts my feet, dropping into the chair they were on, then laying my legs across their lap. It's Mountain.

Hands resting atop my shins, he leans in. "How you doin' over here?" he asks softly, keeping his question between the two of us. "You look a little spaced-out. Are you okay dealing with all this wedding stuff floatin' around?"

"I'm doing alright," I reply with a shrug, "but I can't lie and say it doesn't sting a little."

"I'm sorry," Mountain responds with remorse.

"It's okay." I look down at my companion, and like she can sense I'm sad, she rubs her cheek against mine. "I just need to put on a brave face for everyone else. I'll be fine once all the planning dies down. Once they move on to the set-up in a few weeks, I'll be better."

Crouching down a bit, he puts himself in my view. "You don't have to be brave for me. We can talk if you want."

"Mountain, I—"

"I know." Sitting back, he folds his arms over his chest, letting out a big sigh. "You're not ready."

Feeling a little frustration bubble up, I snip at him. "Are you ready to duke this out?"

That really deflates him. His shoulders slump as his sad eyes meet mine again. "Not really."

"Look, I know we need to talk, and I've already said I will when I'm ready, but right now, I don't know where to start." Trying to explain this is like what I'd imagine walking through wet cement with bowling balls chained to your feet would be like—you get nowhere fast but still want to turn back and hide. "I don't know what to say to you that won't cause a big fight, and I don't want that."

Mountain looks stunned at my admission. All at once, he sits up straight, his eyes get wider, and lets out a small gasp. "Are you saying you don't wanna sort this out?"

"I'm saying I just don't know." I know it's a vague answer, but that's all I can give him right now. Feeling tears begin to well up in the corner of my eyes, I don't know what to do.

"Oh, okay then." I can see the defeat he's feeling, then he stands up, setting my feet back on the chair he's vacated. "I guess I'll leave you be then." Pressing one small kiss to the top of my head, Mountain squeezes my shoulder once and walks away.

A little taken aback at his abrupt exit, but totally understanding the confusion of all the back-and-forth emotions we've been throwing at each other lately, I mostly don't blame him for walking away.

Maybe this is bugging him just as much as it is me, because I've never seen him like this.

But the biggest question is, now what?

One worry begins to wiggle its way into my thoughts, and it's a worry I hadn't ever had until just now. What if we don't ever come back from this? Then what will I do?

CHAPTER FOURTEEN

MOUNTAIN

The cheers that erupted through the clubhouse yesterday morning when all the lights came back on was almost eardrum shattering. We were there for the fourth day in a row, all sitting around the main room, now growing very sick of playing pool, card games, and listening to each other talk, when the television magically turned itself back on.

Hammer jumped out of his chair and practically ran across the room for the long strip of light switches by the front door. Using his giant hands, he flipped all of them on at once and the room lit up. We've been able to have some lights on because of the generator, but the contrast from half to full brightness made me realize we were practically living in darkness.

The storm had cleared by the time we all woke up, but until the roads could be plowed and the electric company made it out to us, the power wasn't back on to the cabins until midafternoon.

Having power again means all the families can go back in their cabins, and everyone else can have their rooms to themselves, but no one is moving out just yet. Whiskey and Hammer said they weren't taking the women and kids back out until the furnaces have warmed the cabins up, and they want to make sure no problems pop up as everything defrosts. We don't need to move everyone in, then have to move them back out if a water pipe bursts when things thaw out. Ring, Steel, and Butch all agreed, so it's now another waiting game.

It's now day five, or day one of life back to semi-normal. The parking lot is plowed clean and all club businesses are back up and running. Rebel Repairs has only had a handful of customers trickle in, a few to get their vehicle's regular tires swapped for snow tires, but the busiest part is the last-minute bike drop-offs. The early snow surprised lots of riders and forced many to bring their beloved motorcycles in earlier than anticipated, our club members included.

Bright and early this morning, before the 'OPEN' sign could be turned around, all my Brothers had to roll their Harleys from the garage and into the heated storage unit we have out behind the shop.

As another way to make money for the club's coffers, we rent out spaces for people to store their bikes for the winter. The large pole barn has room for hundreds of motorcycles, and the spaces sell out fast. In fact, most of our customers are repeats from year to year. Our reputation of keeping things dry, warm, and clean, combined with the fact that our rates are half of what other places charge, we make a ton of money based on volume alone.

I'm in my room, getting ready to head out, when there's a knock on the door followed by a voice booming out. "You about ready to go?"

"Almost. You wanna see me in my skivvies?" I call out to Butch with a chuckle.

"No, thanks," he replies with a laugh. "I don't need to see your tighty-whities."

Getting dressed these days takes a hell of a lot longer than it used to. Having a reason to pay attention to putting your pants and boots on, rather than just jumping into whatever you find laying around, actually takes time.

My new way of getting dressed may not be the way some other prosthetic leg wearers do it, but my physical therapist said there's no 'best way' when it comes to people in my situation.

My lower leg amputation has me wearing what is called a 'below the knee' or transtibial prosthesis. In my three months of living in the rehabilitation center, where I healed from my surgery and basically had to learn to walk again, I got a crash course on my new way of starting and ending my days.

First step is to slide on the silicone liner. Turning it inside out, I roll the liner up my limb all the way to the top of my thigh. Then, while still sitting and bending my knee at a forty-five-degree angle, I insert my leg into the socket of the prosthesis and gently stand.

After setting it into place with my upper body pressure and making sure nothing feels uncomfortable, I slide the outer sleeve of the prothesis up and over the socket, securing everything in place. The top of the sleeve covers the liner as well, the edge resting just below my groin.

Part of what makes my routine different from some others is that I slide my jeans on my legs before I put the prosthesis on. Leaving them bundled down at my ankles, the real and fake ones, I then prep my leg, before pulling up my pants. While some others put their leg on, then pants, then their shoes, I like having my boots on before securing my prosthesis.

After taking a little extra time swapping my normal riding boots for ones with a better tread, I pull up my jeans, and button and zip myself in. I drop my wallet in my back pocket, secure my gun in my shoulder holster, slide my cut on over my sweatshirt, then grab my phone from the charger.

"Let me grab the furball, then we're outta here," I say to Butch as I slide my coat on.

I lift the kitten from the box it's been camped out in for the last hour, wrap her in a fleece blanket, then with one last look around the room to make sure nothing is out of place, we walk out the door. I'm not sure where Blue is right now, since she ducked out of the room just as I was getting out of the shower, so I don't lock it.

Butch and I climb in my pickup and head for town. With the roads finally clear, life seems to have picked up right where it left off. People are out in droves today, seemingly going on about their day like we weren't all just in hibernation for four days.

Our trip out today has two goals, and to save time, we split up the responsibilities.

Stop one on our shopping trip is at a strip mall on the far end of Tellison. After driving through town, I drop Butch off at the front doors of the hardware store so he can get all the supplies needed for the project we have planned.

Late last night, Butch approached me with the idea to make something special for the couples as a wedding gift. Based on a ripped-out magazine picture he snagged from the wedding planning binder Angel put together, he drew up a design we both think everyone will love.

As I pull away, with every intention of driving through the parking lot and over to the humane society across the street, I end up stopping just a few storefronts down. A bright red and green flashing neon sign catches my eye, and I have an immediate change of heart.

Looking down at the bundle in my lap, the kitten picks the perfect moment to lay the softest meow on me, swaying the decision I had set in my mind. It wasn't the easiest decision to make, and I went back and forth plenty of times, but up until this moment, I had my mind made up.

Fuck, I'm keeping the cat.

Swinging the truck into the first spot I find, I tuck the kitten, blanket and all, into my coat. Making sure to cover her head, I slide out and make my way into the pet store.

A blast of warm air hits me as the sliding doors open, so I lift the edge of the blanket, and the kitten pops her head out.

"Oh my gosh! Isn't that the cutest thing!" I look to my left to see a small pint-sized teenager heading my way. "Can I help you find something?"

"Well, to be honest," I start as I pet the kitten's head, "I need everything. I just got this little lady, and I'm not sure where to even start."

"That's all right. Let me grab you a cart and we'll head over to show you what we have. I'll tell you the different options of different brands, and you can pick out what you like best."

Forty-five minutes and a receipt longer than my arm later, I'm loading the backseat of my truck with way too many boxes and bags. Pulling one package from a bag before shutting the door, I take the cart back into the store, then I climb into the driver's seat and open up the package.

When the super helpful young lady asked if I had a name for the "cutie", as she called her, I remembered back to a thought I had the day she showed up. Turns out the name was there all along. I named her Diva.

A jingling sound rattles, drawing the kitten's attention to what I have in my hand. "Since you seem to have conned me into taking you back home, you need a collar, little missy." I clip it around her neck, and she shakes her whole body before laying on the center counsel like it's no big deal. The store has a metal tag engraving machine, so in addition to the black collar with fake sparkly diamonds on it, the jingling is coming from a light blue tag donning Diva's name.

And boy is she ever a diva. She has me wrapped tight around her paw. I bought every single cat toy and supply known to man. I even got her one of those climbing towers that has the built-in scratching posts and cubbies she can crawl into. It looks like a bitch to build, but when the lady pointed to the display options on the top shelf, I had to get the biggest one they had.

Just as I put the truck in drive, the music cuts out and my phone starts ringing through the speakers. Hitting the green button on the steering wheel, I answer. "You almost done playing with your wood?"

"Ha ha, very funny, asshole," Butch's voice booms through. "I'm standin' outside the store and it's colder than a witch's tit. Where you at?"

"I'm right here, asshole," I sling his insult back as I roll up in front of him. Hanging up the call, I throw the shifter into park and unlock the doors.

"Damn, that was fast," Butch says after opening the back door. I watch as he turns back, his hands full of plastic bags, to see the bags already filling the seats, and his jaw drops. "What the hell's all this?" Just then, Diva decides to meow louder than I've heard yet. Eyes popped, Butch shakes his head. "Did you do what I think you did?"

Shrugging, I reply, "If you think I kept the furball, you're damn right, I did."

"I thought you were gonna drop the thing off and run," he continues as he moves bags around to add his to the vastly growing pile.

"That was the plan 'til I saw the pet store four fuckin' doors down and she meowed and gave me the saddest damned eyes. I caved."

"I can't wait to hear what kinda shit the Brothers give you," he says as he laughs.

"Hey!" I try to come up with something to defend myself. Oh, I got it. "At least Opal will be happy. I overheard her and Blue talking and she was sad we weren't keeping it."

"Suuuuure," he draws out before throwing out one more jab, "keepin' it for the grandkid. If that's what you gotta tell yourself."

Just now seeing the pile of lumber Butch also has on a platform cart, I decide to get out and help him load it all in the truck bed.

And sure as shit, when we get back to the clubhouse, as soon as I walk in the front door with my arms weighed down with shopping bags and the kitten still in my coat, all my Brothers in the main room give me hell.

"Got rid of the kitten, I see," Steel snickers as he approaches. "Welcome to the pet owners club."

"I knew you weren't gonna get rid of it." Doc approaches and rubs Diva between her ears, causing her to purr and rattle against my chest.

"Yea, yea, get all your jabs in now, fuckers." I head for the dining area and deposit all my purchases on the first table. "You try and look at this face and say no when she purrs at you. I don't fuckin' think so."

Arms finally free, I unzip my coat and Diva jumps to the floor and takes off running through the crowd. Looking in the direction she went, I spot her through the bodies as Blue scoops her up.

Lifting her to her smiling face, she inspects the kitten's newest accessory. I may not be able to hear her from here, but I can see Blue's lips moving as she reads the tag.

"Well, Mountain, look at you." Bear appears at my side and throws a fake punch, hitting me in the bicep. "You found another pussy on the front porch and decided to keep her. At least you didn't try and shut the door on this one's face like you did to Blue."

That sure gets everyone laughing, myself included. It may sound a little bit harsh, but when you get down to it, it's the truth.

Looking for Blue again, I find her right where she was before, except this time when I see her, she's not smiling. Blue's now expressionless look pulls me back down to the reality of my current situation. I may have been the one to rescue the kitten, but clearly, she's chosen who her favorite person is . . . and it's not me. I guess the two of them have one thing in common—liking each other more than they like me.

After our talk two days ago, I felt defeated. I could see from the stiffness in her shoulders, and from the way she was keeping herself back for the rest of the ladies, that Blue was having a rough time with all the wedding planning swirling around her. I knew she was trying to stay strong but was also occasionally zoning herself out to avoid any questions. So, when I finished the round of poker I was playing, I ducked out and headed for her side.

As quietly as I could, I asked if she wanted to talk but was thrown for a loop when Blue pushed back. She threw a question back, confronting me about whether I was really up for a fight. I had to man up and admit that I wasn't.

My wife has always had this boldness about her, and while that has made me proud of her for being strong, I have to acknowledge the truth in that it still stung to be put in my place by her.

Because we all know pride can be a fickle thing, I let my fear take over. Not wanting to admit defeat, or that as a man I was losing, I pushed again to try and win. I questioned her once more, but all she said was "I don't know," causing the crack in my heart to split just a little more.

It hurt too much, and I needed to walk away.

Karma is kicking my ass, because watching Blue walk away from me now without even a nod hello, or being her normal inquisitive self to question why I brought the kitten back, she did to me exactly what I did to her when she was hurting.

She disappears down the hall and the splinter grows again.

CHAPTER FIFTEEN

ANGEL

A day in the life of a mother of two boys can be summed up in five simple words . . . I need a damn break. Hammer, the boys, and I have been back in our cabin for seven days now, but neither Taren nor Ace will sleep in their own rooms anymore.

Just before the storm hit, I had transitioned Ace from the bassinet in mine and Hammer's room to the crib in the nursery across the hall. He slept two nights in there before we were all confined to one room in the clubhouse, and since I couldn't bring his whole room with us, he went back to the bassinet.

Now, every night since being back home, any time I lay him down in the crib, all Ace does is scream bloody murder. I've tried swaddling, no swaddling, rocking him to sleep before laying him down, putting him down and hoping he'll cry himself to sleep, anything and everything every book or blog I could read says to do, but nothing is working.

And I'm exhausted.

Add a cranky toddler who gets no sleep because his baby brother is howling like a tiny banshee, and I need some "me" time.

It's a little after ten on Saturday morning, and Hammer is currently free of club and Rebel Repairs duties, so I'm leaving him with nap and lunch duty so I can spend some time with my sister. When I called Duchess ten minutes ago with the hope that she could go get some coffee with me, she answered her phone, then proceeded to switch to a video chat, and I knew where she was immediately. My big sister had beat me to the punch and wasn't with her kid or Old Man either.

Walking through the back door of The Cake Butcher, Duchess's bakery, I make a beeline for her office door. It's opened a crack, so I push my way in, then flop my tired backside in the first chair I come to.

"You know, I should be very mad at you right now." I spin myself and kick my feet up on the chair beside me.

Duchess stops typing on her laptop and stares up at me overtop the screen. "And why is that?"

I fold my arms and pout, no shame in my game. "Because you left the clubhouse without asking me to go with you."

A few more clicks and she leans back. "I didn't know you needed to spend the day with me at work. I'm catching up on payroll stuff for taxes. Wanna help?"

"No, thanks." I can't help but be sassy, so I stick my tongue out at her. "As loud as it's been lately, I'm surprised you haven't heard the screaming coming from my cabin at all hours of the night. I don't know who cries more often, me or Ace."

"He still not wanting to stay in his crib?" Her question is met with a sad face. Knowing the mess she and Whiskey went through getting Krew on a livable sleep schedule, I know she feels my pain.

"Nope." Laying my head back, I close my eyes. "I didn't know I could be so tired and somehow still be awake enough to function. Between a toddler and a baby and a sex-crazed Old Man, my gas tank is on empty."

"Have you had any coffee yet?" I hear Duchess's chair squeak, so I know she's headed to get us some caffeine.

"I was hoping you'd have coffee with me when I called you." Sitting up, I spin my chair to follow her around her desk. "That's why I drove straight here. I need mommy go-go juice."

"Let me go make us some cappuccinos. I'll be right back." Duchess disappears from sight, so I lounge back and return to inspecting the inside of my eyelids.

A few minutes later, she returns, and I don't move a muscle except to hold my hand out for the insulated cardboard cup of deliciousness. I feel the cup brush against my fingers, so I latch on, but get no further before my stomach and head both decide now is the time to start disagreeing. I instantly feel like I'm going to throw up what I ate for breakfast. A toaster waffle definitely doesn't sound as good the second time around as it did the first.

Head still spinning, I sit up slowly. "Whoa. How'd it get hot in here so fast?"

After one more whiff of whatever is in the cup, I set the cup on the desk, slap my hand over my mouth, and run for the door. Luckily, the bathrooms are right across the hall, because I'm no more kneeling on the floor before those waffles reappear.

I heave up everything from the last twelve hours before finally feeling my stomach settle. Two minutes of resting my forehead on the tile wall beside me and I'm back to one hundred percent. That's so weird. I may have been sick my fair share of times growing up, and had a few occasional drunken-induced trips to the porcelain throne, but I've never felt anything like this before.

Washing my hands, then rinsing out my mouth, I head back for the office. Sitting back down, I don't get a word out before Duchess chucks something at me, and I fumble to catch it as it bounces off my chest.

"What the hell?"

"Get your boney butt up and go pee on that."

Not knowing what she's talking about, I finally look down at what's in my hands and almost drop it again. It's a box . . . with four big bold letters on it . . . EDPT. Early Detection Pregnancy Test. What the hell?

"What the hell is this?"

Crossing her arms, Duchess raises an eyebrow, looking at me like I'm the dumb one. "What does it look like?"

"Why do I need a pregnancy test? I just have a bug or something."

"A bug, my ass," she says as she laughs at me. "I could recognize your symptoms if I was on the space station. Sister dear, you've got a Hammer bun in your oven."

"No, I don't." Looking down at the box with pink and blue letters again, I start to think. "At least, I don't think I do."

"When's the last time you had your shark week?"

Thinking back, I draw a blank. "Shit, I don't remember."

When I came back to the clubhouse after being abducted, I went to go see my OB/GYN the first chance I got. Having had a miscarriage while all on my own, I was afraid of something being wrong with me. I bled for days in that motel bathroom, then one day, it just stopped.

My doctor suggested I start taking the birth control pill to help re-regulate my cycle, since a miscarriage can send some women's bodies out of whack. Then, once Hammer and I were back together and sexually active on a routine basis, we agreed that me staying on the pill was what was best for us for now.

But then, the boys arrived in our lives, and I guess I might not have been as diligent about taking it as I should have. When you don't wake up at the same time in the morning anymore, one tiny pill can be easy to forget.

"Go pee on the stick and then you'll know either way." Duchess reaches forward and takes away the cup with the offending smell. "More caramel yumminess for me. Now, shoo," she says, waving me away.

No one tells you how hard it is to go to the bathroom on command, so I sit and wait. I've only done this once before in my life, and it doesn't get any easier.

Two seemingly lifetimes later, I'm back in the office, two sticks capped and wrapped in a paper towel. I hand them to my big sister, not wanting to see them. "Here. You look at 'em. I can't stare at that stupid screen without puking again."

Setting the bundle on the edge of her desk, Duchess shuts her laptop, then sits back. "What will you do if you are pregnant?"

"What do you mean?" I sit up, not understanding where she's going with this.

"Are you ready for another one? I mean, I know you've always wanted lots of kids, but going from none to two to three all within a year is a lot."

Thinking about how my family got to be here, I know it's far from conventional. Raising two boys as my own when neither is biologically mine isn't how I saw my start to motherhood, but here I am. Taren, our three-year-old, is Hammer's son from a previous situation-ship with a woman who used to be a club girl before my time.

The shock of that alone was crazy enough, but then to find out Taren had a newborn baby brother was another 'what the fuck' moment. Add in their mother dying shortly after childbirth, and suddenly, neither child had parents. So, after a very serious life talk and some paperwork magic, Hammer and I became the legal parents of two boys.

"If we have another baby, we'll just do what we've always done," I say, giving voice to my possible new life. "We'll adapt and love him or her just like we do the others."

"What's one more when you already have two?" Duchess shrugs like we're picking what color to paint our nails then suddenly deciding to change it. Like adding a baby is no different than buying nail polish remover and cotton balls.

Her nonchalant attitude about this whole ordeal suddenly has me wondering. "Why do you have a pregnancy test in your desk drawer?"

Again, with the *I'm the crazy person* look. "Because you're not the only one trying to grow your family by leaps and bounds," she replies with a smirk.

"Oh my, H-E-double hockey sticks, are you—"

"No, no, no. Not yet," Duchess cuts me off, hands waving like she's directing in a 747 jumbo jet, "but I'm working on it."

"You want another one?" I'm a little shocked. "Already?"

"Whiskey hated being an only child. Yea, he grew up with other kids around, but he wants us to have kids close together in age. We talked about it a lot when I was still carrying Krew and decided we want more sooner than later. So, while we're not *trying*," she finger-quotes the word, "to get pregnant, we're not doing anything to stop it, either."

Well, look at us. Two crazy sisters, marrying two crazy best friends, both raising boys in this crazy world of motorcycles and mayhem and occasional life-threatening danger. We must be crazy ourselves!

"How crazy has this last year been?" I swivel my chair side-to-side as I think out loud. "Just think, a little over a year ago, we were both single, you wanted nothing to do with the Rebel Vipers, and now look at us. We've both got kiddos, maybe more on the way soon, and we're both getting married."

Duchess holds her left hand up, showing off her ring, so I do the same.

"I'm so glad I grew some lady balls and went to the clubhouse to find you."

"I'm glad you came to find me, too."

"Even though you got yourself out and didn't need any of the Brothers' help. You're one badass bitch, little sis," she says with a chuckle. Unrolling the paper towel, the tests fall into Duchess's hand. Her eyes get crazy big and she looks up at me with an ear-to-ear grin. "And you're gonna be one hell of a badass momma . . . again."

"It's positive?" My heart starts beating faster than a hummingbird flaps its wings.

"Looks like I need my baby daddy to knock me up again very soon."

"What the hell is that supposed to mean?" Damn woman won't answer my question.

"I mean," she starts, then flips the tests around so I can read them, "I need to get pregnant ASAP so we can have babies at the same time again."

Staring at the white sticks in her hand, one word, the same on both, is blaring at me like a neon billboard.
PREGNANT.

CHAPTER SIXTEEN

BLUE

Have I ever said I was miserable?

No?

Well, let me tell you.

Let me say it right now for everyone to hear. Everyone including all you haters out there in the back.

I'm miserable.

I'm miserable but don't have the slightest idea how to even begin climbing out of the hole I helped dig myself into. And for a woman of my age to be feeling like a whiny, whimpering teenager who just got her heart broken by her first boyfriend because he slept with her ex-best friend slash head cheerleader slash useless lab partner slash bane of her existence is just fucking stupid.

It's been two weeks since that freak snowstorm hit and I'm growing gloomier by the day. While the clubhouse may be full of happiness, between wedding plans and upcoming holiday cheer, I feel like I'm stranded alone on a deserted island. I've never felt more alone in a building full of people.

All the families are back in their own homes, but everyone has been spending the majority of their time in here to work on wedding stuff. There are homemade flower arrangements in mid-assembly all over the tables, string lights are beginning to be hung from the rafters of the super-high ceiling, and there's even two giant Christmas trees filling the room with the scent of pine and the outdoors.

It should be romantic and sentimental and sweet, but I'm trying to hide my bah-humbug attitude by being as scarce as possible. I'm hiding in my room or keeping my nose buried in my e-reader, which brings up another problem I'm dreading addressing. And even though it should be dealt with, again I'm avoiding it like the plague.

My husband.

Mountain is here in the clubhouse, but not really *here with me*, if you catch my drift. Of the last dozen nights or so, I think he's actually slept with me only half of those. And no, I'm not referring to *that* kind of sleep. Not the fun, sweaty, rolling around, mess up the sheets, can't catch your breath kind of sleep.

Nope, not for me. Instead, I get the boring 'go to sleep alone, sleep for shit because I'm awake worrying and imagining the worst, only to wake up alone, then wondering if he even came to bed last night'.

And to make matters worse, several mornings I've woken to find him sleeping on the couch in our living area again. I don't know what's worse, not knowing where he is or knowing where he is but also realizing he'd rather sleep out there on the cramped couch than be in our extra-large king-sized bed with me.

But what's really the worst is that most mornings I don't even know where he slept based on the fact he's up, dressed, and busy with "club business" by the time I'm up and around. I'm not one to sleep in very late, so he's either up before the sun or not coming to bed at all.

I'm at the point where I don't know what to do. Since he's not making any effort to talk to me either, do I just let things continue as is or do I push the issue? Do I try and talk to him even though I don't know if I'm really ready yet or hope he's feeling as bad as I am and approaches me first?

How long can we continue to live like this before someone else realizes something is wrong and asks one of us about it? Then what would we do? This discussion, or argument, or whatever happens when we finally do come head-to-head, it's definitely not something I'd like to have in front of my family. Seeing as I'm only the Old Lady, everyone would have no choice but to side with Mountain over me. There would be no winning for me.

My biggest fear, above anything else, is that I don't know if the silence and distance is Mountain's way of telling me he's done with us. He could want a way out but not want the confrontation it would take to get there. What if he can't face me to say the words, so he's saying them with his actions and silence?

And that's what brings me right back here to the same place I've been for too long. Alone. Tired. Miserable.

I think it might be time for me to start making some plans of my own.

CHAPTER SEVENTEEN

MOUNTAIN

I'm not going to lie . . . I'm hiding from my wife.
Fuck.

CHAPTER EIGHTEEN

BLUE

Looking down at the handsome little man sleeping in my arms, I can't help but think back and imagine how different my life would've been had I been able to give birth to the baby I lost.

Would he be a strapping young man, a spitting image of his father, and following in the footsteps of his big brother?

Or would she be a beautiful woman, just reaching the age where she wants to spread her wings and driving her Pops crazy with talk of boys and college and what color she wants her bedroom painted?

While there is very little I regret in my life, not giving my husband another baby is right there at the top of my 'what if' list. I'd never admit it to anyone, but the weight on my heart is sometimes too heavy.

That's a big reason why any time I'm near my grandbabies, whether they're related by blood like tiny Krew I'm holding now, or not like Angel's boys Taren and Ace, I give them all my love. I scoop them into my arms and soak up all the young, innocent love they have to give. They know none of the wrong or mean or hurtful parts of life yet, and I want to keep them wrapped in that cocoon as long as I can.

"What do you think?"

I look up and am transformed back to the brightly lit bridal store I've been sitting in for the last hour. Duchess is standing up on a pedestal, trying on her wedding dress for the last time before she takes it home.

I'm here with all the ladies who are getting married next week, getting to see their dresses for the first time. Due to offering to watch the babies, I didn't come along when they came in to buy them last month. But between Duchess, Angel, Sunshine, and Star constantly begging me to come today, I couldn't say no.

They all look so beautiful in the dresses they've picked, but there's something about Duchess that makes me lose my breath. I don't know if it's that I feel a stronger connection to her because she's marrying my nephew, or because I'm holding her adorable son in my arms, but I start tearing up.

"Oh, Duchess," carefully standing, holding Krew to my chest, I step forward to take in the details on the front of this ivory-colored dress, "you look radiant."

This dress looks like it was designed just for her. The sweetheart sparkly beaded neckline leads down into a fitted bodice, then at the waist the material flows out into a skirt covered in lace. And the fit is perfect, like a second skin.

"Isn't it pretty?" she whispers as she runs her hands down the sides.

"That dress is more than pretty. Whiskey isn't gonna know what to do when he sees you."

She looks up, eyes already brimming with tears. "You think so?" Duchess picks up the sides of the skirt and turns to face the three-way mirror behind her. She turns this way, then that way, but her eyes never leave her reflection.

"I know so." I nod. "Do you want me to take a picture for you, so you can remember what it looks like?"

"While I'd love that, if I have any evidence of this on my phone, you know Whiskey's bound to find it and ruin the surprise," she replies with a giggle.

"Then I'll take it on my phone but not send it to you 'til after the big day." I set Krew down in his car seat and pull my phone from my pocket. "Anytime you wanna see it, you come find me."

"Deal." I snap a few pictures, then sit back and watch as Sunshine, Angel, and Star come out of the back room and go to check out.

Since everyone is so close, it was decided amongst the four couples that they wanted to share a wedding day. The ladies are all super excited, and their men will do anything for them, so there was no turning back. The date was set. There will be a giant wedding at the clubhouse on Christmas Eve.

Things are already well in motion, turning the clubhouse into a winter wonderland, and everyone is on board with the transformation. I just wish I could be there to see it, but life doesn't always let us have everything we want.

"What are you going to wear on the big day?" Sunshine asks as she drops onto the couch next to me, snapping me back to the present.

"I have a black dress at home I'll wear." Not able to be completely truthful with her, I cover my real plans with a white lie. "This is your big day, no one will care what I wear."

"That's a bunch of baloney," Duchess calls out from behind us. "You need a special dress too. I don't know why I didn't think about it sooner."

"I don't need—" I try to insist but am cut off.

"Yes, you do." Sunshine pulls me to my feet and leads me over to a rack of dresses that has something of every color of the rainbow. She starts pushing dresses to the sides before settling into the blue section. She pulls out one that's covered in lace and such a light blue, it almost looks silver. "I think you need to try this on."

She practically shoves it into my arms, so I take it and am led back into a fitting room.

Knowing I'm not going to be allowed to leave the store unless I sneak out the back, because let's face it, the Old Ladies of the Rebel Vipers MC are almost as crazy as the Brothers, I give in.

I fold and set my clothes aside then step into the dress. Lifting the material up, it ends mid-calve and I slide my arms into the sheer, lace sleeves. Looking at myself in the mirror, I'm instantly transported back to the planning of my own wedding and the excitement I experienced all those years ago. I remember the dreams I had, the plans I was making, and all the wishes I had for our future.

The recent wedding planning has brought up lots of memories of the events around my big day. While many of them have come true, there's always been a small worry in the back of my mind that Mountain may regret having rushed into inviting me into this life.

I wonder, if he knew how the following few years would turn out, would he have still wanted me?

And with the way he's been acting lately, I wonder if he still wants me now.

TWENTY YEARS AGO

"Can I help you, miss?" Turning around, I see a woman standing just behind the counter of the bridal store I just walked into, smiling at me. "Are you looking for something specific?"

"Oh, yes," I stammer as I pull my purse strap higher on my shoulder. "I need a wedding dress."

As she steps out into the showroom, I notice the woman is impeccably dressed. She's wearing all black and has her hair pulled back into a sharp, crisp bun. Her pants have a crease running down the front of each leg, and there's no wrinkle in sight.

Seeing how neat and tidy she is, I instantly feel embarrassed about how I must look. I'm in jeans with holes in both knees and a t-shirt that has a grease stain on the sleeve from when I was helping Mountain in the shop earlier. My hair is tied up, but after my frantic run to the car in the rain, then from the car to the store in an even worse downpour, it probably looks like I almost drowned.

Running my hands down my damp jeans, I try and make myself look presentable, but it's no use. I'm a damn hot mess and should just turn around and walk right back out the door.

I get halfway turned around before I hear her voice again. "Oh, don't go. You look just fine, honey."

Shaking my head, I point to the door. "But I—"

"You could've run in here butt naked and I wouldn't have cared." The woman waves her finger at me as she approaches. "My name is Phyllis, and this is my shop. I've owned this place for forty-two years and I've seen everything. Now, why don't you come on back and tell me what kind of dress you're looking for."

Not able to argue with her while she's got a grip on my forearm, leading me farther into the store, my feet just follow along. And before I know it, I'm in front of a mannequin dressed in the prettiest light blue dress I've ever seen in my life.

"I like this one." I point at it, unable to tear my eyes away.

"Good gracious, that one is a beauty." Phyllis circles the back of the mannequin and starts unzipping the dress. "I actually just got this one last week. It was too pretty to put on a hanger, so I had to display it."

The bright blue color of the price tag hanging from the sleeve is hard to miss. Pinching it between my fingers, I have to double blink to make sure I'm reading the numbers right. "Is this price right? That seems really low for a wedding dress."

"That's 'cause this isn't a wedding dress. It's actually a bridesmaid's dress," Phyllis says. I lose grip of the tag as she starts walking away, the dress draped over her forearm. "But I know it's gonna look fabulous on you, so you should at least try it on."

Following behind, I try to correct her. "I don't need a bridesmaid's dress. I'm the bride. I need a white dress."

Her eyes swivel to me. "Says who?" She disappears behind a curtain, then reappears seconds later, her arms empty. "Honey, if you're getting married, you can wear whatever color you want. If you love that dress as much as I think you do, the color doesn't matter one bit. You could wear a black dress if your heart so desired."

Honestly stunned by her frankness, I have nothing to say back. But as I think about it, she's right. This is my wedding and I can wear whatever I damn well please. There's no one else here to tell me no. It's not like anything else about our relationship, engagement, or wedding is normal, so why not have a little fun?

"You know what," I say when I get my words back, "you're right. I've made my man wait this long to set a date, he'd be happy if I wore a burlap sack. A little color never hurt anybody."

"That settles it." Phyllis beckons me behind the curtain, which I now see is a large changing room. "Let's get you in this dress and see how it fits."

Kicking off my shoes, I hang my purse on a hook, then undress. Just when I turn around, she has the dress spread open on the floor for me to step into. Once my feet are flat on the floor, she lifts the material, and I slide my hands through the armholes. Disappearing behind me, I watch in the mirror as she zips the dress up, then steps to the side.

As I stare at myself in the mirror, I fall in love even more with the dress, which then flips the reality switch in my brain. "Shit!"

Worry fills her face. "What's the matter?'

"How long is it going to take to order this dress? My wedding is coming up quick."

"When's the big day?"

As I slide my hands down the lace-covered sides, feeling the edge of the trim detail with my fingertips, I see the forlorn expression on my face reflecting back at me from the mirror.

"It's in six days," I whisper.

This dress really is my dream, even though walking in here today, I had no idea what that dream was. But this dress, this is what I want so badly.

With three-quarter length sheer lace sleeves, the almost sky-blue color makes my lightly tan skin glow. The neckline is square and rests just above my cleavage. The bodice is blue lace over a matte-colored material of the same color, and the whole body of the dress looks like one piece. There is no separation at the waist, but between the cut of the dress and my hips, the silhouette is a dream. The bottom rests just below my knees, and the back is a smidge longer than the front, giving an illusion of a train even though none of the material touches the floor.

"Six days? Oh my. You must have one heck of a fella if you're rushing to marry him so fast," Phyllis says as she steps around me.

"If he would've had his way, we would've tied the knot six months ago." Her smile and spunky attitude make me laugh. "He popped the question three days after we met, and he wanted to get married the next day. I told him we had to wait just in case he woke up one day and realized he had lost his mind, but somehow, he never did."

"I've never met your fella, but I like him already."

"He bugged me every day for six months to pick a date."

"Then let's get you out of this dress, so I can put it in a garment bag for you."

"But what about ordering? I can't take this one. You said you just got it in."

Phyllis stops my yammering, grabs my hands, and looks up at me with a very serious expression. "This dress fits like it was made for you. Is this the one you want?"

"Yes, but . . ." I can't even think of what to say to argue.

Taking one last look in the mirror, I try and imagine myself in something else, but can't do it. This is it. This is my dress.

"If you want this one, it's yours. I insist," she says with a soft smile.

"I'll take it."

"When we get back, can I hide my dress in your cabin?" I overhear Angel ask Duchess.

"Me too?" Sunshine and Star echo at the same time.

"That's fine," Duchess replies as she shuts the back door of her truck after clipping Krew's car seat in. "I've forbidden Whiskey from stepping foot in the spare bedroom, and the door has a lock on it, so no one will be able to peek before next week."

"Nice!" Sunshine cheers, holding out a hand for a high-five.

"Ugh!" Star rolls her eyes as she walks around the truck to get in. "If I let Buzz within ten feet of my dress, the asshole will wanna see it and ruin the whole surprise."

"Hammer would be the exact same," I hear Angel say as she gets in the passenger seat.

"See you back at the clubhouse," Duchess calls out as she climbs in. Her truck roars to life and all four ladies wave as they drive away.

Only then do I get in my SUV and really think about what I'm about to do. Looking in my rearview mirror, I see the duffle bags in my cargo area and begin to wonder if this is a good idea. Am I doing the right thing?

How did I get here?

CHAPTER NINETEEN

STAR

For a girl from nowhere Pennsylvania, I sure have made a life for myself, or at least I'm working hard at building that life one day at a time.

Handsome fiancé? Check. Baby belly? Check. Wedding dress? Check. What else could a woman need?

I'm nothing like the girl I was at seventeen, running away from my home, tired of being treated like a glorified punching bag for parents who thought that just because they put a roof over my head and fed me every day, they had the right to treat me however they chose. That's not being a parent, that's abuse.

Parents are supposed to love you, cherish you, build you up and teach you the right ways of the world. Not beat you down, call you names, and belittle you every chance they get, like mine did. I'll never be like that to my child.

Whatever he or she decides they want to do with their life, I will do everything in my power to support them every step of the way. With the strength and support of my Old Man, the father of this precious life growing inside me, anything is possible.

Six months after leaving home, with nowhere to be, I decided to bum along on a road trip that a friend, her older brother, and her older brother's friend were making cross-country. We made it four states to the west before we almost ran out of money and decided to find somewhere to settle for a while and make a new plan.

We were all living in a one-bedroom apartment in Henderson, Wisconsin, for six months when my friend's brother's friend suggested we hit up a party at some place just outside town. Apparently, a guy he worked with at a fast-food restaurant was friends with this biker dude, and they were having an open party for anyone who wanted to come, so he begged all of us to go. I'll be the first to admit the whole thing sounded sketchy as shit at the time, but it turned out to be the best thing I'd ever agreed to do to date.

That wild party in the woods was where I met the Rebel Vipers Motorcycle Club for the first time. As it turned out, the reason Billy wanted to go to this party was because he was hoping to Prospect with the club and join one day, but he turned out to be a flake. A few hours after we got there, the club kicked him out because he was drunk, belligerent, and had tried to feel up the Old Lady of the President.

Big no-no on his part, but I was loving it there. I took a wild risk and asked Blue, the lady my asshole roommate tried to get handsy with, if I could stay. She pulled me aside, under the very watchful eye of Mountain, her Old Man, and asked me what my connection was to the tool bag who was at that moment being escorted outside the fence by two very large, burly, muscly men.

I explained to her my predicament of having no real home, to which she explained the only way a single woman would live at the clubhouse was to be a club girl.

Now, having lived in the area for a little while, I knew of the club's existence, I knew they weren't living on what you would call the "right side" of the law, and from just those couple hours, I got a crash course on exactly what club girls did. I got quite the eyeful when I saw a half-naked woman on her knees between two men, who both had their jeans undone. This woman had her hand wrapped around the dick of one man while her mouth was busy entertaining the other.

That wasn't the only thing I saw happen out in the open that night, and while I may have been young, surprisingly even to myself, I wasn't grossed out or afraid of anything I'd seen. In fact, it excited me. And when I told Blue that, she smiled and laughed and told me if that was my response to what was happening there that night, I just might fit in perfectly. She said to come back the next day and we'd talk about where I might fit in.

The next night, I took myself back to the clubhouse, four duffel bags of clothes over my shoulders, and asked to speak to Mountain, just like Blue had told me to. The man at the gate looked at me like I was out of my mind for requesting to speak with the President, but he escorted me in, staring at my ass the whole way to the front door.

Mountain met me as soon as I walked inside, escorted me into his office, where his Old Lady was waiting for us, and before either of them said a word, I asked him if I could move in. One look at Blue and her smile in response to my boldness, he said I was more than welcome. He then proceeded to lay down the rules and expectations of being a club girl and said that as long as I did the chores that were asked of me and spent time with whichever member requested it, this would be my new home. He handed me a key, then called in a beautiful Latina woman named Cinnamon to show me to my room.

It didn't take me long at all to fall in love with this place. I know it's not everyone's cup of tea, but I knew it's where I belonged from the start. I had a roof over my head and was given a job working at The Lodge, the club's bar and restaurant, which allowed me to quickly save up money to buy my own car. Most importantly, I had the security and reassurance that no one would ever hurt me again and get away with it. Club girls may be at the bottom of the totem pole, sometimes referred to as "club property", but that doesn't mean if someone does something to hurt one of us, that the club won't retaliate.

But nothing could've shocked me more than the life-changing event that put me on a whole new track. Coming up on a year ago now, my life changed in ways I never could've dreamed of. Some might call me crazy or stupid, but I did something even I never thought possible. I fell in love with a Brother.

And as luck would have it, unbeknownst to me, Buzz was developing feelings in return. I can say it was luck now, because at the time, it almost all exploded.

Unsure of how to deal with what he was feeling, Buzz started to pull away from me. And because I thought I had done something wrong, knowing I had no right to question him on why, I retreated as well. I had to admit to myself that I was playing an unwinnable game and back off.

It hurt like hell.

I couldn't say anything to anyone, but unable to hide not wanting to be with anyone else, I closed myself off from everyone and everything, except my job and schooling, and waited for the day they kicked me out.

I knew it wouldn't be long before the single Brothers started talking and realized I hadn't been with any of them in a while, and they would tell me I had to leave. But with nowhere to go and me loving everyone here too much, I didn't want to rock the boat if I didn't have to. So, I just waited.

One night this summer, after a little too much liquid courage, Buzz and I were left alone outside after everyone else went up to bed, and I ended up in his lap, making out. Once I realized what I was doing, falling into his arms at the first moment of weakness, I knew I had to put a stop to it.

When I pushed myself back and got up to walk away, Buzz scoffed and asked me why I'd been so distant lately. I tried to tell him he was imagining things, but he called my bluff. He said he knew something was off and forced me to tell him, his hand holding mine and not letting go.

Again, I tried to insist I was just tired and wanted to go to bed, to which he responded by pulling me into his chest and growling in my ear, "The only way you're goin' to bed tonight is if you admit you wanna be in *my* bed. Only my bed."

My jaw dropped. Looking at his face in the dim, flickering glow from the firepit behind us, it was like I was seeing Buzz for the first time. I'd never seen him without the scowl that's normally permanently etched on his face, but right then, right there in the middle of the backyard, he looked peaceful. His eyes were soft and almost begging me to talk to him.

Knowing I wasn't getting anywhere, I had to say something or he'd chase after me if I tried to run again. I was tired. I didn't have it in me to lie anymore.

With my own desperation probably oozing from every pore, I told him I had developed feelings for him, ones that weren't appropriate for a club girl to have for a Brother, and that I was thinking about leaving.

Without a single word in response, Buzz took off jogging for the clubhouse, my hand still in his, forcing me to run to keep up. I probably asked him a dozen times what he was doing as we hurried inside, up the stairs and down the hall, ending up in his room, but he was silent the whole way.

He didn't say a word until the door was closed and he had me pressed up against it. "I'm fallin' in love with you, but I thought you'd laugh in my face if I said it out loud."

"I'd never laugh at you, Buzz." Throwing my arms around his neck, he picked me up and carried me over to his bed. Once laid out underneath him, feeling his heat, muscles, and very large bulge pressing me down, I told him my truth. "I love you, too. That's why I was pulling back."

From that night on, I slept in Buzz's bed more often than I did my own. We'd had several long talks about what we were going to do about our feelings and when we'd tell the club, but neither of us wanted to rock the boat. Angel had just gotten together with Hammer for real, making her the first club girl to be in a relationship with a Brother, so I was afraid everyone would think I was only with Buzz to copy her.

Buzz worried that since I'd been intimate with some of his closest friends, once they heard, they'd think less of him for wanting to be with me. While we both knew our love for one another was real, we agreed to take some time to ourselves, to make sure this is really what we wanted. And then when the time was right—right for us, not anyone else—we'd tell everyone at once.

It just so happened that two months and a dozen pregnancy tests later, we found out we were connected in the biggest way possible. I am carrying Buzz's baby.

We told the club, who, as it turned out, were happier for us than a pig in a mud hole on the hottest summer day, and things got even crazier from there. I'm in my last semester of online classes, four and a half months pregnant, and in love with the best man in the universe. And I'm getting married!

So here I sit, in the back seat of Duchess's truck, with the other three ladies getting married the same day as me, leaving the bridal store on our way back to the clubhouse. I have my dress draped over my lap, enclosed in its garment bag, and I'm staring out the window, watching the scenery as it rolls by.

Angel is riding shotgun as Duchess drives, I'm behind Duchess, and Sunshine is on the far right, staring out her window with a smile on her face. Krew is nestled between us in his car seat.

It's a quiet ride, none of us needing to fill the space with useless words or humdrum, all seemingly in our own little worlds. Me, twirling my skeleton key necklace, I'm thinking about the man who awaits me at home, ready with ants in his pants to make me his wife.

I don't think life can get much better than this.

CHAPTER TWENTY

MOUNTAIN

"Hey, Mountain?"

I turn my head to see Meredith peeking out the door behind me. Spinning my wheelchair to face her, I ask, "Whatchya need, hun?"

"Are you alright out here? It's pretty dang cold and you've got no coat on."

"I'm fine," I reply with a smile. "Just waiting for the ladies to get back from the dress store."

"Oh, okay. At least let me get you a blanket or something to cover your legs." Stepping outside, she wraps her arms around herself. "If Blue finds out I let you get frostbite, she'll have my hide."

"I doubt that," I mumble, looking out toward the backyard.

"What's that?" she asks.

"Nothing. It's nothing." Meredith really can be the sweetest, but I don't need her knowing my problems. She'd swoop in and make it her mission to try and fix things between me and Blue, and I can't have that. "I was just thinking out loud."

Her scrunched-up expression shows she's not sure if she one hundred percent believes me, but thankfully, she lets it go. "I'll grab you a blanket and be back in a jiffy. Don't try and say no, Mountain. I insist."

Two minutes later, she's back and drapes a familiar blue and black buffalo check blanket over my lap. It's one that's usually on the couch in my living room, so it looks like she just grabbed the first thing she saw. Hopefully, she didn't think too much of the pillows and other few blankets I have folded up there as well, because if she did, she'd realize that's where I've been sleeping a lot of nights recently.

"Thank you, Meredith." I can't admit to her she was probably right about me needing at least something to cover my legs. As the sky grows darker, almost black, the temperature has dropped drastically. "Now, go get yourself back inside. If you get hypothermia because of me, Steel is gonna want *my* hide."

"Yes, sir," she replies with a chuckle. "But if you're not back inside in fifteen minutes, I'm gonna tell Whiskey and he'll come out here and drag you in himself." And inside she goes.

A few minutes pass and the sky is now completely black. I almost consider going in when I see headlights glowing from my right, signaling a vehicle rounding the clubhouse to park in the back lot. All vehicles are accounted for except Duchess and Blue's, so hopefully, it's a sign they're back.

Now, I know absolutely nothing about wedding dress shopping, but seeing as all I was aware they were going to do was pick up the dresses they bought a month ago, I didn't think the five of them would be gone for hours.

Duchess's red truck appears around the corner and parks in the first open spot closest to her and Whiskey's cabin. I wait for Blue's SUV to follow, but as the seconds tick by, it doesn't appear.

The women are chattering as they all get out of the truck, then Star hands Duchess a big white bag before reaching back in the cab and lifting out Krew in his car seat. I don't think they've noticed me yet, half hidden in the shadows of the back porch's overhang, so I stay silent as not to spook them too much. All four ladies, Duchess, Angel, Sunshine, and Star, head straight for the cabin, then disappear inside.

Where in the hell is my wife? Shouldn't she have been right behind them? She went to the same place they did, right? I try to remember hearing her tell Belle that she was accompanying them to the store. In fact, I know I did. Sitting in my wheelchair for the first time in almost a month, since I decided not to put on my prosthesis and just sit like a lazy fucking bum on my ass all day, I couldn't chase my lady out the door. And she didn't even give me one look before she walked out.

Now, I realize things these last few weeks have been bad, really bad, but to not even acknowledge my presence before leaving, that's something Blue has never done before. She's given me sad eyes, she's looked at me like she wants to murder me, I've even seen her footsteps falter in hesitation as she's walked away, but she's never not shown me her sky blues before leaving.

I hear a door open and close, followed by a screen door, and look up to see Star walking down the cabin's front porch steps and heading my way. Not wanting her to be startled when she runs into me once reaching the patio, I call out, "Hey, Star."

I see her jolt a little at the sudden words, but she deflates just as fast when she realizes it's me. Hand over her chest, she lets out a sharp breath, a puff of vapor dissipating quickly into the air. "Mountain, don't be scarin' a pregnant lady like that. If I was further along, you might have been delivering it right here, right now."

I've always liked Star's spunky attitude and easy comebacks. She fits into our not so little family perfectly. I'll be honest, I never saw the switch from club girl to Old Lady coming, but now that I see her and Buzz together all the time, the match couldn't have been more perfect. Watching Buzz grow up alongside my son and Hammer, I always wished the best for the boys, but for them to have all found happiness in such a short period of time is good for an old man's soul.

"If you had your baby on this porch, we'd both end up in the hospital, 'cause this old fart would be having a heart attack."

That makes both of us laugh.

"What are you doin' out here in the cold? Shouldn't you be inside spoiling the crap outta your grandbabies?"

"I was earlier but needed a little break from the crazy. I don't know who's worse at whining, babies or their dads when they hafta change poopy diapers."

"We've both been around this bunch long enough to know the answer to that question." Star rests a hand on her hip. "Those men may be badass bikers with zero tolerance for bullshit, but when it comes to those kiddos, they turn to mush."

"No kidding," I reply, letting out a deep laugh of my own. I look around again, just to make sure Blue didn't get back before I came out here and maybe parked in a different spot and I missed it. "Hey, so was Blue still with you when y'all left the dress store? I haven't seen her come back yet."

"She was," Star replies with a nod. "She said something about having to stop at the pharmacy for some stuff. It shouldn't be too much longer before she gets back."

Before I can ask anything else, the door opens behind me, spilling light out from the hallway. Star looks behind me and her face comes to life.

"What are you doin' out here? You're gonna freeze to death. Get your pregnant butt inside this clubhouse right now." I hear Buzz's deep timbre call out. "Oh, hey, Mountain." He finally notices me after playfully scolding his lady. "Why are you out here?"

"I was waiting for my Old Lady," I say with a shrug.

"Well, don't be out here too long. There's a wind chill advisory for tonight. Don't need your other leg gettin' frozen and fallin' off."

"Ha, ha, very funny, asshole." I flip him the double bird. "Get your lady inside and quit worrying about my gimpy ass."

"Don't say I didn't warn you."

"You're the third person to scold me for bein' out here, so get in line, fucker."

They go inside, and I pull out my phone to call Blue.

First call, it rings, but there's no answer. Second call, again, no answer. This is getting ridiculous. Third call, after one ring, it goes straight to voicemail. No fucking way. She's screening her calls and just ignored me.

What the fuck? My thumbs thump across the screen so hard, I wouldn't be surprised if it cracks as I type out a text.

Me: Answer your phone right now!

Fury building, I call Blue one more time, and this time, she picks up.

"What?" she asks, a little snap to her tone.

"What do you mean, what?" I snap right back.

"Mountain, I'm not in the mood to talk right now," she says, her voice softer this time. "Can't I just have a few moments of peace and quiet?"

"Where the hell are you that you have peace and quiet?" Around here, quiet is hard to come by, so I'm curious as to where she is. "'Cause this clubhouse is anything but those two things, so you must be somewhere else."

"I can't tell you that right now."

"What do you mean, you can't?"

"I just can't." She sounds dejected.

Taking a deep breath, I ask a question I'm not sure I want the answer to. "Can't or won't?"

There's a pause before her answer. "Both."

Fed up with this, I need to know where she is so I can go get her. "Blue, you tell me where you are right now or I'm gonna ask Cypher to track your ass down. Then, I can't help that the whole fucking club will be in on our business. Is that what you want?"

"No." Her reply is quick.

"Then tell me where you are." My words seethe through my clenched teeth.

"Fine," she replies, a sigh mixing with her word. "I'm at the girls' house in town. I came here to get away."

"Away from me?"

My response is only met with a sniffle. I knew this was bad, but to need to be away from me? Fuck.

"That's it. I've about had it with this back-and-forth bullshit," I growl into the phone. "You either get your ass back home right now, or I'm comin' there myself."

"No, Mountain. I don't wanna talk to you right now. I just need some space. These last few months have been too much. I just can't—"

"I'm on my way." I hang up the phone before tucking it back in the pocket of my cut.

I heard her words but don't care what she thinks she wants. If she thinks she needs space from me, if she thinks this is the end of us, she's got another thing fucking coming. I've dawdled and hemmed and hawed way too damn much these last few months around her, but no more. I'm going to that house to confront this bullshit head-on, and I'm not coming back home without her.

Rolling my ass inside, I head straight for our room to ditch the wheelchair and grab my crutches. I don't have the time or energy to deal with putting my leg on, so I'll just have to go without it for now. Hopefully, when I get to the house, I can convince her things will get better, and before we know it, she'll be back in our home, and we can take that first step together to rebuilding us. To getting us back to the way we should've been all along. Together.

I pull up to the house and see the brand-new, summit white Chevy Blazer I bought her this summer parked in the driveway. Parking beside it, I grab my crutches from the passenger seat and slowly make my way to the front steps. Hobbling up to the porch, the second I raise my hand to knock, the inside door opens and I'm met with the first sight of my wife in almost five hours.

Fuck, she's beautiful. But if I never see the hurt and tears in her eyes again, I'd die a happy man. Is this what I've done to her? Did I do this?

"Get your stubborn ass in this house right now," she scolds as she pushes the screen door open so I can come inside. "And why the hell aren't you wearing your prosthetic? You know the physical therapist said you should never leave the house without it."

As soon as I'm clear of the door, I slam it shut behind me, then crutch my ass toward Blue. She must see something in my expression she knows means business because her eyes go bug-wide as she backs away from me one step at a time. But too bad, so sad for her, I follow her backward steps with forward ones of my own.

"I will go wherever I damn well please, whenever I damn well please, and not wear that damn hunk of titanium whenever I damn well don't want to... whether you like it or not!" I bark my words at her with no care whatsoever of the way they come across.

Her back finally hits a door leading to what I know is a coat closet, so I press my chest to hers, pinning her in place. We stare at each other, both our breaths labored as we wait to see who breaks and speaks first. I win, because it's her.

"What do you want, Mountain?"

"I wanna know why you left me. That's what you did, right? You left me?"

Blue's gaze drops, and I know I hit the bullseye on the first shot. She left me.

As if I have no control of my extremities, my arms somehow walk my crutches back a few steps without me falling flat on my ass. If it's possible to be breathing without your heart beating, that would be me right now. I don't feel my heart thumping in my chest, but I do hear it pounding in my ears. It's like I'm in surround sound mode and every sound my body makes on the inside is coming in loud and clear inside my head.

"You don't want me anymore?" Blue stumbles forward a step, but I raise a hand to stop her. "Tell me right now if we're over, Blue. I can't handle this bullshit another minute. Tell me the truth."

"Let's sit down and I'll tell you everything." Blue walks toward the living room and sinks into the couch cushions. When she sees I haven't moved, she looks back at me. "Please?"

"Fine," I mumble with a harrumph. Finally sitting on the chaise part of the sectional, I wait for her explanation.

Blue folds her hands, straightens her shoulders, and once her eyes are on me, she begins. "I don't know how else to say this, so I'm just gonna say what's on my mind and not hold back."

Straightening myself, I prepare for whatever daggers she's about to throw. "I wouldn't expect anything less."

"My feelings have been hurt way too much lately and I couldn't be in that clubhouse anymore. We've been tiptoeing around each other for months, and I can't do that anymore. If I have to wake up one more morning not knowing if you slept beside me or out on that fuckin' couch again, I might scream the whole place down. I just can't do it. I can't, Mountain. I can't." The more words she speaks, the louder she gets, and by the time she stops, there are tears rolling down her cheeks.

If this was any other instance where I saw her so emotional, with tears and hurt and pleading pouring from her, I'd have her wrapped in my arms, whispering in her ear, and telling her everything will be okay, but I know this isn't a time for that. Hell, me doing that is probably part of what led us here. We've been brushing tiny problems under the rug for so long, an unavoidable bump finally formed, and now we're both tripping over it, trying not to fall and cause irreparable damage.

"Why didn't you tell me you were leaving?" I have to ask. "We both know things have been bad, and we've been pushing everything back, but I had no idea you were thinking of doing this."

"Honestly, I didn't either until a few days ago."

"What pushed you here?"

"I've been slowly packing a bag for a week now, putting a few items in it every day, and you never noticed. The bag was on the bench in our closet, and you either didn't notice it or were ignoring anything that was mine, but you never once said a word about it."

I'm trying to think of what bag she's talking about, but I'm drawing a blank. She's right, I didn't see something she was doing right in front of my face, when normally, I would've seen the bag in the spot it wasn't supposed to be and asked her about it right away. But I didn't. I didn't see the big blinking sign right in front of my face, and I let her walk out the door.

"I'm sorry for that, Blue." Scooting forward, I rest my hand next to her leg, unsure if she wants me to touch her or not. "I hate that you were trying to show me you were hurting and I ended up looking right through you."

Blue's hands slide over mine, and I instantly flip mine so our palms are flat against each other's. Like instinct is more powerful than either of us, our fingers link together and I feel her tension.

"It wasn't until this morning, when the bag was too full to put one more thing in and I zipped it shut, that I realized today was the day. I finished getting dressed, set the bag on our bed, then went about the start of my day." Her voice is raspy and weak, but I let her continue even though every nerve in my body is screaming.

"When lunch was over and it was time to leave, and you still hadn't said a word about the bag, I knew this was my time to go. Meredith is staying the week at the clubhouse because of the weddings and the house was going to be empty, so I knew this was the perfect place to go to get some time alone. I never even thought you'd realize I was gone so fast."

I have to give it to Blue, her plan to get away was almost foolproof. Meredith is renting Duchess and Angel's family's house in town, and with the wedding activities, the house is vacant and a perfect place to hide from the craziness. I just wish I had seen the signs of Blue's impending take-off so I could've stopped it from happening. Another failure on my part as a husband.

Thinking about how I was waiting outside for her for the first time in who knows how long, only for this to be the day she had no intention of coming home, is kind of ironic. I feel a harsh laugh in my throat but try to cover it with a cough.

I obviously don't fool Blue, because she pulls her hand from mine and barks, "What's so damn funny about my pain?"

"No, no, no, no," I repeat, reaching back for her hand. "Your pain isn't what's funny, it's what I was doing when I called you that's actually funnier."

"What do you mean?" Her head cocks in curiosity.

"I was sitting outside on the back porch in my wheelchair, waiting for you to come home so we could talk." Squeezing her hand, I lay it all out on the line. "When I watched you leave for the dress store, and for the first time in twenty-one years you didn't look back at me before you walked out the door, I knew something was really wrong.

"I was sick and tired of pussyfooting around the problems we've been having, trying to give each other time to build up our arguments, and needed to get your attention the only way I could think of. I knew if you came home and found me sitting outside without a coat or a hat or anything on to keep me warm, you'd yell at me for being an idiot. I knew that no matter how mad you were at me, you'd have no choice but to at least say something to scold me and that would be my opening.

"I figured you'd gripe at me to put a coat on, then I'd say something back like 'only if you make me', to which you'd probably push my stubborn ass back inside yourself, and then that would be my in to start the conversation we're having right now."

"Oh" is her only response. Blue is staring at me, apparently stunned into shock by my truth.

"Blue, please say something more than 'oh'."

Her head shakes a little and her eyes blink like she's waking from a trance. "Well, you're right about one thing, mister." Now that's she's awake, her eyes are shooting invisible laser beams at me. And if they could, I'd imagine her ears would have steam rolling out of them too. She looks pissed. "You have no business being outside with no coat on. Your immune system is compromised from those meds the doctors have you on, and you need to get a grip when it comes to the fact you only have one damn leg left. If you do anything to injure yourself, you won't have any choice but to live the rest of your life in a wheelchair. Is that what you want for yourself? 'Cause I sure as fuck don't."

Hearing her words of concern for me, knowing she only wants what's best for me, I know we're not anywhere near done yet. If Blue was really done with me, I have no doubt that she'd push my broken ass into a snowbank herself and watch me shrivel up and die from the cold. But, no, her first concern when hearing I put myself in a situation I really should've been smart enough not to was to be worried about my health.

Needing to show her that this is far from over, I take her unaware and pull her into me. Her shock at the sudden jerk causes her to lose her balance and she falls against me, knocking us both flat on the couch. The chaise portion we're laying on is extra wide, so my back and head land on the cushion below, softening the blow to my chest as Blue crashes on top of me.

Her arms are pinned between our chests, so Blue wiggles her hands free of mine, then wrestles herself onto her hands and knees, her whole body braced over mine. Eyes peering down in anger but lips trying to hold back a smile, Blue begins interrogating me.

"What do you think you're doing pulling me around like that? You could've hurt yourself."

I frame her face with my giant hands and pull her head down. I smash our lips together and devour her whole. Pressing my tongue to the tight seam of her lips, she gasps in surprise, giving me the entrance I need. Blue tries to pull herself back, but I don't let her.

I keep her attached to me as I kiss the living daylights out of her, showing her who the boss is now. She's had the leash for too long, and now, it's time for me to take it back under my control. I didn't convince this woman to marry me in three damn days without some balls, and I'm not about to let her end it now.

Rolling our bodies to the side, I let us both suck in the air we desperately need, but quickly tell her what's about to happen next.

"When we get up from this couch, you're gonna go get that bag you packed, put it back in your car, and drive your happy ass back to the clubhouse with me following you the whole way."

"No, Mountain," Blue protests as she wrestles free from my hold to sit up. "Stuff is still all screwy between us. Things aren't gonna be back to what they used to be just because you say I have to come home."

Mirroring her, I move to her side so our legs are touching, then interrupt her. "I don't care that everything isn't perfect, Blue. All I'm saying is I want right now to be the start of us fixing what's broken. I know it won't be all done overnight, but we have to knock down the walls we've built between us and start somewhere. Why can't that be now? Hell, we've talked more in the last ten minutes than we have in the last three months."

"I want that more than anything," she says softly, but I can hear the doubt in her words, "but I'm scared. What if we try putting ourselves back together only to find we're too broken? I wouldn't be able to handle that."

Grasping both her hands in mine, I lift them to my lips. Kissing her knuckles, I rest our joined hands on her lap. "Our pieces will never be too broken to put back together, do you hear me, Blue? I waited too many years to find you, then spent so many more doing everything I could to keep you, I won't let one bump on our timeline make everything fall apart. You were made for me, just like I was made for you. I believe that with my whole damn broken heart. Because that's what I'd be if I ever was without you. Broken."

Untangling our hands, Blue then pulls my face to hers, as if I'd give any resistance to her kisses, and she presses her soft lips to mine. Pulling back, she rests her forehead against mine, eyes closed as she holds me in silence.

Needing more of a connection, I take a huge risk and lift her into my lap. As if on instinct, Blue straddles me, positioning us the closest we can be with our clothes on.

Blue finally opens her eyes and rests back on my thighs. Her hands still bracket my face, holding my gaze to hers. "I'd never want you broken. I watched that almost happen once, the day you woke up from your accident, and I will never allow it to happen again. Whatever you need from me, I will give to you with every fiber of my being."

Turning my head to the right, I kiss the palm of her left hand, the one still wearing the ring I gave her that spring day so long ago. "Does that mean you'll come home with me so we can start rebuilding us?"

"I'll follow you to hell if that's where this life takes us," Blue replies with strong conviction. "I love you too much to let go now."

I can't help but smile at her tenacity and strength. "Then let's go home so I can lay with you in our bed for the first time in too long. I need to show you how much I love you. Can we do that?"

"Please do."

CHAPTER TWENTY-ONE

BLUE

I know everything wrong won't be miraculously fixed just because I agreed to come home, but seeing the need, vulnerability, and hurt in my husband's eyes made me realize he finally wants the same thing I want—us. He wants us, and so do I.

The whole drive, I watch my rearview mirror more than I look out my windshield but somehow manage to make it back through the compound gates in one piece.

I'm parked, out of my SUV, and halfway to the back door when Mountain slides out of his truck and yells, "Damn, woman, if you drove any faster, I woulda pulled you over myself." Every word brings him closer to me.

Pressing my back to the door, I reply, "Oh yeah, then what would you have done?"

Stepping into my bubble, his lips graze my ear. "Then I would've bent your ass over and fucked you on the side of the road, frozen balls and all."

On wobbly legs, I reach for the door handle behind me, turn it, and back away from his heat. "I guess it's a good thing we've got a big bed you can bend me over just inside. I wouldn't want you to lose your manhood 'cause of me."

"Get your ass in our room and get naked," Mountain growls. "Now."

So, I do. After closing the back door, I pray for no interruptions but all I hear is voices in the main room. Ignoring all of our family, I use my key to open the door to our private space. Stepping inside, I shuck my coat and Property cut, kick off my boots, and head straight for the bedroom.

I have every intention of following Mountain's order of getting naked but make it no further than tossing my duffel bag on a chair in the corner before I see Diva staring up at me from her sprawled-out perch on our bed.

"What are we gonna do with our new little friend?" I ask as Mountain presses his front to my back, resting his chin on my shoulder.

"She'll probably be scarred for life if she sees what I wanna do to you right now."

"Let's move her and her litter box out into the living room," I suggest, heading for the bathroom, where the box has been since Mountain brought Diva home for good. "Then she won't be sticking her paws in places they don't belong."

I barely have the kitten nudged out the door and start to close it when a hand appears beside me, slamming it shut. My right hand is grabbed, I'm spun around, and my back is pressed against the door. Mountain's crutches crash to the floor with a clatter, but neither of us pay them any mind because his lips crash down on mine and we become too distracted by each other.

Mountain has his hands braced against the wall on either side of my head, so I take advantage of the perfect position he's put himself in to do something I haven't gotten to do in a very long time. We may have been intimate not so long ago, but I didn't get my chance to admire and devour one of my favorite parts of him.

Resting my hands lightly on his chest, I grab hold of his leather cut and slide it off his shoulders. Knowing to never just drop it wherever, I look to my left and see the series of hooks Mountain hung on the wall for us to hang items such as this one. Reaching out, I'm just close enough for the metal to catch the cut as I let it go.

Attention back on my Old Man, I feel for the buttons of his flannel shirt. Unbuttoning him from the top down, I pull the material, untucking it from his jeans. Once it's open, I push it over his shoulders, and he shrugs out of it. Next comes the t-shirt, which he takes off all on his own, showing the tight muscles, soft skin, and beautiful lines of the tattoos he's had since before we met.

Across his broad chest, from shoulder to shoulder, are feathers of a bird's wings spread out like they're about to take flight. Tracing the top line from his shoulders, inward over his clavicle, and down the center along his sternum, my fingers ghost over his skin as we continue to kiss. Our lips only separate when we need a quick break for a gasp of air, then we're right back to it. But not for long.

With both hands, I get his jeans unbuckled, unbuttoned, and unzipped in no time flat. Pushing the denim out of my way, they're over his hips and exposing his backside. As I push them down, I pull back from his lips and drop to my knees.

I don't have much room between him and the wall behind me, but I'm still flexible enough at my age to fit in cramped spaces when what I want is important enough. And what I'm looking at right now—black boxer briefs encasing the manhood of the beast holding himself up above me—is very important.

"What are you doin', Blue?" Mountain pants. "Are you tryin' to unman me?"

I look up to see every one of his muscles straining, trying to keep his arms locked straight and remain standing. "I was hoping to get reacquainted with this," I run my finger down the swollen bulge in front of my face, "but if you want me to stop, I can."

"I'd love nothing more than for you to suck me dry, but I'm shaking way too much to let you do it while I'm up here on one leg." As fast as lightening, Mountain grabs hold of my hair with one hand and pulls me to standing again. He presses his weight into me while his eyes blaze with hunger. "Help me to our bed and you can do whatever you want to me 'til the sun comes up tomorrow."

"As you wish."

Helping him shimmy hop backward, until the back of his legs hit the bed, I then pull down his jeans and underwear and help him sit. Once I untangle everything from around his ankles, I toss the denim and cotton to the side without a care.

His angry-looking dick slaps up against his abdominals, and I go to reach for it again, but Mountain stops me by grabbing my hips and yanking me into the space between his legs. "Now, it's time for you to get naked."

As I lift off my sweatshirt, followed by my t-shirt flying who knows where behind me, Mountain pushes my leggings and thong down in one fail swoop. I untangle my feet from them by stepping on whatever chunk of material I can, turning them inside out as I work them off. Finally free of the stretchy material, I rest one hand on Mountain's shoulder to support myself as I pull off my socks, then drop straight back down to my knees on the fluffy carpet that runs along the end of our bed.

Needing to continue my admiration of my Old Man's impressive body, I trace my fingertips down the ridges of his ab muscles, counting all six of them as I go. When I get to the tip of where his twitching dick is resting, I come to the three circles of ink around Mountain's belly button. I missed seeing this the first time we made love, but the next morning, I found it while exploring and made him tell me the embarrassing story.

Apparently, many years ago, Mountain lost a bet to Skynyrd about some football game, then had to let him tattoo something on him without knowing what it was until it was done. So now my man is rocking a biohazard symbol mere inches above his cock, but I secretly love it.

Leaning in close, I press a kiss just above the swirls, then lower my lips to the one thing I've been dying to touch for too long. Sliding my left hand up the inside of Mountain's thigh, I feel his entire body go taut, then I wrap my fingers around his cock before licking a bead of precum from his tip.

One bead disappears on my tongue only to be replaced by two more. Needing the taste of him, to remind myself this is all real and not just a crazy, out-of-control dream, I suck him in as far as my throat will allow. Mountain's length is too much to take it all, so I slide my grip down to his root and pull up as I rock my head back.

Between my hand and my lips, I begin to work up and down his length, over and over, until two hands thread themselves into my tied-up hair.

"Enough!" he shouts. I had no intention of stopping until I got him so worked up that he came down my throat, but my man has ideas of his own. Mountain pulls me up, forcing me to get to my feet even with his hands still in my hair.

I grab hold of his knees as he has me bent over, ass sticking out behind me, and meet his glare. "I wasn't done," I try to complain but am met with a sharp yank as he pulls me even closer.

"The only way I'm gonna come in you is if your tight pussy is wrapped around my dick, not your mouth." I have no chance to respond because Mountain kisses me, probably bruising my lips in the process.

Just as fast as he grabbed hold of my hair, I'm let go, only to feel a slap on my ass. "Oww!" I cry out.

"Oh, quit your bitchin'," Mountain growls. "Get up on this bed and lay down. I need your pussy now." And he smacks my butt again in the same spot.

"Shit," I mutter but crawl up the bed anyway, feeling the tender spot on my backside as I do as he says. All other worries disappear as my knees are pushed apart and the bulk of my man crawls between them.

Peppering my skin with kisses, licks, tiny nips, then a full-out bite to the underside of my left breast, all I can do is squirm, hands clutching the comforter below me, as I'm assaulted with sensations from every direction. The hair on his thighs scratches against the inside of mine, and the heat and weight of his body appears and disappears from my chest every time he moves to a different spot. The scrape of his beard brushes against my skin as he drags his lips from one spot to another. It's too much and not enough all at once.

"Please," I hear myself beg as I press my head deeper into the pillow. "I need you, please, Mountain."

The bed shifts around me, but I pay it no mind until the second I realize Mountain's kisses have stopped. Opening my eyes, I'm met with his face right above mine. "Is this what you want, Blue?"

Just then, he rocks his hips forward, rubbing the length of his dick into my folds, causing my center to throb and weep. "Yessss," I hiss as he does it again.

"You're so wet and hot for me," he continues to tease, then finally finds my entrance with his blunt tip. "You want me right . . . here?" With that one word, he slams forward, entering me in one quick thrust.

"Yes!" I shout, eyes rolled back and seeing stars. "More!"

"I'll give you whatever I . . ." each word out of Mountain is met by another driving-forward drop of his weight, "damn . . . well . . . please."

Over and over, his hips come crashing down into the cradle of mine, and I'm sent deeper into a space I don't think I've ever been in before. Up here, I'm floating above my body as I'm ravaged from the inside out.

I feel enough of my body to let go of the comforter and wrap my arms around Mountain's shoulders, pulling him closer to me. He drops his weight onto his forearms, then presses his lips to mine. But it's not a kiss. In fact, it's anything but. Both of us are panting into each other in sync with the rhythm of his dick slamming in and out of my sopping wet pussy. I can feel and hear how wet he's making me with every slap of our skin connecting.

It's dirty, it's nasty, and it's heaven all mixed into one. And if it weren't for the feeling building inside of me with each thrust, about to explode all over both of us, I'd be begging my man to never stop. But unfortunately for me . . . nope, I take that back . . . fortunately for me, my man knows exactly how to please his woman.

I hold on to him as tight as I can, digging my fingertips into his shoulder blades as I come so hard, and so long, my vision starts to fade out in the corners. I hear grunts, a few 'fucks' along with a moan so loud it'd put a ship's foghorn to shame, then Mountain pushes inside me as far as our bodies will allow before holding himself to me tight.

"Fuckin' A, Blue," Mountain mumbles into my shoulder before pushing up onto his hands to give us both room to breathe. His chocolate eyes meet mine, and I don't think I've seen this deep shade in a year. He looks almost a decade younger, the lines around his eyes are less sharp, and his cheeks are high and flushed as he smiles down at me. "How did you do that to me?"

This is what we both needed, even more than I think we realized. I know I didn't until just now. We may have been excited and anxious to get to this point, where we're finally open and honest about what we need from each other, but it's almost like this first time really reconnecting put back the first piece to our puzzle. The first piece to reconnect us.

Unable to hold back, I laugh out loud, shaking both our bodies and sending a few more jolts of pleasure through us. "How did I do what to you?"

Mountain slowly pushes up onto all fours, then falls to his right, settling on his back with a thump. I roll onto my left so I can see his face.

"How did you drain me like that? I wanted to love on you for hours, but ten minutes in and I'm sixteen again, losing it like a one pump chump." His reply sends both of us into hysterics.

My cheeks hurt from smiling so big, and now laughing, I'll probably never be able to un-move my face from this position. "You're welcome?" I reply in a half shrug, half asking answer. Tracing some of the feathers on his chest with my right hand, I prop my head up with my left, then kiss his bicep. "I should really be thanking you for all that, Mountain. We wouldn't have gotten to this point if it weren't for you."

Rolling to his right, Mountain lifts my right leg over his hip and presses close. "What do you mean? I like where we are very much right now. Don't you?"

"I do," I reply as I continue tracing his chest, trying to put my words together right, so I can tell him what I'm feeling. Once I think I have it all unscrambled, I move my hand up to his cheek. Lightly scratching my nails along the scruff of his beard, I finally admit my weakness. "I need you to know that I'm still scared out of my mind."

"No!" he exclaims, but I hush any further protest with a finger to his lips.

"Listen, please," I beg him. "I'm scared because I know deep down in my soul that had you not called and chased me today, the bridge between us would have been too damaged to repair. It crushes me to say it, to admit it, but I had every intention of never coming back to this clubhouse again.

"I had a plan to wait a few days, whether you tried to reach out to me or not, and then I'd find a new place to live. I'd planned to go out and look for a job, find an apartment, and try to start to build my life without needing you. I thought you and I were past fixing what was so broken, and I needed to get away from this place."

"Blue, please let me speak. I need—"

"No, please." I sit up and wipe the tears rolling uncontrollably down my cheeks. Mountain sits and pulls me into his embrace, but I continue. "I had to be away because these walls hold too many good, happy, loving memories, and I couldn't be here one day longer. The house was the only place where I knew I could go and still be safe."

"No, no, no, no, no." Rocking me side to side, Mountain whispers over and over again, repeating his devastation to my words, then like the flip of a switch, I'm pushed back. His hands are back holding my face to his, and with one long, harsh kiss, I'm let free. "You will never leave my side again, do you hear me, Blue? Never. I'll never let you feel as weak as you did this afternoon when you walked out those doors. We will never be there again, I promise. I promise on my mother's grave, on my children's lives, on our grandson's life, you will never again go one day wondering if I love you. Because I do, Blue. I love you more than life itself."

Mirroring Mountain as much as our sweaty bodies allow, I climb back into his lap to straddle him. "I love you more than anything in this world. I never meant for my words to scare you, I just needed you to know everything." Pressing my lips to his, I hope to show him the gratitude I have for pushing through my walls and making me see we weren't done yet.

"Our journey is far from over, love," Mountain coveys his truth. "We have so many more days and years together. We have more memories to make, more grandbabies to love, and probably more fights to have which will be followed by moments like this of brutal honesty and making love. I wouldn't want to do this with anyone but you."

Tracing his cheeks with my fingertips, I stare into his soul. "Please promise me that as we start to unravel the mess we let our relationship become, we will always remember this right here? I know the fight is far from over because we still have bumps to iron out, but if it ever gets to be too hard, we stop whatever we're doing and come right back to this bed."

"If I ever feel either of us is having a weak moment, I'll pull us into this room and onto this bed," Mountain presses kisses to my cheeks, nose, forehead, and chin after every line, "and drape your pretty little legs over my lap, hold you in my arms, and we will take a deep breath. Is that what you want?"

"All I want is you, my strong, handsome, amazing, loving husband. You and our family are all that matters."

"I love you, Blue."

I try to respond, but before I can, my body falls forward as Mountain lays back, pulling me with him. I quickly become preoccupied with our commitment to use this very bed as the space to reconnect whenever life becomes too rough.

Our hands and bodies speak for us as we give everything we have to each other. This is our new beginning.

CHAPTER TWENTY-TWO

MOUNTAIN

If a man could survive on sex and sleep alone, this weekend would've built me up enough residual energy to store in order to live another sixty-some-odd years.

Blue and I didn't leave our room all weekend, only getting out of bed to feed our new kitten, play with her for a few hours intermittently to stop her insistent meowing at the door, take a few soapy showers that ended up with us dirtier than when we started, or to find something to eat to replenish the calories we were burning between the sheets. Or on top of the sheets. Or against the wall. Or on the floor. Or on the couch she says we now have to replace because it reminds her of me sleeping on it.

If a new couch is what she wants, a new couch is what she's going to get, just as soon as this wedding week is over and our clubhouse is brought back to some semblance of its former self. In a matter of a month, the converted meat processing plant the Rebel Vipers have used as a clubhouse for over thirty years has turned into a wedding warehouse for anything and everything that the brides have wanted.

As soon as the announcement was made, letting everyone know of the four brides getting their lucky day, there has been no turning back. There are lights and lace and something called tule everywhere you look. There's been plans drawn up for what has to be moved where to make room for the rows of chairs that need to be set up to make an aisle for everyone to walk down. And the craziest of all, every damn biker in this place is on board for the shindig. Not one Brother has raised a stink about their precious clubhouse being turned into a winter fairytale land for the Christmas Eve nuptials.

And that leads me to the mission I'm on right now. I need to hunt down my son and see what it's going to take to try and cut in on a little bit of the action of the big day. But I need to get out of this room, and away from Blue, to do so.

"Blue, I told you," I say as I pull her close by our joined hands and give her a quick kiss, "I'm just gonna go see if the guys need any help with their jobs for the wedding. It's Monday, the big day is on Friday, and knowing those four yahoos, someone's bound to have forgotten something."

"Why don't I come with you?" Her eyes beg me to say yes, but I need to put my one foot down. But that doesn't stop her from trying. "I'll show you how much I appreciate you helping the guys later if you let me come help too."

"Dammit, woman, I'm trying to be a good Pops to my son and you're raining on my parade," I lay on the excuse thick. "If you step one foot in that office with me, no one is gonna believe it was my idea to offer my help. They're gonna think you dragged me in there with you, and then they'll never let me forget it."

"Okay, fine," Blue says with a sigh and a roll of her eyes. "You go do your secret man stuff. I'll go find the brides and gossip with them about how stubborn the men of this club are."

"Love, that's not gossip, that's the truth. We're stubborn, we know it, and we're damn proud of it." Puffing my chest out like a peacock, I strut toward the door. I no more get my cut over my shoulders when I'm ambushed with a kiss so tempting, I debate locking us in this room for just one more day. "That's enough outta you, you sex fiend. I'll give you all the lovin' you need tonight, I promise."

"Is that a promise or a threat?" Blue winks as she backs away.

"Both," I reply with a growl. "Now, go get dressed and hang out with your ladies. I'll come find you in a little bit."

"Love you," she says with a smile.

"Love you, too," I tell her for the thousandth time in two days. With one last head scratch for Diva, I head for the hallway, making sure the surprisingly fast furball doesn't escape.

Whiskey's office is directly across the hall from mine and Blue's room, so all I do is turn right, take a half dozen steps, then turn left into the open doorway. "Morning, fellas. What's crackin'?"

"Holy shit, it's alive!" Whiskey gasps as he leans back in his chair. "We were beginning to wonder if the two of you were ever gonna come up for air."

"Don't you worry about me and my Old Lady's air," I reply back with a short laugh as I take a seat in the empty chair next to Bear. Hammer is also in here, but he's kicked back on the couch against the far-left wall, feet propped up on an upside-down milk crate. "I gave her all the *air* she needed."

"Oh fuckin' jeeze Louise, I didn't need to hear that, Pops," Whiskey whines as he throws a balled-up piece of paper at me.

"Just because I know it happens, don't mean I need to hear about it."

"I didn't know old people could even still do that," Hammer speaks up. "Aren't your bones too brittle?"

"Fuckin' right we can still get the job done." Bear holds out his fist and we bump in agreement, both grinning like the cat who ate the canary. Or maybe the bikers who ate the pussy, because I sure did my fair share of that this weekend. Fuck, just thinking about it makes me hard.

"That's enough outta you two old bastards." Whiskey shakes his head. "Was there something you needed, Pops? Or did you just come in here to rub in how much you got laid?"

"That's just a side perk of my drop-in," I reply, straightening my cut like I'm posturing. "But no, that's not all. I wanna run something by all the grooms, and Bear too, since he's in here."

"You want me to call Buzz and the Sunshine gang in here?" my son asks, picking up his phone. "It's Monday, everyone should be around."

"If you wouldn't mind." I no more than say the words and his fingers are flying across the screen of his phone.

A series of dings later, he tosses it back to the desk. "They're all on the way."

"So, you gonna leave us in suspense, Brother?" Bear turns his chair toward me. "What's the big news? You gonna leave this merry gang of misfits to join the circus?"

"Yea," Hammer chimes in. "I'm sure they'd love a one-legged man who can juggle."

"Fuck you, Hammer," I reply with a middle finger. "I've juggled once in my life and I was half drunk when I did it. Those broken beer bottles weren't my fault."

"Not 'til poor Blue stepped outside with no shoes on and walked right through the pile of glass shards," Whiskey says with a groan. "I don't think I've ever heard any woman scream so loud in my life."

"She still gives me grief for that scar on her foot." I think back to the day I had to hold her in my arms as she screamed and cried, Doc removing the pieces of glass in her foot one at a time, and then stitching her up.

"Where's the fire?" Ring walks in, Steel right behind him. I turn to see Buzz not a few seconds later.

"Come on in and join the party," Whiskey calls out. "Pops has something he'd like to run by us."

"What's up, Mountain?" Ring leans against the wall full of bookshelves to my right. Everyone else finds a spot to sit.

"Everything alright?" Steel asks from his perch on a short file cabinet off to the side and behind Whiskey.

"Everything's fine." I raise a hand to sate any worries. "I just need to ask y'all a favor."

"Anything you need, we're here for ya," Buzz replies.

Looking around at the six of them, I know I can trust them with the major kick to the ego I went through. "I don't know if any of you have noticed lately, but things between Blue and I haven't been going so good. We went through a little bit of a rough patch and tried to keep it out of everyone's way, but long story short, we made up this past weekend. Things aren't back to one hundred, but I need to do something to show her I'm all in, and that's where I need everybody's help."

Leaning forward, Whiskey props an elbow on his desk, chin resting on his knuckles. "I can't lie. I've seen a little tension between you two but never knew it was bad."

"I take it things didn't go so well after our little porch chat?" Bear asks.

I shake my head. "Nope, not so much."

"But things are better now, right?" Looking at my son, I see a flashback of his ten-year-old self sitting in this very office as I told him the news that I wanted to marry his aunt. His blue eyes stared at me like I was off my rocker, much like hers did when I held out my momma's ring to her and asked her to marry me. The look he's giving me now is filled with more emotion than it did that day, but I feel the same pride to be his father, maybe even more.

"Things are much better now," I reply with a nod. "Hence calling you all in. I want to know if before you all get hitched, if you wouldn't mind me stealing a little of your spotlight and renewing my vows with Blue? She never got a real wedding 'cause I snuck her off to the damn courthouse, so I think, I hope, she'd love to take part in the big day."

"Hell yea," Ring replies with a shout. "I'm all for it."

"Me too."

"I'm in."

"What's one more?"

Whiskey finally gives his decision when the ruckus dies down. "I'll give my stamp of approval as long as you let me be the one to give her away."

"But I need this to stay between the seven of us 'til the morning of," I practically plead as I look at my Brothers all around me. "If even one woman hears of this, it's gonna spread like wildfire, and my plans to keep it a secret will go up in flames."

"Mum's the word from us." Buzz mimes zipping his lips and tossing the key.

"Same here," Hammer adds. "I can't wait to see Blue's face when she walks down that aisle."

"Me too, Brother. Me too." My words are met by a rolling round of laughter.

"Need us for anything else? Or can I go back to cartoons with my munchkin?" Steel asks as he points to the door.

"Nope, you're all free to go." I wave him off. "Only people I need now are my son and the preacher man."

The newcomers all head out, including Hammer, so I'm left with Whiskey and Bear.

"Whatchya need from me?" Bear questions as he kicks one boot over the other knee.

"I need you to run through the vows you'll be using with all the others with me. I have no idea what to say to remarry someone. I've never done this part before. The babble the judge had us saying all went in one ear and out the other. I'm out of my element here, man."

"I hate to be the bearer of bad news, Mountain," Bear shakes his head at my predicament. "All the other couples are writing their own vows."

Jerking my head to Whiskey, I see him nod. "He's right, Pops. If we all gotta write some flowery lovey-dovey shit, so do you."

I lean back in my chair and rub my eyes with my thumb and pointer finger. "Fuckin' hell."

"It'll be okay, Brother," Bear says with a laugh as he slaps my shoulder. "Just tell her how you feel. But no talk about sexy stuff. She'll be bound to leave your ass at the altar for that."

"Remember," Whiskey adds with a chuckle of his own, "children will be present. Keep it PG."

"Yea, yea, yea. I'll figure something out."

"Now, what'd you need from me, Pops?"

Remembering perhaps the second most important part of what I hope to be a very happy day, I get down to the brass tacks. "I need to get Blue a gift."

"Any thoughts on what to get her?" Whiskey asks as he leans back in his chair.

"Oh, I have the perfect idea, but I'll need your help to pull it off."

Hands linked behind his head, he asks, "Whatchya got in mind?"

"You know how you . . ."

CHAPTER TWENTY-THREE

MOUNTAIN

"Driver! Turn this shit up!" Hammer shouts across the bus as the next song comes through the speakers.

All my Brothers let out some form of happy acknowledgment as the steady drumbeat and vocals of "Cum On Feel the Noize" by Quiet Riot fill the rectangle party room on wheels we're currently cruising down the highway in. A few seconds in, as soon as the guitars kick in, we're all singing along.

We may sound like screaming, howling monkeys, but none of us care one bit. We're all a couple beers in and starting to feel the beginning of what hopefully will be a great buzz for the rest of the night. It's just after eight o'clock on Thursday night, the night before Christmas Eve, and we're on our way to a strip club.

We probably should've done this a night earlier in the week, but everyone has been so wrapped up in planning the actual wedding, somehow the bachelor party got pushed off until tonight was our only option left. So here we all sit, in a party bus on our way to a club called Scores Gentlemen's Club. It's a little over an hour away from the clubhouse, and we happen to know the owner, so he promised to hook us up with some VIP treatment.

Now, that's not to say those of us who aren't either married, getting married, or are taken have any plans on doing something to jeopardize our relationships, but sometimes looking is acceptable. A few of the Old Ladies weren't the happiest when they heard the news about our strip club destination, but that's part of club life.

I kissed Blue, promising to keep my hands to myself, even offering to sit on them if that's what she wanted me to do. Then, I slapped her on the ass before I walked away and climbed on the bus. It wasn't until we pulled away that I noticed the inside pocket of my cut was a little bulkier than normal, so when I pulled out an impressively large folded stack of dollar bills, I realized my wife is one sneaky devil. She knows I'd never stray from her, so she contributed to my night of fun fund.

We just left a restaurant where each of us chowed down on steaks bigger than our heads, so filled bellies are checked off the list, and we spend the next twenty minutes or so drinking beer, munching on snacks, and shooting the shit as we listen to too loud music.

I recognize the building as soon as we slow down to turn into the parking lot. Being just off the nearest highway, there is parking for semis and larger trucks, so we circle the lot until the driver finds a space. From the number of cars and rigs in the lot, it looks like there's going to be a large crowd tonight. Thank God for VIP.

As we disembark and are out from behind the tinted windows of the blacked-out bus, the club's sign shines brightly from the building's front and side facade. A large white square is backlit, making the silhouette of a woman dancing on a hockey stick stand out. The words 'Scores' is written in a black flowing font, but pops because of the red neon lights glowing behind it.

Having been here before, we know the club's interior and exterior has a sports theme. The building itself is matte black, but there are vertical white lines painted along the front that mimic the yard lines on a football field. Inside, the booths all have tables depicting the layout of different sports fields. Baseball diamonds, soccer goals, hockey rinks, football goal posts—if you can think it, there's a table that's got it.

Following the group, with Butch and Bear at my sides, I almost crash into Tiny when he comes to an abrupt halt in front of me. "Whoa, what's the hold-up?"

"Dunno," Tiny mumbles with a shrug.

Murmured voices start to pick up, but a few raised ones at the front of the group grab my attention. Circling our crowd, I make it to the front to see Whiskey glaring at his phone. "What the fuck?"

Steel's starts to ring just then, so he pulls it from his pocket to answer. "They have *what* at the clubhouse?" he yells into the phone.

Hammer reads whatever is on Whiskey's cell from over his shoulder. "Oh, fuck no." He moves to grab it, but it's pulled out of his reach.

Steel is walking in circles but suddenly faces us and snaps into the phone. "Goddamnit. We're on our way back."

"On our way back where?" I can't help but ask, several Brothers echoing my confusion. We haven't even stepped foot in the club, and now, all of a sudden, these two want us to leave. Not without a damn good reason.

"Our Old Ladies decided it was a good idea to bring male strippers dressed as cops into our clubhouse," Steel explains, causing my jaw to drop at his ire.

"And no one tried to stop this from happening?" I step toward my son, intent on getting some answers. "Where the fuck are the Prospects? Aren't they supposed to be watching over the ladies?"

"When Ray and Diego tried to stop the douchebags," Whiskey's fingers move quickly over his screen as he talks, "my soon-to-be wife threw down her 'I'm the President's Old Lady, so I'm the boss while the Brothers are gone' card and insisted the fuckers be let in."

"They did what?" I feel my pulse racing but can't seem to care. "Blue never would've agreed to that." And she wouldn't. At least, I think she wouldn't. She handed me money for me to spend tonight, but maybe that was convenient because she had gotten her own stack to shower on strippers as well.

Steel lifts a finger, silencing our group as he continues listening to whichever Prospect got stuck calling their VP on a night like tonight. I wouldn't have wanted that to be me. Steel can be an angry motherfucker when he wants to be. "One sec." He pulls the phone away from his ear to speak. "Apparently, every single woman we left at the clubhouse is throwing dollar bills around like confetti at the New Year's Eve celebration in Times Square. Ray's words, not mine . . . Your wife included." Those words, he aims at me.

For goddamn motherfucking heaven's sake, what were those ladies thinking? If my instincts are right, I know exactly who's behind this, and three women are fixing to get their asses handed to them when we get back.

"I bet those strippers are puny as fuck," Ring comments as he flexes his bicep. "No one has real muscles like us."

"I say we head back to the clubhouse and remind our women what real men look like." Hammer's posture reads 'ready to fuck some shit up' as he stands with his boots shoulder-width apart and his arms folded across his chest.

"That's not fair!" Cypher calls out as he points at the building in front of us. "What about us seeing strippers?"

Gunner's complaint follows. "Yea! Just because you guys wanna yell at your ladies doesn't mean the rest of us should have to suffer."

Butch shakes his head as he mirrors his son, arms folded and mean-mugging the whole lot of us. "I'm not leavin' without seein' titties."

Whiskey and Steel exchange looks, seemingly having a conversation without words, before turning to me. "What do you think, Pops?"

"What do I think about what?"

Whiskey points at the bus. "Should we head back or stay?"

Thinking for a second, I realize there's not one answer that will work best for everyone. Maybe it's best we split up. "I say whoever wants to stay can stay. Those of us who wanna go home and show our women the error of their ways can head back. The bus can take us home, then come back at closing to pick everyone else up."

Whiskey's eyes glaze over for a second as he thinks, then blinks the fog away. "Everybody goin' home, get back on the fuckin' bus!" he shouts.

There are fist bumps, back slaps, handshakes, and 'have funs' passed around to people on both sides of the coin before Whiskey, Ring, Steel, Hammer, Smoke, Haze, Buzz, and Bear climb back on the bus with me and head for home. Everyone else has chosen to stay, so who knows what time in the morning they'll be rolling in. Skynyrd decided to stay in an attempt to be some semblance of reasoning, but knowing him and his crazy ways, he'll be right in with the fray.

An hour later, we pull in through the compound fence and see a van parked off to the side in front of the bay door of Rebel Repairs. I don't know whose van this is, but they need to take some pride in their shit. Having driven some vehicles in my life that probably belonged alongside the Flintstones, even I wouldn't drive this hooptie. It's a faded red color, but one of the side doors looks to be spray painted a turquoise blue, and not one body panel is without rust spots or holes along the edges.

The second I hobble my ass down the bus steps, I hear music blaring from inside the clubhouse, even with all the doors and windows closed.

"Let's see what our ladies are up to." Whiskey stomps forward but is brought to a stop when Buzz runs ahead of him, stopping him at the double doors.

"Before we left, Cypher downloaded an app on my phone so I can access the sound system inside. Maybe as soon as we open the door, I shut the music off."

"That'll bring the party to a crashing halt," Whiskey replies with a laugh and a fist pump to Buzz.

Like we're about to embark on a stealth mission, we all line up on the porch, then slowly open the doors. Looking around, I see the ladies are too preoccupied to notice our arrival. There's so much giggling and cheering and whistling going on, I doubt they'd be able to hear a bomb going off behind them.

All of the ladies are facing to the right of the main room, where three men who are currently wearing nothing but banana hammocks and bow ties are dancing in an open area. The dining tables have both been pushed out of the way and all of the furniture has been rearranged to face the strippers. Couches, recliners, and a few tables, now holding blinking cups with what looks to be straws shaped like penises in them, litter the room like this is a midnight matinee.

Whiskey makes a quick mime of slashing his throat, signaling Buzz to cut the music. The room almost echoes as the bass stops booming and a song about anacondas not wanting none unless you got some, but it cuts out before we hear what that is.

"Good evening, gentlemen," I call out, eyes locked on the fuckers who are now frozen in place. They're all standing still with their hands cupped over their tiny peckers, looking back and forth from each other to the nine of us who crashed the party.

Gasps fill the room as every single woman jumps up from her seat and turns to face us.

"Oh fuck," Duchess mumbles. "We're in trouble."

My eyes move to my wife as I hear Whiskey say from behind me, "You bet your sweet ass you're in biiiig trouble."

"Everybody who doesn't live or work here," Steel's voice booms out, "get the fuck out of this clubhouse. Right. Now."

The entertainment goes scrambling for the miscellaneous discarded items of clothing scattered on the floor, along with a small duffel bag each, then I follow them in my periphery as they book it around the room and out the door being held open by Buzz.

I turn back to see Blue heading straight for me. Her steps are slow but steady, and she stops just inches from my chest. "Mountain," she says hesitatingly.

Cocking an eyebrow, I look down into her baby blues. "Yes, wife?"

She rests her hands on my crossed forearms, then breathes out a big sigh. "I had no idea this was happening until you guys all left."

My head crooks a little to the right and I try to get a read on if she's lying or not. "Did you do anything to stop it?"

"Well . . ." Blue looks around at the other ladies who are now also paired off with their men before turning back to me, "no."

Her continued hesitancy is making me feel a mix bag of emotions. On one hand, I know I should be really mad at her for taking part in stripper-gate and not calling me as soon as she found out, but on the other, seeing the look on her face is making me horny as fuck. I don't know if the innocent act is all a ruse because she has been known to play sneaky to get what she wants in the bedroom, but whatever it is, it's working.

Dropping my arms, I take a step back and turn to address the crowd of couples. "I think the party is over and it's time for everyone to go to your rooms."

Angel spins around in Hammer's arms, resting a hand on her hip. "But I'm not—"

Hammer crowds behind her and slaps a hand over her mouth. "You're not a kid," he growls in her ear, "but I'm about to teach you a lesson you'll never forget."

"Oh!" Angel mumbles as her eyes go big. Even behind Hammer's big mitt, I can tell she's smiling by the roundness of her cheeks. She pushes out of his hold and takes off running out the back door.

"When I catch you," Hammer shouts as he's hot on her heels.

Taking that as some sort of sign, every single woman goes running in a different direction, all except my woman. She stays right where she is, standing right in front of me.

I take a step forward, coming back to where I was before I ordered the party over, and lean my head down just a bit to whisper in her ear. "Aren't you gonna run off like a scared bunny rabbit too?"

"Nope." Blue plants a soft kiss on my cheek before taking a tiny step back. "I know you can't run with that leg, so I'll just let you lead me to my lesson."

Can you say 'perfect fucking woman'?

"Bedroom. Now." I point to the hall a ways behind her.

"Yes, please."

CHAPTER TWENTY-FOUR

DUCHESS

"There's no way in hell that Whiskey signed off on this." Ray points at the man standing outside the front gate.

"I never said he did," I reply. My arms are folded across my chest, hands rubbing up and down my biceps. It's fucking cold out here, and since these asshole Prospects won't let my guests through, I had to come outside to try and straighten things out.

His back turned to the fence, Ray asks, "You want me to open this gate and let these three yahoos dressed as mall cops into the clubhouse? I'm gonna lose my head for this."

Diego is standing beside me, eyes locked on the van idling out by the road. "If I lose my cut because of some low rent strippers, I'm gonna hurt someone." I spin on my heels to face him. His arms are crossed and he is seething mad. If I could fully see his expression in these shadows, I imagine his whole face would be red.

No longer caring if I'll freeze, I drop my hands to my hips and glare at Diego through squinty eyes. "I respectfully don't give a fuck what happens to you. This is our bachelorette party, and we want some entertainment."

Ray throws his hands up, flabbergasted. "But why does it have to be strippers?"

I turn my scowl on him. "Where are the Brothers right now?"

"That's not the same." Diego's words sound like a mixture between a whine and a protest.

"It's not?" I question, one eyebrow lifted so high, it's probably in the middle of my forehead. "Are they not on their way to see women take their clothes off?"

"Yes, but—"

I stop him before he can say anything else stupid. "But nothing, Prospect. The second the Brothers left this compound, I became the person in charge. My Old Man is the President of this club, so that makes me the highest-ranking person here."

"And as the woman who's been here the longest, I back her up," Belle, Skynyrd's Old Lady, pipes up from behind me. I had no idea she came outside, but I'm more than thankful for the backup. "Hell, I'm the one who called them. When the Brothers come back, do you want me to tell my Old Man and my son, who are both your superiors, that you didn't give their women what they wanted?"

Ray glances between the man standing silently, waiting to be let in or told to go away, then at me and Belle. "It's your fuckin' funeral." He heads for the guard shack, and seconds later, the gate rolls open.

Pointing toward the clubhouse, I tell the man, "Drive your van on up and park just to the left of the front doors, then I'll show you guys where to set up."

Walking up to the front doors, I follow the van carrying the three strippers that Belle, Angel, and I arranged to have here this evening. I'm not exactly sure where Belle found them, but based on their vehicle of choice, they need the money big time.

Showing the men around the main room, they step into the bathroom to change, while us ladies, minus the pregnant ones, and the irritated Prospects manage to move the furniture around to accommodate the evening's activities. As soon as the last recliner is slid into position so Sunshine and her growing belly have a front and center view, the party begins.

Music kicks on at a volume that's *this* close to too loud, and I see two men approach the area we cleared for them from the left, then one more from the right. They line up, backs turned toward us, dressed in knock-off policemen's uniforms. Once the crescendo builds to the top, the beat drops and they spin around and rip open their shirts. All you see is bare chests, two showing tattoos, and gyrating hips doing coordinated moves. Either these men have been working together for a long time, or they have a very good choreographer.

We spend the next ten minutes, or three songs, watching as the strippers remove one article of clothing at a time. There are pants flying through the air toward us followed by dollar bills being tossed in the opposite direction at them. By the time the fourth and fifth song hit, they decide to start dancing closer to us, and the only thing they're wearing is neon-colored G-strings.

As stripper number one, whose name I believe is 'Thunder', stands in front of Angel with his legs braced apart and his abs and hips doing these crazy twirly moves, she sits back and just watches with an almost bored expression. "They have nice muscles and bulges, but my man's are way better."

"Mine too. Times two." Sunshine lets out a crack of laughter as she holds out a few bills to the stripper who's dancing in circles around her chair.

Her laughter, along with her funny rhyme, makes all of us laugh along. Girl's got some spunk today, and I love it. I can't even imagine what it's like to be carrying two babies at once, and Sunshine is doing it like a champ. Putting her in the spotlight to be spoiled is well deserved.

"It's a good thing we sent the kids away for the night," Sara calls out from a few seats to my left. "There's no way in hell we could've done this with all the munchkins running around."

"No kidding. Thank God for three mothers-in-law," Sunshine yells out.

"Steel's moms are seriously the best. We owe them soooo big," I holler back at her.

Sunshine sure lucked out in the partner family lottery. Between having two moms himself, and an awesome half-sister, Steel also has a bonus mom. When Steel's biological father slash pseudo sperm donor married Kathy, and they had Meredith, his moms brought her into their circle and include her in everything. So, when Janie and Helen offered to watch all the kids and babies so we could have a ladies' night, Kathy and Meredith joined in. I have no doubt that all four women are spoiling them rotten.

"And I'm glad Ray took outside watch duty. If he had to stand in here like Diego, I'd be toast." Sara's words make us all look back at the grump who's typing on his phone while standing guard at the entrance to the far hallway. I have no doubt he's texting with Whiskey or one of the other officers about what's happening here right now.

"We might as well get our looks in now, ladies," Raven hops up onto her knees on the couch to my right, "'cause the second those

Prospects get off the phone, we've only got an hour until the men get back and put the kibosh on our party. I just know they're both squealing on us as we speak." She then tucks a couple bills in the G-string of the guy shaking his butt in her face.

"Maybe we can just all take our clothes off when they get here," Sunshine says with a laugh as she waves a fan of money up in the air. "The makeovers and waxes we all got this morning will make the men forget they're mad at us."

"Sunshine," Angel is losing her mind in giggles, "just because your men like to pull you into the bathroom and fuck you silly with the door unlocked, doesn't mean the rest of us like to be voyeurs."

All Sunshine can do is shrug. "What can I say, my men like to watch me get off."

"I like the naked idea." Blue smiles as she throws a few bills out on the floor to the man who's grinding on his knees. "Mountain loves my smooth legs." She stretches out her leg, pointing her toes and showing off her freshly painted white toenails in her open-toed heels.

"No offense, Blue," I chuckle and throw a dollar at her, "but I don't wanna see your waxed lady bits."

She crumples the bill and throws it back at me, "I didn't mean get naked in front of everybody, you nympho."

When we start throwing more money at each other than at the strippers, the laughter grows so out of control, I can't help but fall into a snorting fit. Then, as soon as I do it, Angel can't help but fall into her own hysterics. I swear, it's a family curse. God help our children, and hopefully, they won't inherit that trait from us.

The next half hour or so passes in a flash, and before you know it, everything comes to an ear-pinching halt. We're taken by surprise when the music is cut off, and every single one of us jumps up from our seat and spins to face the firing squad.

We come face to face with a bunch of grumpy, grouchy, irritated, sexy, muscle bulging, sex on a stick group of bikers.

"Oh fuck. We're in trouble." I look at Whiskey, very familiar with the pissed-off look he's aiming at me.

"You bet your sweet ass you're in biiiig trouble." Fuck, he heard my mumbling.

"Everybody who doesn't live or work here, get the fuck out of this clubhouse. Right. Now," Steel shouts. Immediately, I hear rustling from behind me, followed by the strippers running out the front door, clothes and bags in their arms.

My eyes are locked on my Old Man, so when he curls his finger, beckoning me to him, I can't help but do as he orders. As if they know exactly where to go and what to do, my feet make their own way until I'm standing in front of Whiskey. My brain is stuck between 'oh shit' and 'fuck me' modes, and I have no control over my movements.

"Start talking, Duchess." Whiskey's words are accompanied by crossed arms, furrowed eyebrows, and just a flash of heat in his eyes that makes me hope this won't be all bad.

Looking down at the floor, I have my fingers twisted in knots, and I scuff my tennis shoe against the floor. I know this is bad, this is really bad, but how do I get out of this trouble? Do I apologize? Do I try and be flirty? Do I just tell the truth and see what happens? Tomorrow is our wedding day, he can't be too mad at me, right?

Grabbing hold of the courage and balls I had to get those strippers into the building, I buck back up and face whatever happens next. I meet Whiskey's eyes head-on, lift my chin high, throw my shoulders back, and puff my chest out . . . like the boss bitch I am.

"We were just having some fun, is all."

"Fun?" Whiskey's right eyebrow lifts. "You call bringing strippers into my clubhouse fun?"

"Well, yea," I reply, attitude still on high.

"And who gave you the permission to hire them?"

"Who what?" This is his first question that starts to tip my scales in the other direction. Worry starts to drop just a little bit as anger begins to sneak in. "Who gave me the permission? No one. I didn't know I had to ask permission to have a little fun with my girls. Isn't that what tonight was supposed to be before y'all just ran in here and crashed the party?"

"You're right," Whiskey growls as he takes a few steps toward me, then presses his bulk into my chest. He grabs hold of my hips, leans down, and bites on my earlobe. "Tonight *was* supposed to be fun."

His lips move to my neck, so I tilt my head to the side. He nips at the spot he knows drives me wild, and right then, I know he's not really mad, at least not all the way mad. My man is horny and needs to use it as a way to work out his frustrations. And luckily for me, it'll be me who he works over.

Whiskey's attack on my senses is making it hard to stand, let alone breathe. "So, then, what's the problem?" I ask with a sigh as he licks up my neck.

"My problem is," he grunts as he thrusts his denim-covered hardness into my stomach, "what do I do with you now?"

"I think the party is over and it's time for everyone to go to your rooms." Mountain's powerful voice snaps me out of the slow burn I was building.

Whiskey spins me in his arms and wraps himself around me in a way I've always loved. His chin is tucked into the crook of my neck and shoulder, his arms are encompassing my torso like a boa constrictor, and his feet are spread apart so my ass settles right back into the groove of his hips. He's touching me with every bit of himself that is physically possible, and I love it.

But there's someone in the room who's not so happy with Mountain's order.

Angel works her way free from Hammer's arms and spins around. A hand on her hip, she sasses back, "But I'm not—"

Hammer pulls her into his chest and covers her mouth with his large hand. "You're not a kid," he growls in her ear, "but I'm about to teach you a lesson you'll never forget."

"Oh!" I watch as Angel's anger fizzles out, and that's when she begins to understand what's really going on. Hammer must be feeling much of what Whiskey is and wants to teach his lady a lesson in permission versus forgiveness. Again, she squirms her way out of Hammer's grasp and starts running.

She gets halfway to the door before Hammer snaps out of his surprise and chases her. "When I catch you . . ."

And like a green flag at the Daytona 500, everyone takes off, but instead of running in circles, we all head in different directions.

Me? Where do I go? I push out of Whiskey's python arms and book it straight for the hallway on the right side of the main room which eventually leads outside and straight to our cabin. It's empty right now, no screaming infant to disturb us, and I very much look forward to not having to be quiet and careful of the noises I make as I'm ravaged and pleasured all night long.

I make it out the door and maybe five steps before I'm compressed between a large square porch post and the hot, heaving body of my Old Man.

"Well, miss 'I'm the President's Old Lady, so I'm in charge', where the hell do you think you're goin'?"

"To bed, so you can punish me." Holding the post I'm being pressed against as best as I can with my hands, I grind my ass back into a very hard package.

"You got that right." Whiskey grabs hold of each of my bent elbows and proceeds to march me toward our home.

Not caring one bit that my feet can barely keep up, his forward momentum makes my shoes scrape and skip across the path leading to our porch. He lifts me clean off my feet as he climbs the steps, then sets me back down in front of the door. Between the two of us, we get the door open and we're through the opening before he attacks.

Whiskey spins me to face him, then proceeds to literally take my breath away. His lips come down on mine so hard, I have to scramble to clutch the front of his flannel, so I don't fall backward and land on my butt. His hands are holding my face in place, tilting my whole body into the position he needs so he can devastate me.

But just as quick as he spins me to face him, I'm spun back around and suddenly facing the living room. His hands on my hips, Whiskey forces me forward, and next thing I know, I'm bent over the arm of the couch, face first into one of the fluffy decorative pillows.

"Stay there," Whiskey orders before wrestling with my waistband to unbutton my jeans and pulling them down. "Don't move!"

SLAP! A hand comes down on my right butt cheek, then immediately again on my left.

"Fuck!" I scream into the pillow.

"I told you not to move," Whiskey says with no emotion. His hands grip hold of my butt cheeks, and I feel his fingertips bruise my muscles. "No panties, huh? I think I can work with that."

"Oh, please." Just hearing him talk about my ass makes my hips wiggle, but two seconds later, another slap comes down, this time on the side of my hip.

"Dammit, Duchess." My body is on fire, but Whiskey's fingers are icicles against my skin as he traces two fingers up the inside of my thigh, "I need this pussy." Then, with no preparation, he slams both fingers into my channel and begins fucking me with them like a train with no end in sight.

This time, when my muffled scream fills the room, it's in extreme pleasure instead of pain. Between the twist of his wrist, and the rubbing of his knuckles, I'm thrown straight into heaven with no plan on stopping before I see the stars.

"Fuck, you're so wet," Whiskey remarks as he continues to handle me. "I need you on my dick."

Hell, no argument from me on that. His fingers disappear, and right away, I have a hot, hard dick hitting just the right spot, slamming my insides. I grab hold of the pillow, screaming profanities into it even I've never heard myself say, as my ass and Whiskey's thighs clap against each other with every single one of his thrusts.

Turning my head to the side so I can breathe, I call out, "Right there. Right there. Please."

"Do. Not. Come." Whiskey orders each word with a forceful jolt to my hips. And I think he goes crazy.

He grabs hold of my hip in one hand, threading the other into the hair at the back of my head, then turns my face back into the pillow. I feel myself so close to coming, I expect to go off at any second, but when Whiskey lets out a growl to rival a lion, I know my chance is gone.

Whiskey uses this moment as a way to punish me for my hiring the male strippers, by fucking me like a damn ragdoll and not letting me come before him like he usually does. He's always said that I'm to 'get mine' before he does, but this one time he didn't, I can't even find myself being mad at him for it. That was hot as hell . . . and I want to do it again.

Letting me go everywhere he has hold of me, Whiskey slides his dick out of my pussy, then lifts me up to standing and turns me around. Pants still around my ankles, he drops his shoulder into my torso, tosses me over his shoulder, then proceeds to march down the hall to our bedroom.

Tossing me down on the bed, I land with a bounce as he pulls my shoes off, followed by my jeans, then steps back to start disrobing himself.

"Clothes off," Whiskey orders.

Like I'm going to protest. Items go flying, and right as I pull off my last sock, Whiskey grabs hold of my ankle and pulls me down to the end of the bed. I'm lying flat on the comforter as he pulls my hips to the edge of the mattress. He spreads my knees apart, lifts my legs up so my toes are pointing to the ceiling, and presses my thighs to his chest.

Sliding his dick between my swollen folds, I feel the ball of his Prince Albert piercing rubbing my clit as he teases me with his tip. I must've seen this curved beauty a thousand-plus times in the little over a year I've known this man, but every single time he undresses in front of me is like the first. The glint of the two steel balls attached to the head of Whiskey's penis is like a magnet to my cervix. Every slide of his dick into me, they hit me so deep, there's probably an indent somewhere up there.

Having enough of his teasing, I reach for his forearms. "Fuck me, Whiskey."

"What's that, my Duchess?" I swear Whiskey's eyes sparkle as he glances up from where our bodies are about to be joined.

"I need you," I say with a lift of my hips, "to put that monster inside of me."

Whiskey lets go of my legs and drops forward, folding my body almost in half. My knees are closer to my face than they've ever been. With his hands, he cups the sides of my breasts and pinches my nipples with his fingertips. My own piercings pull with his assault on my tender skin as he tugs the barbells I have through my nipples.

"You've gotten so bold with your words, love," Whiskey practically purrs before nipping my earlobe.

"You did this to me."

"I sure did." Rocking his hips back once, Whiskey drives his cock back inside me in one thrust.

"Shit." I try to squirm but can't move.

"Is this what you wanted?" Suddenly standing back at his full height, Whiskey holds my legs just above my knees and begins fucking me again.

In and out. In and out. Over and over and over, his hips drive into the round of my ass and I take off again.

Throwing my arms out to the sides, I hold on tight as my head flies back and I cry out repeatedly, "Yes! Yes! Yes! More!"

"Will you ever bring strippers into my clubhouse again?"

"No," I cry out, shaking my head.

"What do you need, Duchess?"

His question makes me slam one hand down on the bed in anger and need. "You, dammit."

"Tell. Me." Whiskey thrusts forward even harder with every word. "What. You. Need."

Having had enough of whatever theatrics he's trying to pull, I tell him my heart's most deepest desire. The one thing I've been asking of him for the last month since I got the all-clear from my doctor. "Put a damn baby in me already, goddamnit!"

"If you insist."

Oh, and I sure as hell do. Whatever he does to me next better make me grow another one of his babies. I love the one he gave me already so much, Krew needs a brother or sister pronto.

With one slight twist to both of my nipple piercings, everything building in my core explodes at once. I come so hard, I lose both my hearing and my sight and have no recollection of what's happening until I realize I'm lying on my side, head on the pillow, wrapped in Whiskey's arms.

"Are you in there, Duchess?" Whiskey asks as I blink up at him.

"I think so." Rolling onto my back, I stretch my arms and legs out in every direction, finally feeling like my body is mine again.

Once I'm back in his embrace, Whiskey tips my chin up to lure me in for a gentle kiss. "Do you think I gave you what you wanted just now?"

Scratching my fingernails down the scruff of his beard, I pull a little on the end at his chin. "I hope so."

"What do you want this time? A boy or a girl?"

"We don't get to pick that." His innocent question makes me snicker as I snuggle into his chest. "It's your swimmers that determine which one we get."

His whole body jerks. "My what does *what*?"

I rest my chin on his chest and look up at his confused face. The two lines between his eyebrows make him look so adorable and innocent, rather than the hard-edged killer he is inside.

"Did you not know that it's your sperm that makes the gender of the baby? Didn't you listen to anything you were taught in sex ed?"

"Nope." He pops the 'p' as he lays back. "I was havin' too much fun flinging condoms at Hammer from across the classroom."

"Of course, you were." I roll my eyes as I nuzzle into his heat.

"Did you just roll your eyes at me, Duchess?" Whiskey pulls me on top of him by my arms and sits me up, resting his hands on my thighs.

My butt is cradling his dick, which is hard again, so I wiggle a little to feel it jump. "Maaaaay-be."

"Just for that, I think you need to show me what I missed out on by leaving my bachelor party early." His hips thrust up once, bouncing both of us.

Dropping my hands to bracket his head, I lean down to whisper, "Connor, I may not be as skinny as I used to be, but I'll treat you better than any of those strippers you were going to see would have."

"Prove it."

"You're on." Sliding my slit up his cock, I show him what I've got.

"Fuck, yea."

CHAPTER TWENTY-FIVE

BLUE

Tugging the tie on my robe tight around my waist, I flip my hair over my shoulder and open the bathroom door. Stepping out into the bedroom, I make it three steps before I come to an abrupt halt at the sight of Mountain's profile as he sits at the end of our bed.

If I had a nickel for every time I told myself I was a lucky woman for somehow tying this man down, I'd be very rich . . . and have a whole truckload of nickels.

Even from the side, I can tell he's wearing the two things he knows I love seeing him in the most. Mountain's backside and muscular thighs look damn edible in those black Wrangler jeans. And that black t-shirt . . . well, butter my buns and call me a biscuit, because the way that cotton hugs his biceps should be illegal. Combine those guns with the taut pectoral muscles I use any excuse to touch, and I've died and gone to heaven.

"What's got you lookin' so spiffy, mister?"

My question makes Mountain turn his head toward me. He holds his hand out to the side, so I grab it, and he leads me around to stand between his boots. His smile is so wide, it's infectious, and I can't help but beam back at him.

Mountain lets out a wolf whistle. "How did I get so lucky to marry you?"

"I was just thinking the same thing." I rest my hands on his shoulders as he holds onto my hips. "Is this what you're wearing to the weddings?"

"Oh, this old thing," he says as he chuckles. "I've got a few more things to add to my outfit for the day. What are you wearin'?"

"The other Old Ladies made me buy a new dress while we were at the store last week. I didn't really want to, especially with how crappy things were going with us at the time, but now, I'm glad I did."

"I'm glad you did too." Mountain's reply is paired with a smile that's half smirk, and there's this look in his eye that I can't place.

I knit my fingers behind his neck and lean in a little closer. "What's going on with you today?"

Hugging my hips tighter, he looks up at me, his smile full-out now. "I've got an idea I need to run past you before the day starts."

"What's that?"

"What if I told you I want to renew our vows today?"

"What?" I step back, dropping my hold on him, only for Mountain to catch my falling hands in his.

"Blue, it's been twenty-one years since I was lucky enough to convince you to marry me," I can't take my eyes off his as he stands, "and I think it's time I tell you again how much I love and appreciate you. But this time, I wanna do it in front of all our family and friends, not just a judge and a few random witnesses."

"Mountain, I—"

"Please say yes, Blue. Please?" Mountain cuts me off before I can finish.

I pull my hands free and set them on his chest. Leaning up on my tiptoes, I lure him down for a quick kiss. Looking up into his beautiful brown eyes, I try again. "Mountain, I would remarry you every day for the rest of my life if I could."

Arms around my waist, Mountain picks me up and spins both of us in a circle. When I'm finally set back on my feet, his hands settle on either side of my neck to hold me steady as he kisses me deeply.

Coming up for air, he rests his forehead on mine. "You won't regret givin' me another chance, Blue. I promise."

"I can't believe we're doing this!" I cry out in laughter.

"Well, you better believe it." Mountain spins me around and nudges me forward. "Now, go get that new dress you bought, and anything else you need to get ready, 'cause you need to get your butt out to the cabin with the rest of the brides."

"Getting ready there was already my plan!" I shout over my shoulder as I disappear into the walk-in closet. "I want to be nowhere near this room when all your Brothers come traipsing in here to get ready."

I quickly swap my robe for sweats, fuzzy socks, and a pair of moccasin boots, then grab a small duffel bag from the shelf. I drop in my heels, undergarments, and a box holding the jewelry I plan on wearing.

Heading for the bathroom, I'm met by Mountain leaning against the door frame, arms folded. "I can't wait to see you walk down the aisle since we didn't get to do that the first time."

"You're too much sometimes." I kiss him, then shimmy past.

After adding all my makeup and hair essentials to the bag, I loop it over my shoulder, then head back to the closet to grab the dress. Once I have my coat on, I drape the dress bag over my arm, give some love to Diva, who's set up camp on the back of the couch, and make my way to the door.

"Hold your horses there, little filly," Mountain calls out as he takes his sweet time walking around the room. "Where's my kiss?"

Feeling so excited for today, and a little cheeky, I open the door and turn back to say, "Your kiss will be waiting for you at the end of the aisle."

But before I can lift a foot, I'm spun around, bent backward over his arm, and kissed like we're separating for a year. Standing me back up, he slaps my butt and pushes me out into the hallway. "And don't come back 'til you're ready to say 'I do'."

Laughter and applause fill the narrow space as Whiskey and Hammer step out of the office and I can't help but blush a little.

"See you fellas later." I wave and head outside.

Hustling down the path and up the steps to Duchess and Whiskey's, where all the brides are congregated to get ready together, I wrangle the door open with my empty arm and head inside.

Walking into the cabin, I'm met with what I can only call organized chaos.

"Good morning, ladies," I call out.

'Good morning' echoes through the wide-open living and kitchen space.

"What's got you smiling so big this morning?" Duchess asks from a chair at the dining table.

Sunshine appears at the entrance to the hall, waving a paper accordion fan at her face. "I think someone got a little morning delight."

"You're all nuts," I reply as I take off my coat. Hanging my dress on a rack that's just to the left of the entryway, the same one holding everyone else's, I lift my duffel bag off my shoulder and head for an empty space at the table.

"Something's up," Angel adds to the craziness. "You look a little flushed. Like Mountain kissed you within an inch of your life."

Throwing my hands up, I let them in on the news. "Fine, it's not like you're not gonna figure it out anyway."

"Tell me, tell me, tell me," Duchess chants as she claps fast.

"Mountain and I are going to join all of you in the celebration by renewing our vows today."

"Oh my god!" Duchess jumps from her chair, leaving Angel standing with her hands up and a clip hanging from her mouth. She was in the middle of pining her sister's curls up but was left in the dust as I'm bombarded by a tight hug. When Duchess finally lets me go, she steps back and gushes. "I'm so happy for you."

"This is so exciting!" Sunshine is next in for a hug, followed by Angel and Star.

"Not exactly how I saw this day going, but if there's one good thing about it, it's that Mountain can't leave me at the altar," I say with a laugh. "We're already legally married."

"Speaking of the altar," Angel grumbles as she rolls her eyes. "I understand how some people like the tradition of not seeing the bride before the wedding, but since when has anything we've done been traditional? Hammer took it one step too far when he snuck out of bed this morning before I opened my eyes."

"Oh, you poor thing," Duchess playfully mocks, hand braced over her heart. "Whatever will you do?"

"And then when I finally tracked his behind down, he refused to give me a kiss."

"You heard Hammer bellow through the office door." Duchess turns in her chair to face her younger sister. She's got her finger waving like she's scolding her, but the whole time she's fighting back a smile. "We aren't allowed back inside the clubhouse until the ceremonies. Otherwise, he's gonna blindfold you."

"Who's getting blindfolded?" Meredith's voice makes us all look toward the front door, where she's standing, holding a couple white rectangular-shaped boxes in her hands. "I like the sound of that."

"Meredith!" Sunshine joins the 'scolding little sister party' even though they're only about to be sisters by marriage. "Don't let Steel hear you say something like that. He'll lock you in your room until you're forty."

"How's he gonna do that when I live by myself, huh?" Meredith sticks her tongue out before walking toward us.

Ray enters the cabin behind her, one arm carrying even more boxes and the other over his eyes. Sara is right on his heels, steering him farther into the kitchen space. "Honey, you don't have to cover your eyes, you're already married."

"I know," Ray says back. "I just don't wanna be seeing any parts of the brides that I shouldn't be. Their about-to-be-hubbies would kick my ass."

She stops him in front of the island. "Set those boxes down right here, and we'll be on our way. Congrats, ladies. See y'all soon." And with that, Sara and Ray are gone.

"What is all this?" I ask as I count the six assorted sized boxes now piled on the island.

"I come bearing gifts from your men," Meredith begins handing them out, "but don't open them yet. I'm under strict instructions to take pictures as you each open your box, so wait 'til I say it's your turn."

"But why am I getting a gift?" I'm not really getting married today. What could this be? Mountain must have been preparing for this longer than I thought.

"I don't know." She shrugs as she hands two boxes to Sunshine. "It was on the pile I was told to bring in here, so here it is."

We all find a chair and sit in a circle to watch as each of us sees what our amazing, thoughtful, crazy men got us.

Duchess goes first and opens her box to find a pair of light dusty pink Converse tennis shoes. Pulling a rolled-up piece of paper out of one of the shoes, she unrolls it and reads out loud. "To replace the ones you lost on the day I almost lost you. Thank the heavens, I got you back. Love, Connor. P.S. I can't wait to see you wearing these . . . and only these."

"Oh goodness." If I could make a wish to keep Duchess here but forget all about that day, I'd wish on a hundred tossed pennies. Watching Whiskey in agony as he realized his love was missing, I lost it. Even though I know Mountain wanted to go along to help rescue her from her kidnappers, he had to stay behind and deal with my inconsolable self.

"What's the meaning of the shoes?" Meredith asks.

"I had another pair just like this," Duchess says with a smile as she pulls on one of the laces. "They were the first thing Whiskey saw when I jumped out of my truck the day I appeared at the gate."

Angel reaches out her pinkie and Duchess hooks hers in, connecting the sisters in a way I've seen them do a few times before. After wiping her cheek, Angel turns to the group. "Okay, who's next?"

"Why don't you go," Meredith tells her.

Angel's box is the smallest of the bunch, but knowing Hammer, it probably packs a big punch. She rips the lid off and pulls out two square velvet jewelry boxes along with a card that she reads. "So you always have our boys close to your heart. Yours, Hammer."

Opening the first one, tears glint in the corners of her eyes, then she turns it to show us. "It's a charm with Ace's birthstone.

It's called a peridot." A yellowish-green circle gemstone sparkles in a silver setting. Opening the second box, Angel turns around another charm, this time a frosty blue color that almost looks like water. "And this is aquamarine for Taren."

"How in the world are we supposed to look any kind of presentable after all this," Sunshine waves her hand in the air, "insanity? These men don't play fair. And I have two boxes to open."

"And that's why we're leaving you for last," Meredith replies with a chuckle.

"Last? That's cruel and unusual punishment." Sunshine crosses her arms and pouts.

Star looks at me and asks, "You or me first?"

"Go ahead," I respond. "Pregnant lady first."

A little gentler with her box, Star opens it from the flap on the side and slides out something flat and rectangular wrapped in gray tissue paper. She shakes it and a small rattling sound comes from inside the bundle. Carefully tearing the tape, she unwraps a picture frame and something drops into her lap. Picking it up, it's two keys on a skull keychain.

Flipping over the eight-by-ten frame, she starts bawling uncontrollably. "He didn't!"

"Didn't what, honey?" Duchess is up and at her side in seconds. Star hands her the frame, and whatever it is, it causes Duchess to gasp. She peels a Post-It note off the glass and reads it for Star. "I found this listing starred in the favorites on your laptop. I bought it. It's ours. Love always, Buzz."

"He bought my dream home," Star says between a hiccup and some sniffles. Duchess hands her the frame back, and she turns it around to show us. It's a picture of a brick tri-level house with black stutters. "It's a block away from Raven's Gram's house in town. I saw the 'For Sale' sign the day we helped move Raven back here, and I couldn't stop thinking about it."

"It looks like someone was doing some snooping on your computer," Duchess says with a laugh as she sits back down.

"We'll miss you living here, but we're so happy for you," Angel adds.

"Thank you all for accepting me like this." Star uses her sleeve to wipe her cheeks. "I'm so happy I found this family."

"We love you too, honey." I blow her a kiss.

"That means it's your turn, Blue." Meredith holds her phone up at the ready to capture the mess my face turns into when I open whatever Mountain found to give me.

My box is the second smallest, but it's long rather than square, like some of the others. If I had to make a guess off the shape alone, I'd say it's a necklace. I lift the top off and flip it upside down to get the black velvet box into my hand.

A slip of paper is wrapped around the box, so I carefully cut the tape with my nail and unfold it. "We fit together, much like a puzzle piece, our hearts are made for each other. Always yours, Jethro."

Fighting the resistance of the box's hinge, I see that my guess was right when it snaps open and a silver skeleton key is laying inside.

While every Old Lady, starting with Duchess, has gotten a skeleton key necklace when she received her Property cut and patch, none of us older women have had one until now. I never thought of asking for one, as I saw it as a new generation type of tradition, but seeing that Mountain was so thoughtful to think to get me one, I'll wear it with pride.

I take the necklace out and hold it up for the ladies to see. "Looks like I get to join the necklace club."

"What design is on yours?" Duchess asks as I clip it around my neck.

"Two interlocking hearts."

The words of his note were a clue to what was inside. From the very beginning, Mountain and I said we were like two puzzle pieces looking for their matching piece. And the hearts on this necklace are just like that—one rests just on top of the other, completing each other.

"Okay, last two," Meredith calls like she's the host of a game show. "Open the flat box first."

"Leave it to my two weirdos that I have to open them in a specific order," Sunshine comments as she pulls a manilla folder out of the box. She flips the folder open and proceeds to drop it back in her lap. "No, no, no, no. He didn't."

"Didn't what?" All five of us ask in unison.

Papers still in her lap, Sunshine begins turning page after page of what looks to be some sort of legal document. Suddenly, she lifts the bundle and hugs it to her chest. Rivers of tears pouring down her cheeks, she looks up and smiles. "They're adoption papers for Opal. He wants me to be her mom."

"Was there a note?" Meredith asks. Based on her standing still, phone in hand, I think she's recording a video.

Flipping the folder closed, she reads from a yellow piece of paper taped to the front. "My Sunshine, since she already calls you 'momma', how about we make it official? I'm the luckiest dad in the world. Love, Steel."

"Holy moly." Angel breathes out a sigh. "Leave it to the tough guy to make a woman's heart melt."

"No kidding." Sunshine's words are a mix of joy and laughter. "And I still have one box to open. I don't think I have any more tears left to give."

"I guess there's only one way to find out," Duchess replies.

This box from Ring is the tallest of the bunch. The box is a square, probably twelve-by-twelve, and is held shut by a narrow orange ribbon. Sunshine somehow manages to wiggle it off without breaking it, then loops it around her neck like a necklace. Pulling the folds open, she throws her head back and starts laughing hysterically.

"What's so damn funny?" Meredith walks around the circle until she's behind Sunshine, then looks over her shoulder. "Oh! Well, good for you, sister."

"What is it?" Angel calls out in frustration.

Sunshine digs in the box, pulling out a piece of paper in one hand and a bunch of colorful fabric in the other. "He got me a box full of panties."

Duchess leans back in her chair. "I sense a story here, but I'm not sure I wanna know the answer."

"Let me read the note and you'll get it." Sunshine giggles, then starts to read. "Since I knew nothing could beat Steel's gift to you, I had to make mine something extra fun. I look forward to ripping each of these off of you, just like the ones I did on the day I made you mine. I can't wait to call you my wife. Love, Ring."

We spend the next few minutes laughing and crying and sharing our love notes with each other. Some are sweeter and more sentimental, like Hammer's to Angel, or funny like Ring's to Sunshine, but not one is less meaningful than another.

As the five of us get ready to walk down the aisle to our men, we laugh and sing and take way too many selfies. This day started out as one I'll never forget, and I have no doubt the next few hours will be exactly the same.

CHAPTER TWENTY-SIX

RAVEN

It's amazing how fast a space can transform when everyone pitches in to get a job done. Because on a day like today, it's all hands on deck. It's not only Christmas Eve but also Rebel Vipers wedding day . . . times five!

Between all the Brothers, Prospects, Old Ladies, club girls, and a random mix of family members here to help, we somehow managed to change the clubhouse main room from the mess it was in for last night's bachelorette party fiasco into a Christmastime magical fairytale land.

Under guidance from myself, Belle, Sunshine's aunt, Jane, and Opal, of course, we took all the supplies that the brides put together and have everything in place in a matter of hours. Angel had a map and a very shockingly detailed picture drawn out of where everything was to go, so all it took was just putting everything in its place to zhuzh the place up.

There are several Christmas trees of various sizes spaced out in three corners of the room, all decorated in white lights and green and black ornaments. Small globe-shaped lights mixed with string lights are draped from every beam and corner of the room, giving the illusion of a twinkling clear night sky. Battery powered lanterns surround the bases of the trees and are also lining the center aisle leading up to an amazing wooden archway that the couples will stand under to say their vows.

Before we could even start decorating this morning, Butch and Mountain surprised us all by bringing in the archway they built as a gift for all the couples. It's currently sitting in front of a partition we have blocking off a corner of the room. Using black drapes hanging from the rafters above, we hid all the couches, recliners, and tables that usually fill the room.

To make it seem like part of the décor, the drapes are decorated with what are called curtain lights, which are basically strings that hang down to create the illusion of a wall of lights. Once the couples say their "I do's", the dining tables we have stashed back there will come out, and all the chairs currently set up in rows with an aisle down the center will be rearranged around the tables for everyone to sit down and eat a meal together.

Now that everything is set up, I'm taking a few minutes to myself to take in the calm before the storm. Standing in the far corner, in the opening of the smaller hallway, I have an almost panoramic view of the whole main room. Everyone else is either up in their rooms or the cabin of their family members getting ready, so I'm enjoying the last bit of quiet this day will have.

I have to say, I think we did a damn good job turning this converted factory that's been a man's land of living room space for thirty-plus years into an almost tranquil setting. The overhead lights are dimmed to their lowest, so all the lanterns and hanging lights are creating this glowing effect to the space, and the real Christmas trees make the room smell like we're actually outside in nature.

How I lucked out in getting to live here is really a miracle in itself. I've been here officially for less than two months, but these four giant walls, and the two men who I get to share the rest of my life with, make this the only real home I've ever had.

Hearing footsteps coming down the stairs, I take a few steps forward and see both Smoke and Haze looking around. Speaking of my two men, I see both of their eyes light up when they find me across the room. We all head for each other and meet in the middle, right in front of the row of bar stools.

"What are you doin' down here by yourself?" Haze asks as he wraps an arm over my shoulder, pulling me into his embrace.

"Just soaking in the quiet before the craziness begins," I reply before giving him a kiss.

"This place is unrecognizable." Smoke looks around like he's seeing it for the first time, even though he was part of the set-up crew. Pulling me away from Haze and into his arms, he drops for a kiss before spinning me around to hold my back to his front.

"I wish we could keep this stuff up all year round," I say as I lean into him.

"I highly doubt Whiskey and the others would go for that." Smoke's chuckle shakes me along with him. "This is a motorcycle clubhouse, not a wedding venue. We're not gonna start renting out the space to paying customers."

"Could you imagine?" Haze joins in on the laughter. "Some hoity toity lady coming in here to tour the space while planning her nuptials. Next thing you know, someone comes stumbling into the room with a gun in one hand, dragging a beat-up and bloody bad guy behind him in the other. I don't think we'd get many customers that way."

"You guys are such weirdos." I turn and smack both of them on the chest.

"Hey," Smoke holds up his hands, "if someone wants to pay for a rustic wedding, they can go to The Lodge or brewery and pay for the spaces there."

"The clubhouse is sacred ground to this club. Only reason this got by the officers is because most of the grooms are officers themselves," Haze goes on to rant. "They're bending over backward for their Old Ladies on this one."

"As they should," I sass back, arms folded over my chest.

Haze's serious face drops and he backs me into Smoke's embrace again. He pulls my hands into his and links them together down at my sides. Crowding into my chest so I'm sandwiched between them, he looks down at me with a soft smile. "Is this what you would want?"

Confused at what he's asking, my eyebrows furrow. "What do you mean?"

Smoke tucks his head into my neck and kisses right behind my ear. "Is this the kind of wedding you would want?"

"Oh!" Oh, now I get it. "You mean . . ."

"Yup," Haze replies with a nod. "Would you wanna get married here like this, or maybe somewhere more like a church? Tell us what you'd want one day."

Trying to put together my thoughts is a lot easier than I thought. With all the planning going on lately, I can't lie and say I haven't thought about what I'd wish for my wedding day, but I never imagined it'd be brought up so soon.

"While I love you both so much," I untangle one hand from Haze and pull one of Smoke's into my grasp, then pull all our hands into one bunch, "I don't think a clubhouse wedding would be my speed."

"Then where would we get to make you ours," Smoke kisses my temple, "legally?"

Turning to face Smoke, I untangle all our hands, but just like every other time we're within arm's reach of each other, we all end up intertwined back together immediately. "I've never been a church kinda girl, so that's out of the question. Not that I could get you two yahoos into one anyways," I add with a laugh. "But I'd be all for an outside shindig."

"Outside, like in a park?" Smoke's eyes light up like the Christmas lights all around us. "Or maybe in the backyard here, so all our friends would be in one place?"

"If you two asked me nicely, I could be talked into a backyard clubhouse wedding." Rocking on my toes, I lift up to kiss his cheek. "It's not like everyone who lives here isn't our family anyway."

"I like the way you think," Haze growls in my ear before starting to kiss down the side of my neck.

As romantic as this all sounds, I start to wonder if this is them trying to tell me they want to get married now, or them just getting all wrapped up in the goings on and the fog of happiness everyone has been floating in for the last month.

Hearing more footsteps come down the stairs, I pull out of the bubble we've gotten ourselves sucked into and step back. The main room on Christmas Eve is not the time or place for a discussion like this, so I need to wrap up this conversation before things get way too out of hand and we start making promises I don't think any of us are ready to keep. Life may happen in super speed around here, but it's way too soon to be talking about a wedding for us.

"While I love you both more than I ever could tell you," one hand in each of theirs, I take a step back, "now is probably not the best time to be talking about us taking the next step. Being together, the three of us, has been a huge change all around, and I'm not ready for a wedding yet."

"You're not saying never," Smoke says with a half-smile, "just not yet, right?"

"Exactly," I reply with a smile of my own for both of them. "You two had your attractions to each other for so damn long but really have only been open and honest for less than half a year. Then, just when you get together for real, I fall into the picture and add a whole new spin to everything. I think we need to take some time to just be us, like this, as three committed and happy people, before we take the giant leap into deciding who marries who and who takes whose name. I just want to be us for a while. Is that okay?"

"Raven, if this is all we ever are, I'd die a happy man." Haze lifts both mine and Smoke's hands to his lips. "But if waiting is what you want to do, we'll wait for you to be ready."

"Just don't wait *too* long," Smoke adds with his deep chuckle. "One day, I want you to wear our ring and carry our babies and be our wife."

"I want all of that too."

"Me three!" Hazes declares. "But when you're ready for a change, can you at least give us a head's up so we can start planning right away?"

"I will," I promise them. "Now, let's get our butts upstairs and get changed for this wedding. We've got lots of celebrating to do in the next twelve hours or so."

"Yes, dear." Smoke laughs out loud, pulling me toward the stairs. "Whatever you say, dear."

Each of my hands is being held by one of my men, and I take one last look at the main room as we make our way up the stairs. Thinking about the happiness and love that's about to fill the room makes me extremely grateful for my life, and I can't wait for whatever the future holds for me and my troublemakers.

CHAPTER TWENTY-SEVEN

MOUNTAIN

"Listen up, you fuckers." I spin on my heel and see Whiskey standing in the door to mine and Blue's space.

The fellow grooms and I have taken over the room and back hallway, along with Whiskey's office to get ready. The women are all out in the cabin, so there's no chance we'll be crossing over or accidently running into someone we shouldn't be seeing yet, and the clock is ticking to the moment we all get to see our brides.

"We've got about a half-hour before things get rolling. Make sure all your flies are zipped because there's an impressionable young lady right outside the door who insists on coming in to see us."

"Impressionable, my ass." Whiskey is shoved forward, forcing him to catch himself before he falls flat on his face, and Meredith comes waltzing into the room like she didn't just almost knock over a man three times her size. All the others, including myself, laugh at her spunk while Whiskey tries to posture up and smooths down the front of his shirt. "I return with gifts from your ladies.

Fair warning, you all are getting the same thing, just with a personal touch signifying your relationship, so no fighting over who got a better present."

As she walks around the room, she hands a box to each of us, myself included.

As I take mine, I lean down to ask softly, "How did Blue get me this? She didn't know about us doing the vow thing 'til this morning."

"I may have overheard one birdie talking to another birdie," following her finger pointing over my shoulder, I see Whiskey and Steel both opening their boxes, "about your surprise, so I did some digging of my own. I found out what the ladies were getting the grooms for gifts and bought one for you with Steel's credit card."

"Ha!" I laugh. "I'll make sure to pay him back for that."

"Nah! He probably won't even look at the statement to see something was charged on it. He's more of a 'just pay the bill' kinda guy."

Pulling on the end of the bow, the black ribbon wrapped around the matte black box comes undone. I remove the top to find a black leather cuff with a light blue metal buckle laying inside. While I'm not normally a jewelry man—though I did replace my dog tags with a silver link necklace a few years back—this is something I can see myself wearing every day. Looking around the room, everyone else is putting theirs on, so I do too.

"Does Blue know about this?" I ask Meredith, who's still at my side, snapping a few pictures of us.

"She does. I pulled her aside after giving the ladies their gifts and filled her in. She even got to take a peek at it before I brought it over."

"Thank you for this, Meredith." I pull her in for a quick hug and kiss the top of her head. "I'm so glad you're in this family too."

Hugging me back, she whispers, "Thank you for letting me be part of it."

"Anything for a Brother's little sister."

"Now, that's enough of the sappy talk. It's time to go get you hitched." Meredith pulls back and cocks her head to the side, making a funny face. "Or is it re-hitched?"

"A little bit of both," I reply with a laugh.

Going around the room, each of my Brothers holds up a wrist to show off their cuffs. Whiskey has a red buckle and is sporting his on his left arm, while Steel and Ring have matching orange buckles on their right. Hammer's buckle is yellow and on his left wrist, and Buzz's is a shiny silver on his right because he's wearing a watch on his left.

Meredith has us huddle up for a group picture, and while she keeps telling us to smile, taking what must be fifty pictures, we're saved when Bear ducks his head in to say it's time to line up. One more round of well wishes and celebratory handshakes, fist bumps, and back slapping hugs, we line up in the hallway.

This morning, all grooms were given explicit instructions on where to stand according to the clipboard in Raven's possession. She claimed to only be telling us what was written on the paper, but I saw her cheeky grin. She was getting a kick out of telling all of us ornery bikers what to do.

Last in line, I follow Steel, Ring, Hammer, and Buzz, down the hall, then head to my spot under the archway. Blue and I are starting the ceremony with our vow renewal, so I'm front and center first. Whiskey is going to be walking her down the aisle, so once he does that, he'll be joining the group to wait for his turn next.

Soft music fills the room, and all the guests stop their chattering and turn to the back of the room.

Bear is officiating, so he makes his way up the aisle before coming to stand under the arch. Black leather binder in one hand, he claps me on the shoulder with the other.

Jamie was asked by the ladies to be the ring bearer, and he accepted. He's making his way down the aisle with a small wooden box holding all of our wedding bands inside. His expression is stoic and purposeful. He's taking this job very seriously, not smiling or waving at anyone, which of course causes the room to chuckle at his bravado. Taking his place in the first chair of the first row, directly to my left, I hold out my fist, and Jamie bumps me back with his much smaller one.

Opal is the flower girl and she's next. Coming down the makeshift aisle, she's got the biggest smile of anyone. Carrying a basket of flower petals, she throws them in the air so they cascade down all around her. Wearing a pale pink dress with a puffy skirt, she stops halfway down the aisle to do a spin and the skirt flows around her, making everyone ooh and ahh over her. Opal definitely is loving the attention, but she should be because this is a big day for her too. She takes her place to the left, in the first chair next to Meredith and Steel's moms.

The music then begins a transition to something more dramatic. I recognize the melody as a song I used to hear in church during Christmas mass when I was a little boy. While we weren't a super religious family growing up, my mother would make my father, brother, and I dress up and attend services on every holiday.

Just thinking of my mother, Sheila, I hope she's looking down at us from heaven, proud that I'm finally doing the right thing and giving Blue a proper day. She was so upset when I called to give her the news that we had tied the knot, she flew out the next day and slapped me with her purse the second I arrived to pick her up from the airport. Blue, of course, thought it was the funniest thing, but my mother berated me for years, saying when she gave me her wedding ring to pass down to my future bride, she would've at least liked to have met the lady before I signed on the dotted line. Mom and Blue were instant friends, but I still wish, like with many other things, she could be here to see this.

I turn to look at Bear, but his wink and head nod tell me I need to be looking someplace else. That's when I look to my left and see her.

My wife. My bride. She looks just as stunning as she did on the day I married her the first time. Maybe even more. Definitely more. Every day, she's more beautiful than the one before.

Right now, she's on the arm of my son, taking part in the wedding I should have given her all those years ago. But unlike our marriage before the judge, today Blue actually gets to walk down the aisle, in front of all our friends and family.

I thought I knew what this moment was going to be like, but I was so wrong. I imagined she'd appear at the end of the aisle, then she'd magically be at my side and I'd pour my heart out to her. I forgot about the part where I actually have to wait for her to walk down the aisle. *This is absolute torture.* There are a fair number of rows between where she started and where I'm standing, and it seems like it's taking forever. I wish like hell they'd start walking faster.

Before I know it, she's finally by my side, and I let out a relieved breath.

As Whiskey places Blue's hand in mine, I pull it to my lips and kiss her palm. "Fuck, you're beautiful." It's probably not the time or place to swear, but my life has never been what a lot of people think is right, so I don't care.

Her cheeks turn pink as she blushes. "You're not so bad lookin' yourself."

"You ready to be mine all over again?" I ask as I take both her hands in mine.

"More than anything."

CHAPTER TWENTY-EIGHT

BLUE

"Are you ready for this?"

"Dang, Blue," Whiskey whistles as he turns from where he's standing in front of the kitchen island, "you look amazing."

With my bouquet of white roses, baby's breath, and a little greenery for decoration in one hand, I wrap the other around his waist as he pulls me close for a hug. He presses a kiss to the top of my head, then steps back.

"You don't look too shabby yourself all spiffed up like that," I tease him as I pat him on the chest.

"Nah." Whiskey tries to wave off my compliment, but I can see the blush flood his cheeks. "I just put on what Duchess left out for me."

Deciding to give the poor guy a break, I can feel the nerves rolling off him, so I move on. "Today's the day, huh?" I ask him with a cheeky smile.

"It sure is." His response is mixed with a chuckle. "I was just trying to figure out how to tie this damn thing, but I'm ready to give up." He grasps the long black tie in one fist and slides it from the collar of his maroon button-up.

"I think you look just fine without the tie." I set my flowers on the island and adjust his collar. I unbutton just the top button, then smooth my hands across his shoulders, brushing out a few imaginary wrinkles. "Duchess will marry you no matter what you wear, tie or no tie."

Shaking out his hands, he replies, "God, I hope so."

"I know so," I say as I grab my bouquet again and we head for the hall.

All of us brides, minus Duchess, who's still hiding in the cabin until Whiskey escorts me away so he doesn't see her, came inside the clubhouse and were immediately led into the kitchen so no one sitting out in the main room could see us until it's our time. Each of us paired off with the person assigned to give us away today. For me, that's Whiskey.

Finding our place in line behind Bear, Jamie, and Opal, Whiskey turns to me and holds my hands in his. Whatever he's about to say must be serious because he straightens his shoulders, takes a big breath, then lets it out slowly. "I've been thinking about this for a while now, but I've got something I need to tell you."

"What's wrong?"

"Nothing's wrong, and that's exactly why I need to say this. I need you to know that I love you very much. I don't know if I've ever told you, but I'm so glad you were the one who helped raise me. Everything I have now is because of you and Pops. I finally know what true love is because of you two."

"Oh, Whiskey." I somehow manage to stop the tears forming by blinking really fast and sniffling a few times, but I get myself together and pull him in for another hug. "I'm so damn proud of the man you've become. I had no idea what I was getting myself into when I came here, but I want you to know I don't regret one single minute of knowing you since."

"Even when I climbed a tree to get away from you after seeing you makin' out with my Pops?" he asks with a wink.

I can't help but let out a loud laugh. "You may have been a rotten, grouchy ten-year-old when we met, and you definitely still have your moments, but I'm so proud of you. And thank you for doing this for me today."

"Anything for Krew's BeeGee. Now, let's get you re-married." Whiskey holds out his left arm, and I hook my right hand into the inside of his elbow. "Then, it's my turn."

A soft song starts to play through the surround sound speakers, and one by one, Bear, Jamie, and Opal take their turns walking down the aisle. Unable to see what's going on, I hear a few laughs and know right away that Opal must've done something cute and funny. She has got to be eating up the spotlight.

The music changes to a tune with more of a full sound and some bells, and I know that's our cue. With a nod from Raven, who's taken charge of telling each bride and her escort when to go, my walk down the aisle begins.

We step into the main room and I get my first look at the fairytale land all of the morning's helpers turned the clubhouse into. It's spectacular. There are Christmas trees all around the room, various strings of lights hanging from everything you can think of, and just as we turn at the end of the aisle, I see Bear and

Mountain standing underneath a beautiful wood archway. I can't be certain, but something tells me this was made specifically for today because I've never seen it before.

One slow step at a time, I make my way past all our friends and visitors, and closer and closer to the man I married so many years ago. I never thought I'd have a day like today, but I'm so glad I get to be a part of it. This is truly magical.

Mountain is standing straight, hands clasped together, and he looks so handsome. He's wearing a long sleeve, white button-up shirt with a light blue bowtie and his cut. I can't help but smile when I see he's wearing what will forever now be known as my favorite pair of his black jeans. Paired with his cleanest black riding boots, everything else fades away as I step closer to my husband.

As the music begins to fade away, we stop right in front of Mountain, and Whiskey takes my hand before placing it in his. Mountain lifts it to his lips and kisses my palm.

"Fuck, you're beautiful."

I can't help but blush at his words. His charm comes out in spades when he's in a good mood, and today is very much a good mood day.

"You're not so bad lookin' yourself," I whisper before I pass my bouquet off to Opal.

He takes both of my now free hands into his much larger ones. "You ready to be mine all over again?"

Looking nowhere but into his chocolate brown eyes, I tell him the truth. "More than anything."

"First of all, I'd like to welcome everyone to the Rebel Vipers clubhouse on this crazy Christmas Eve that I don't think any of us will ever forget," Bear begins, making the room fill with chuckles from his funny but truthful statement.

"While many of you may be thinking, why are these two crazy people up here in front of us, making us wait to see who we really came here for when they're already married, believe me when I tell you, I thought this was nuts too. But when Mountain brought up the idea of renewing his vows with Miss Blue here, I knew it had to be done. Plus, what's one more set of 'I do's when you already have four?

"Let me tell you a little story about how this all started, many, many, maaaany moons ago." That gets everyone laughing again, a little louder this time. Mountain squeezes my hands and I look up to see him roll his eyes, but he's smiling the whole time. "This couple decided to rush off to the courthouse and get hitched without tellin' any of us first. They said 'who cares what our best friends think, let's not tell anyone 'til after we tie the knot, then go back home and surprise 'em all at once.'

"It was a Wednesday afternoon and we'd all just gotten off work. We bikers were tired, hot, cranky, ready for some ice-cold beers and a night of being lazy bums, but we were all in for a huge surprise when a certain someone's Harley came flyin' into the parking lot and almost ran my ass over." Bear's arms are waving in the air like he's directing an airplane in for landing, very much overexaggerating what happened that day, but the continued laughs he's getting egg him on even more.

"It's not my fault you weren't watchin' where you were walkin'," Mountain calls him out with a snicker, punching him in the bicep.

"I didn't know the parking lot was hostin' a demolition derby that day. But anyway, Mountain climbed off his bike, scooped Blue up into his arms, and headed straight for the front doors. He marched right over the threshold, set her down right back there," Bear points to the back of the room, "and swooped her low into a deep kiss. When they finally came up for air after what seemed like an hour, he announced to the room that he and Blue had just gotten married and it was time for a party. I had never gotten so drunk before in my life, and I don't think I have a day since."

"I have," Skynyrd calls out from his seat in the back, causing another round of laughs.

"But anywho, my point is, this whole slew of weddings is gonna go down a little bit different than what y'all might expect, but that's okay. Why start doing things normal now? When will you ever be at another wedding where there are five brides and six grooms?" That earns a round of applause and a bunch of boot stomping from the aisles. "So, let's get this show on the road. Blue, you're up first."

"Me?" I look back and forth between Mountain and Bear. They both smile and nod back, so I guess it's my turn. "Oh, boy. Okay. Not like you decided to give a girl time to plan to get her thoughts together. I only just found out about being part of this six hours ago."

"I couldn't give you a chance to tell me no." Mountain squeezes my hands as he shrugs, a lazy smile on his face.

Looking up at him, I wink. "As if I could say no when we're already married."

"Very true."

"But anyways, vows, okay." I take a few seconds to collect my thoughts, then begin. "Mountain, I love you. I probably loved you about an hour after meeting you. When I just showed up at your front door, and you tried to shut that door in my face, my walls went up sky high. But when you immediately apologized, the first brick came right back down, and it was my turn to be knocked off my feet.

"I was totally unprepared for the bomb you were going to drop on me. After you told me my sister was gone, you were nothing but kind and sweet and gentle, even though you had no reason to be. You had no idea who I was, but you treated me so kindly, I couldn't help but fall in love with you. You explained everything as simply as you could, then welcomed me into your clubhouse. You gave me time to sort my thoughts out. You gave me a place to rest. You gave me a home.

"A certain ten-year-old boy may have wanted to run me off the second we met," I turn to see Whiskey's big smile at my reference to him before coming back to Mountain, "and I myself wanted to run a few times over those first couple of days, but you stood by my side and welcomed me in.

"Then," I can't help but chuckle at myself, "you threw all of us for a loop when, just three days in, you asked me to be your Old Lady and put your momma's ring on my finger. I never in a million years saw that coming. You knew practically nothing about me back then, but you insisted that we had a lifetime to learn about each other. We sat at that picnic table, the one you still refuse to get rid of even though it's crumbling to pieces and needs to be firewood, pulled out the ring, and asked me to marry you.

"And somehow, for some crazy reason I still don't understand to this day, it was easier for you to get me to agree to be your wife than it was for me to be your Old Lady. I argued with you about not being ready to be an Old Lady in a lifestyle I had no clue about, but the second you asked me to be your wife, I knew it was the right thing to do.

"I guess what I'm trying to say is, thank you, Mountain. Thank you for seeing something in me when I had no idea what I was myself. Thank you for embracing me into your life and showing me what it meant to have a family.

"Thank you for giving me a family. You allowed me to step in and help you raise your son. You let me stand at your side over the years as you built this club into the amazing and powerful thing it is today. But most importantly, you held my hand and let me stand by your side for all of these years.

"Together, we have watched the group of men and women around us flourish in their own lives, and all of that is because of you. You brought us all together, because none of us would be here without you.

"Your son has a son because of you.

"Your daughter has a very rapidly growing family because of you.

"I am who I am because of you. And for that, I have to thank you.

"Thank you for being my husband. Thank you for being my Old Man. But most important of all, thank you for being my best friend. I look forward to whatever the next forty years hold for us. Who knows, maybe we'll be blessed with a bunch more grandbabies to spoil rotten." That gets the crowd laughing again.

"I just know that no matter where life takes us, or whatever happens to us along the way, as long as I'm with you, everything will be okay. Wherever this winding road leads us, I'll always be at your back, holding on tight to you, as you lead us through the twists and turns of this crazy life. I may have been the one to drive fifteen hundred miles to track you down, but just know, every mile I have spent with you since has been worth it. And until we meet again at whichever gates welcome us in, I'll follow your lead until the very end.

"I love you, Mountain.

"I love you, Jethro.

"No matter the name I call you, I will always love you."

MOUNTAIN

"Mountain, it's your turn." Bear nods my way with a smirk. "Good luck trying to beat that."

He may be a smug bastard, but he's right. How am I going to follow that up? I took the time to write out vows that I thought were what I needed to say. I thought I needed to be sweet and poetic, even though as a biker I have no idea what those things are supposed to sound like, so I'll admit right now that I looked up some stuff on the internet. But as I stand here, holding the hands of the woman who's stood at my side for the last twenty-one years, I realize poetry and fluff isn't what I need to shower her with. It's the truth I need to say. I have to switch gears.

Blue is standing here, looking phenomenally hot in a light blue, long sleeve dress, lace covering every inch of her from her arms to her knees. There's a hint of cleavage teasing at the neckline, but only just enough for me to see, which I appreciate. The only person who needs to be thinking a bride is this drop-dead gorgeous on her wedding day is the groom, and that's me.

As I continue to take her in, I realize this dress looks strikingly like the one she wore at our first nuptials. While this dress may lean more toward the side of silver than sky blue, both dresses have the same shape and lacy look. But one thing about this dress that I notice is different, is that it makes her clear blue eyes shine so bright.

Whether it's the lighting or just the happiness of the day, Blue is sparkling.

Knowing I need to quit standing here, just staring at her like a fucking creep, I clear my throat and take a deep breath. Time to put myself out there for her, laying it all on the line. Here goes nothing.

"Lana Renee Hill, I have failed you.

"I have failed you in every aspect of our marriage.

"I didn't keep true to the vows we pledged to each other, and for that, I apologize.

"Twenty-one years ago, we stood before a judge and made promises to each other to always remain faithful. We made promises to one another and said we'd forever forsake all others and that we'd never stray from each other.

"As I stand here today, in front of all our family and friends, I have to tell you that I wasn't truthful.

"I didn't stand by your side through sickness and in health.

"I admit that sometimes, many times in fact, I made things worse than better.

"And I admit that I broke one of our sacred vows. I didn't forsake all others.

"I put *myself* before *you*. I put my worries and my concerns and my insecurities before yours. I was too prideful.

"As your husband, I'm supposed to be the rock on which our relationship lives, and I wasn't.

"I wasn't your support when you needed me.

"I didn't keep our foundation solid.

"I failed.

"One day at a time, I let both of us down. I let the pieces of our puzzle crumble apart. And when you tried to put them back together again, I withheld some of them from you.

"I didn't put you first. I didn't put *us* first.

"I let the worries surround me and drown me in the maybes and what-ifs. I was weak.

"But somehow, through all my shortcomings and all my failed promises, you continued to stand by my side and hold us both up.

"You started to put our puzzle back together with the pieces that you had, and you forced me to see the pieces that I withheld, forcing me to give them back. You, my amazing, beautiful, sometimes cranky and crazy wife, put us back together one piece at a time.

"Had you not done what you did, taking a stand for yourself and making me see what my life would've been like without you in it, the final missing pieces never would have fallen into place.

"I stood before you one week ago and saw my life flash before my eyes. Because when I thought I was losing you, I felt a pain worse than I ever had before.

"I knew I was nothing without you, because I'm not.

"I knew I'd never be anything without you, because you're my strength.

"I knew I had to do whatever it took to keep you as mine, to keep you by my side, because life without you would be too painful to bear."

Working my hands free from Blue's, I slide them up her arms, over her shoulders, and my palms come to rest, softly holding her cheeks. I drop a kiss on her forehead, then one on each cheek. I pull back but hold her face up to mine, not letting our eyes unlock.

"This right here, right now, is our new beginning.

"This is our fresh start.

"My lovely, tenacious, brave, and loving Blue, I promise from this day forward to always let you lean on me as much as you let me lean on you.

"I know 'I love you' will never be enough to show you what I feel in my heart, so with that, I will just say thank you.

"Thank you for loving my son.

"Thank you for loving my daughter.

"Thank you for loving me.

"Thank you for being you."

Pressing my lips to hers, I pour every feeling and emotion and gut-wrenching need I have into her. I tried to lay all of my truths and weaknesses at her feet, so now, I just hope Blue can love me back as much as I love her.

What I feel for her is so much more than love. It's life.

CHAPTER TWENTY-NINE

DUCHESS

Once I got the all-clear that Whiskey was out of the kitchen and escorting Blue down the aisle, my Uncle Howard and I made our way into the clubhouse. Not wanting Whiskey to see me before I could make my own entrance, I decided to stay back in our cabin until he was out of sight. So now, at the end of the aisle myself, I'm suddenly feeling very nervous for what's about to come.

My steps falter, and I see the flash of concern across my Old Man's face. He immediately looks as worried as I feel inside. Is this the right thing to do? Are we getting married too fast? What am I doing?

"You got this, little lady," Howard whispers down to me as he pulls me back to the present. "Your momma and daddy would be so proud of you."

And just like that, as fast as the worry set in, it all disappears with ten words.

While I would give anything in this universe to have my parents here today, I know without a doubt they're sitting side by side up in heaven, watching down on me and my sister as we get ready to pledge our love and devotion and lifelong commitments to the men we were blessed to find. Sometimes, I wonder if they played some part in us finding our soulmates, because that's just the kind of parents they were, selfless and giving until the bitter end. They lived together and died together, always putting Angel and me first.

"Thank you, Uncle," I whisper in Howard's ear as he leans down to hug me after we stop in front of Whiskey.

Not only is Howard the husband of one of my employees at The Cake Butcher, he was also my father's best friend. Asking him to give me away today was my way of showing him how much I appreciate him being in my life, and at the same time, having a piece of my dad with me. The two of them grew up together, met their wives within days of each other, and lived in the same cul-de-sac as us my entire life. If anyone deserves the right to give me to my husband today, it's Howard.

"Take care of her for me now, ya hear?" Howard passes my right hand to Whiskey, then takes my bouquet with him as he takes his seat in the second row with his wife, Angie.

Whiskey pulls me so we're standing under the arch, facing one another, then he links his fingers through mine. "Ready to be my wife?"

"Nowhere else I'd rather be," I reply with a smile so big, I feel it in my cheeks.

Whiskey is looking so handsome in his long sleeve maroon button-up, I don't know if I'll be able to say my vows without drooling. This man always looks good enough to eat, but there's just something about him today, all cleaned and spiffed up, that's pushing my need for him over the top.

The top button of his shirt is undone, and I can tell he took some time cleaning up his cut. Add in his tight black jeans and shined-up cowboy boots, and Whiskey is looking fine as hell.

"Miss Duchess, why don't you go first?" Bear asks as he gestures my way.

Giving all my attention to the man in front of me, everything and everyone around us fades away. Everything I have to say today is for him, so he is all I care about.

"Connor Aaron Hill, I love you more than I can put into words. The happiness and blessings that meeting you have brought into my life are impossible to list, but I'm still going to try.

"First, I need to thank you for loving me. If it weren't for the sparks you said you felt the moment we met, ones I have to say I felt too, none of this would be happening. I barged into your life that day, but you threw my sass right back in my face and knocked me clean off my rocker. I drove away that day so mad at you, but at the same time wishing I could come back and kiss that smug smile off your face.

"Next, I need to thank you for everything you did to find and save me. When I should've stayed in bed with you that morning, I put myself in danger, scaring the bejesus out of both of us. Every minute that I was gone, I knew you were out there looking for me. I knew you would do everything in your power to find me and bring me home. It was when I was in that rundown shack that I told myself the moment you found me, I would agree to be your Old Lady. You were more than patient with me, waiting day after day for me to agree to start our lives together, but the moment I realized I just might lose you forever, I knew you were born to be mine.

"I will wake up every morning by your side and thank you for giving me a son. Having Krew, being the mother to your child, and hopefully many more, will always be my most important job. Together, we will raise our children to be strong, loving, and generous human beings. With help and guidance from our friends and family, we will build the next generation together.

"I also need to thank you for giving me a home. When my parents passed away, leaving me and my sister all alone, I never expected to leave the house I grew up in. I was in the mindset that one day I'd meet someone, continue to plant my roots within those four walls, and live out my days right there. But when you took me in and introduced me to this life, you showed me that change is okay. A family and a home don't have to be in a neighborhood, in a house with four walls and a roof. It can be wherever you make it. We will grow old in this clubhouse together. We will raise our children in the cabin out back. We will be a family wherever this journey takes us, and I'll be by your side every step of the way.

"I thank you, I love you, and I adore you.

"Today, I will put a ring on your finger and claim you as mine. Just like your cut on my back shows the world that I'm yours, my ring will tell the universe that you belong to me. My husband."

I forgot to put Whiskey's wedding ring in the ring bearer box earlier, so I pull it out of the pocket of my dress. That's right! This thing has pockets . . . and I love it!

The ring I chose for him is a plain, white gold band. When he heard I was going shopping, Whiskey had asked that I find him something simple. He's really not a jewelry kind of guy, minus his adorned manhood that's only for me to see, so I chose a ring without much muss or fuss for him. And just like him, it's straightforward and unpretentious, showing the world that he belongs to someone. It shows the world that he's mine.

After sliding the band on his left ring finger, I look up at him and see the smile he saves just for me.

WHISKEY

I'm a very firm believer in the saying that once in every man's lifetime, they should fall in love with a redhead. I just happened to be one of the damn lucky ones because I found my soulmate when I did. It took me just moments to start falling for her, and within a matter of days, I knew she was the one I wanted to make my Old Lady.

In the last fifteen months, this woman has changed my life and put it on a track I never imagined possible. I always thought I'd maybe find a woman to settle down with, possibly pop out a few hellions, and just deal with whatever life threw my way, but the life I'm living now is so much more than that.

I love Duchess, and I'm flat out crazy about the son she's blessed me with. Krew is the light of my fucking life, and I can't wait to knock his momma up over and over again, giving him more siblings than he'll know how to handle. And with how she's looking right now, if she's not pregnant already, she definitely will be before this night is over.

Duchess is standing at the end of the aisle on the arm of her pseudo-uncle when I catch my first sight of her. I was whispering over my shoulder with Hammer, and when he stopped midsentence about some part he'd ordered for his Harley, I knew something was up. I turned back forward and there she was. Fuck me. Right now is probably not the time to not being wearing underwear—my dick is getting serious zipper pinch.

Everything is going as well as expected—considering all I want to do is rush down that aisle, pick her up, and drag her to the nearest room with a door—until she stops walking about halfway to me. I feel all the blood drain from my body, and my heart drop to my stomach. I freeze. What's happening? Is she having second thoughts? After all this time, has she finally seen me for the crude asshole, killing, bad attitude, monster that I am and regretting agreeing to be mine?

Watching Howard whisper in her ear and then seeing the smile come back to Duchess's face, I'm able to breathe again and my heart climbs back up to where it belongs in my chest. She finally reaches my side, and I take her hands in mine, then listen to the sweet words of her love and thankfulness for me. It really should be me who's thankful for Duchess, because she's the one who saved me.

"Whiskey, please say your vows to Duchess," Bear says as he claps me on the right shoulder. "And make them good, son."

Standing before me in a dress like I've never seen before, I lose all train of thought as I take her in. I had words I planned to say but now can't remember a single one. Duchess's dress is an off-white color, almost a cream, and it fits her like a second skin. The strapless top is pushing the curves of her tits up sky high, and the entire front is covered in lace and sparkles. A belt of crystals in a snowflake pattern is knotted around her waist, then the material of her skirt flows down to a tiny train pooled at her feet. Everything is covered in a layer of lace, and if I'm not mistaken, I see a flash of pink peeking from the bottom edge. She's wearing the shoes I gave her.

Duchess's fiery red hair is all pinned back and up, but not tightly, and her natural curly waves give the look an intentional messy vibe. I know next to nothing about hairstyles, but something tells me it was done this way on purpose. I see an extra sparkly surprise when I notice the tiny tiara tucked into her curls, the same one she wore with her costume that first Halloween. She's really pulling out all the sentimental cards for this day, and I love it. I love *her* so fucking much.

Duchess holds my hands tight and smiles up at me, bringing me back to the room. A slight chuckle leaves her lips, so I swoop down for a quick kiss to silence her. If I don't start talking now, we'll never get this night of weddings done, and I'll have to wait even longer to figure out how to get her out of this dress.

"Kiana Marie Hayes, anything in this lifetime you want, it's yours.

"Anywhere on this Earth you wanna go, I'll take you there.

"Anyone who threatens you or our son, you tell me and I'll ride to the ends of the universe to teach them a lesson they'll never forget . . . then I'll wipe them from existence and turn them into dust.

"It doesn't matter to me how big or small something is, when it comes to keeping you and our son safe and protected, I promise to you that I'll fix it, solve it, find it, or kill it with my bare hands. Because to me, you're worth the fight. No matter the price, I'll pay it for you and Krew.

"You, my gorgeous, smokin' hot Old Lady, have made me the man I am today, and I'll never let anyone take you again. One time was enough for me. So, while it may seem like I'm being an ass, always keeping you close to my side and never letting you out of my sight for long, I'm only doing it for us. I'll do whatever it takes, and use everything in my power, to never have you go through pain like that again. You're too precious for anything bad or evil, so you're stuck with me now.

"I love you, Duchess. I live for you. I live for us."

"Jamie, rings please," Bear asks our ring bearer.

I'm not sure how Duchess ended up with my ring in her pocket, or how a wedding dress even has pockets, but leave it to my woman to find a dress where she can carry all the things she needs . . . even on her wedding day.

I take the wedding band that completes the set to the teardrop-shaped engagement ring I gave her months back, then ruffle Jamie's scraggly hairdo. He immediately tries to smooth it down as he goes back to his seat while everyone chuckles because of his angry face.

Before I slide the ring on her finger, I hold it up to show her. "See this, Duchess? This is the first gift I'll be giving you as my wife, but I want you to know that it won't be the last. Not every gift will be diamonds, but the value of the gift comes from my heart rather than the price tag.

"I'll give you my love every day, and I'll definitely be showering you with so much more, but just know, there's nothing I could give you that is more valuable to me than you."

The infinity band of diamonds nestles perfectly beside its partner, then I drag her in for a kiss.

And that makes it official . . . Duchess is finally my wife.

CHAPTER THIRTY

STEEL

"How the hell'd we get so lucky?"

"I've got no idea, but I ain't lookin' back now," I reply to Ring as we stand at the front of the aisle, watching our bride walk toward us.

On the arm of her father, Mountain, Sunshine takes one step at a time, each bringing her closer and closer to us. Paired with the tallest heels I've ever seen our woman wear, Sunshine's dress is perfect for her.

Wide straps cover her shoulders, then lead to a deep V cut between her breasts, giving us just a teasing hint of her cleavage. It's classy but fun, just like her. The skirt billows down from a tight belt and almost flows around her like a curtain in the wind. The hem stops a few inches above her ankles, showing off those killer heels I mentioned before. I plan on keeping those on her as long as possible tonight, maybe even when we get to bed later. Her shoes behind my ears sounds like a meeting I need to arrange.

As Mountain kisses Sunshine's cheek, Ring steps forward to take her hand. The two men shake hands before Mountain turns to me and I shake his hand as well. Ring turns Sunshine so she's standing between the two of us, him to her left and me to her right.

"I'd like to welcome everyone to the third act of our five-ring circus," Bear calls out to our guests with a laugh. "These two crazy knuckleheads somehow managed to convince this lovely ray of sunshine to marry not just one but two of them today, so let's get them started on their journey into unholy biker matrimony. Steel, you go first, my friend."

Ring kisses Sunshine's hand before she turns to face me. "Hi, there," she whispers, a big, beautiful, bright smile on her face.

"Hi, there," I parrot back. "You ready for this?"

"Sure am." Her reply comes with a wink and a secret only she, Bear, and myself are in the knows of.

"My dearest, lovely Sunshine. I don't know how I managed to be one of the two men you picked to be yours forever. I'll probably never understand, but I definitely know how lucky I am. I wake up every day knowing I'm one lucky son of a bitch to call you my Old Lady, and in a few minutes, I'll be even luckier to call you my wife.

"Since the day we met, you've been a light to my darkness, and I hope your brightness never has a chance to go dim. I'll spend every day by your side, fanning your flames, building you up higher and higher until you've reached every goal and made every dream you've ever had into a reality.

"To the world, you may be just my Old Lady, but you're so much more than that.

"To my daughter, you're her mother.

"To my best friend, you're the best partner.

"And to your family, you're the best sister, daughter, and cousin ever.

"But to me... to me, you're everything." I lift our joined hands and kiss Sunshine's knuckles, then work one hand free to wipe a tear rolling down her cheek.

"You're the sunrise at the start of every day, you're the bright sun giving me warmth during the longest hours, and at night, you're the setting sun as our days unwind and we lay in bed beside you.

"Calling you Sunshine is for far more than just the color of your hair or the smile on your face. It's what you bring to everyone around you. You show love and kindness to everyone you meet, you go out of your way to help a friend in need, and you take care of us all in even the smallest of ways.

"You brought light into my life when I needed it the most, and I'll do whatever it takes to be the same light for you.

"From this day forward, I vow to be your rock, your strength, and your steel, until the day I take my last breath, and hopefully, even after that. You're so much more to me than an Old Lady, or a wife, or a mother. You're my other half. I look forward to the opportunity to stand by your side for many, many more years.

"I love you, Penelope, from now until eternity."

"Sunshine, it's your turn." I hear Bear speak, but my eyes never leave Sunshine.

She takes a deep breath, rolls her shoulders back, and lifts her chin even higher. Something tells me I'm either about to be put in my place or she's about to turn me into a puddle of mush, but either way, I'm excited and nervous all at the same time. Hell, I'd probably listen to her sing the phone book and think it's the best song ever.

"My handsome, strong, loving, amazing Steel. What do I say to a man who's given me everything I've ever wanted or needed?

"I tried to think of how to make my vows meaningful and something that neither of us could ever forget, but everything I came up with paled in comparison to just telling you the truth. I need to tell you everything that's in my heart, and hopefully, my words will show you how much you mean to me. So, that's what I'm going to do right now.

"You, my hardheaded, relentless, and crazy man, may act like you're made out of steel, but to me, you're really just a marshmallow wrapped in aluminum foil. I know you're not like that with anyone else but your daughter, but that's what I love about you most. The way you treat me . . . treat us . . . is better than any words can describe. You take care of us, love us, and would die for us, and that makes us the luckiest girls on this planet.

"When I met you almost two years ago, it wasn't under the most ideal of circumstances. You were injured, avenging crimes for both my father and my brother, which I don't ever really think I thanked you for, and I just happened to be at the right place, at the right time, to meet you. I was just doing my job when they rolled you in for me to bandage your leg. It was my job to help put you back together, but what I don't think either of us realized was, at the time it was really you who was saving me.

"At the time, I was barely holding on to my sanity, but those few hours with you were a light to my darkness that I needed so desperately. I latched on to the way you made me feel, and as I tied your last stitch, I think I ended up leaving a little piece of myself behind with you. I never thought our paths would ever cross again, but somehow, the forces around us were stronger than anybody realized. You carried that piece of me with you until the day we met again, right here in this room, and you gave it back to me the second I realized you had come back to me.

"You were barely home an hour when you came marching out of Church on a mission. You walked right over to me and grabbed my butt, not recognizing me from that angle."

"How could I have been so blind?" My input makes everyone who knows me laugh. Because let's be real, a woman with an ass like Sunshine's is a magnet for my eyes. I could pick her backside out of a line-up.

"That's a very good question," she asks, her cheekiness coming out to play. "But anyway, back to what I was saying. The truth is, I may have sewn up your injury that day, and you eventually gave me that piece I left with you back, but it was you who left an even bigger piece of yourself with me. You left an impression on my soul, and I hope that never, ever fades away.

"And with these two little gremlins growing in here, our bond is only going to grow stronger. These boys will look up to you and Ring and think you hang the moon."

"Wait! What?" Did she say what I think she just said? I look over Sunshine's shoulder at Ring and his eyes are bugged out and wide. "Did you hear that too?"

"I think so." Ring is standing still, but his head is wobbling like a bobblehead.

I look back down at Sunshine, whose smile is a mile wide. "Did you say boys? Are our twins both boys?"

"They are," she responds with a nod, "and they're identical."

"WHAT?" Ring shouts before placing his hands on her hips and spinning both of them in a circle. Her back is pressed to his chest as he spins her around, her dress flowing out like a fan in front of her. I hear cheers and whistles erupt around us, but my attention is all on my woman and Ring enjoying the moment of celebration.

When they're back to standing still, he turns her to plant a big 'ol smacking kiss on her lips, then she's back facing me in seconds. I grab her hands to steady her on her wobbly heels, then kiss her myself. "Are you for real? Two boys?"

"As real as the sun is setting right about now, according to the ultrasound that neither of you looked at too closely, these babies are going to come out looking like we hit the copy and paste button. They'll be each other's best friends, just like you and Ring are, and I can't wait to meet them."

"Me too, Sunshine."

"Me three," Rings adds with his hand raised like we're in Church.

"But before these boys can get here, we need to finish this wedding," Sunshine says with a snicker. She grabs hold of my hands and gets back to the brass tacks. "Thank you for letting me love your daughter as much as I love you.

"Thank you for your part in helping me put myself back together. Without you, I'd still be in pieces.

"After I lost my mother, I was floundering, looking for a new port to call home, and you and Ring did that for me. In addition to my newfound father and brother, the two of you took me into your lives and gave me the greatest gift anyone could ever ask for. A family.

"I love you, Colt James, and I can't wait to watch our family continue to grow."

"I love you too, Penelope." I pull her close for a quick kiss, then take a step back, ready for the surprise I was actually in on.

"And speaking of family . . ." Sunshine turns around to face Ring.

RING

Hearing I'm going to be the father to identical twin boys? Day fucking made.

Watching my best friend marry the love of our lives? While the average person would be insanely jealous, I'm the happiest man in this room. I'm not usually the go-lucky kind of guy, but I'm happier today than I've ever been.

"And speaking of family . . ." But just when I think I have my head wrapped around one surprise, Sunshine turns to face me to finish her sentence. "What would you say if we do this thing, you and me?"

"What are you doin', Sunshine?" I link her fingers into mine and step as close to her as our feet allow. "It's not my turn yet."

"Yes, it is," she replies with a nod.

"What's going on?" My gaze volleys between her and Steel. "You didn't say 'I do' to him yet."

"That's because I'm not marrying him today." Sunshine peeks back at Steel, then sets her hands on my chest. "I'm marrying you today, Ryan."

My brain instantly shuts down. I could hear the words that just came out of her mouth, but I don't understand them at all. What she's saying could be a foreign language for all I know, I'm damn clueless. "What? How?" I finally manage to get a few cells to fire and say some words.

"Ring, when this whole wedding talk started, you were the one who said I should marry Steel, and while we both appreciate the selfless and honorable move you were trying to make, you need to be selfish today."

Not understanding, I ask, "Selfish how?"

"When two people get married, it's normally the joining of those two people, two families coming together as one, but our situation is anything but normal. I'm standing up here pledging my love to two men, who both love me back for some crazy reason, and I had no idea how I was supposed to pick which one I was going to be legally marrying. It's not an easy choice for a girl who loves both of you equally, but you tried to make that choice for me.

"You tried to make that choice for me, and while I appreciate that, I just can't let it happen. I need you to be selfish and decide that marrying me yourself is what you want, because giving you a family is what I want."

"You already are giving me a family. These babies—"

"These babies will be yours, mine, and Steel's no matter whose DNA made them, but this wedding is about building us, the three of us."

"Can I butt in here for a sec?" Steel steps close behind Sunshine. "I think what our lady is trying to say here, though she's missing the point because she doesn't want to sound crass or hurt anyone's feelings, is that you have no biological family, Ring. You're a lone wolf who needs a pack, and by asking you to be her legal husband, Sunshine is giving that piece of herself to you. She's making her your family, in name and in love."

Holy shit, I never even thought of that. Not having a family, being abandoned by my birth mother, is something that Sunshine and I talk about more often than I'd sometimes like. She seems to have this sense of knowing when I'm having a rough day and gets me to open up to her about what I need. Though the only thing I ever need is her.

"But what about Opal?" The plan was for Sunshine to marry Steel so she could adopt Opal, to give her a mother who actually loves her more than the bitch who gave birth to her, then overdosed and died on the drugs that were more important to her. It was supposed to be for the paperwork to keep Opal safe legally, just in case something happens to Steel.

"Someone pulled a little bit of magic again and got us the paperwork we needed to make it happen without me marrying Steel," Sunshine answers before winking at Hammer, who's standing behind Steel.

It looks like I've got a few Brothers to thank, along with a certain Cartel leader, for pulling some strings to make this all come together.

"But what about your last name? Doesn't it need to be the same as Opal's?" I have so many questions, I don't know if I'm trying to talk her into or out of hitching herself to me for life.

"The plan is that I'll hyphenate my name to be both yours and Steel's, just like we talked about doing for the babies," Sunshine answers. "And we'll change Opal's too when we do her paperwork."

"She'll have my name too?" And here's where I think I shed my first tears. I feel my eyes get very heavy and I pinch the bridge of my nose to try and hold them off. "Really? Are you sure?"

"Opal needs her Papa too." Steel reaches forward and claps me on the bicep.

I nod at him, hopefully showing my thankfulness for his part in all of this. He really is the best Brother, partner, and co-Old Man any biker could ask for.

"And that would make it your turn to say your vows."

Bear's words snap me to attention, and I get back to the matter at hand. I guess I'm marrying my Old Lady today.

"Oh boy. Okay. I guess it is. Wow. This is totally not what I was expecting to happen." That earns a chuckle from the crowd.

"Is this okay? Do you not—"

Sunshine tries to interrupt me, but I cut her off, needing her to know what this means to me. "I want this more than can be put into words. Let me just get my head screwed back on right and tell you everything I need you to know."

"Okay." Her shoulders sag in relief. She holds her hands out to me, and I link them tight with mine.

"Back less than a year ago, I was my own worst enemy. I lived and breathed this club, not caring about what happened to me outside of staying above ground and watching over Opal when she came to visit. Other than that, I was wild and lost, and for the most part, reckless.

"But then one day, out of the blue, you came into my world and built me up from nothing. You not only know all the right words to say when I'm having a tough day, but you don't just say them as a way to brush over my problems. You use them to build me back up, helping me to become a better man. You make me a man worthy of the love you show me every day.

"From this day on, I promise to always be that rock to you in return, because you are the foundation of our family. You are our heart.

"The day you drove up to my gate, I have to admit I was in a pissy-ass mood. I thought being relegated to a Prospect-level job was way below my standing and I was mad. Plain as day fucking livid. Then, this big ball of brightness pulled up and knocked me clean off my feet.

"You may have taken me by surprise, but once I had my faculties again, it only took me minutes to realize what I needed to do. I needed to do whatever it took to make you mine, including potentially pissing off my President. I may have had to endure a few punches and kicks from your father, but every bump and bruise was worth it.

"Your hunt to find your missing family brought you here, and that's where we began.

"Your words about finding a family are the same as mine, and I think that's what you were just trying to say. We all know I didn't grow up with really anyone at all, but the day I found the Rebel Vipers, I'd finally found my place. I had friends, I had Brothers, and while she may not be my blood, I was blessed with a little girl who calls me her Papa."

"That's me!" Opal exclaims.

Turning my attention to the little one in the front row, I hold my arms out and she comes running. Picking her up, I set her on one hip and kiss her on the cheek. "Yes, it is, munchkin."

I reach one hand out to Sunshine, and she takes mine in her left and Opal's in her right. "It took a little bit of time, but you welcomed the three of us into your circle, and we'll always be so damn grateful for that.

"Now, our little family is growing by two more munchkins," I smile and look down at the bump I know is growing seemingly by the day under the poof of that dress, "and no matter whose blood runs through their veins, they will be just as much my children as they are Steel's and yours.

"I promise to love you forever.

"I guarantee I'll love our family forever.

"And believe me when I say," I step in close, "I'll never let a day go by without kissing you like I own you.

"I love you, Penelope Jet. You'll always be mine."

I pull Sunshine in, and she tilts her head up for a kiss. Opal's tiny arms hug both of our necks at the same time I feel her kiss my cheek.

SUNSHINE

Listening to Ring profess his love is almost too much. Combine my doubled-up hormones and this parade of multiple weddings all in one day, and who could blame me for shedding a few tears. Whose crazy idea was this again? Oh, that's right, I played a big part in it.

As Ring puts Opal back down, I dab under my eyes with a tissue from Meredith.

As the three of us adults get back into our circle, I take in the similarities and differences in my guys' attire. Not shockingly, both of them are wearing their cuts, but that's not where the similarities end.

They're both wearing black button-up shirts, but where Ring's is a long sleeve, Steel's has short sleeves and his biceps are straining at the seams.

Both men are wearing black Wranglers, but their feet look a little different. Steel is wearing his favorite pair of Lucchese cowboy boots, while Ring has chosen a black pair of what he calls his "shit kickin' boots".

Ring is rocking a long, skinny black tie, while Steel has no tie and has the top two buttons of his shirt undone.

"Sunshine, you ready to do this again?" Bear asks. "Just remember, if you wanna rethink your choices, I'll pretend to lose the paperwork, or maybe fill it out with the wrong name. It's not too late to change your mind."

"Shut up, ya old fart," Bear's Old Lady, Peanut, hollers out. "Let the woman be and quit your yappin'."

I watch as Belle gives Peanut a high-five, then there are four thumbs up in our direction. I can't help but smile at the two of them. They really are the epitome of badass biker Old Ladies, and I hope to one day to have some young, new women look up to me like I look up to them and to Blue.

Turning my attention to Ring, I give him everything.

"I can't wait to tell our children about the day I met you. I drove up to your gate, rolled down my window, and practically drooled all over myself at the sight of your black hair, black clothes, and skin covered in dark tattoos. I may have even wondered how far under your clothes that ink went, but let's just leave that between us, okay?"

That earns me laughs from everyone.

"I'd never met anyone like you before, with your gruffness and yet gentle side, but something about you pulled me in like magnet. I was hooked from the moment you tucked me into your side. I gravitated to you from the second I arrived, and you stood at my side as I sat in the office shaking like a leaf as I had to explain to virtual strangers who I was.

"But it was you, Ring, who lent me a supporting hand when I needed it. It was your wink to me as I walked out the door that floated around in my mind for days after. And while you may not have been the reason I was there that day, you were for sure part of the reason I kept coming back, whether I wanted to think that at the time or not.

"When I watched the way you supported your Brothers when they needed you, when I watched you dote on a child who wasn't your blood, when you rescued me from that pit of hell, I knew you were everything I never even knew I was looking for.

"And for that, I promise that I'll always stand by your side when you need me, I'll always be your rock when you need someone to lean on, and I'll always hold on to you when the road gets rough.

"If you kiss me like you own me every day, I'll give you as many babies as you want. I love you, Ryan Bell."

Ring shines a deep, wide smile that even I only see once in a great while. "Damn, I'm a lucky man."

"And now, it's time for the rings." Bear nods to Jamie, who jumps up and holds open the box he's been in charge of.

Steel, Ring, and I each take turns taking out the rings we picked out, then I turn to Steel first.

Holding his big hand in mine, I slide a silver band with three diamonds embedded onto the fourth finger of his left hand and say, "With this ring, I give you my life and my love forever."

Steel returns the favor, placing a plain silver band on my left hand. He tucks a wild piece of my loose hair behind my ear, then leans down to lure me in for a kiss. It's nothing wild or inappropriate, merely a meeting of our lips, sealing our love and commitment to one another. While he may not legally be my husband after this, I will call him so forever.

Turning to Ring at my left, I slide a solid black band on his hand. "With this ring, I give you my life and my love forever." His has no embellishments like Steel's, but it's solid and unbreakable, just like him. And for a man who only ever wears black, this band called out to me the minute I saw it in the jewelry store.

Now, this kiss can only be described as Earth-shattering. In typical Ring fashion, he wraps one arm around my waist, bracing my cheek in the other, and proceeds to dip me backward so far, I have to hold onto his neck so tight to keep from falling down. Sky-high heels and Ring kisses are a dangerous combination.

"By the power vested in me by the Rebel Vipers MC... and the state of Wisconsin... I now pronounce Sunshine and Ring, man and wife!" Bear's words echo through the room but are quickly drowned out by the applause and hooting and hollering from the rambunctious crowd.

When everyone settles back down, he calls out again. "And I also pronounce Steel and Sunshine man and wife as well!"

The crowd cheers again, but this time continues as Steel scoops up Opal from her chair. Then, with one hand in Ring's and the other holding Steel's, I lead the four of us back down the aisle.

We walk just the same as we live our lives, all together as one.

CHAPTER THIRTY-ONE

HAMMER

If you would've told me three years ago that I'd be getting married today, I probably would've called you crazy before punching your lights out. Me, getting married? No fucking way. But here I am, standing at the front of the crowd, waiting for my very own angel to be escorted down the aisle by my dad.

And that too is something I never imagined happening. I don't ever in my entire life remember Butch attending a wedding, even for someone he knew, so when he asked my permission to ask Angel if she'd allow him to walk her down the aisle, I almost blacked out. I didn't see that coming from a mile away, but I'll never forget the day, that's for sure.

I told him I'd be honored if this was something he wanted to do, but only under the condition that it also had to be what Angel really wanted. He came to our cabin one night for dinner, and before the food was even on the table, he asked her if he could give her away at the wedding. And when she started crying the second the question left his mouth, I knew it was the right thing to do . . . for both of them.

Even before we were together, Angel was never really close to my dad, but since Taren and Ace came home to us, my dad has been around a fuck ton more. I don't know if someone said something to him or not, because I'm not about to look a gift horse in the mouth, but thankfully, he's cut way back on his drinking.

When I asked him about it one day, he said he'd rather spend as much of his free time with his grandsons as he can, instead of hiding out in his cabin all alone. It's almost like he has a new lease on life. Watching him have his hands full of Matchbox trucks and mini motorcycles instead of a bottle of who knows what is a strange feeling, but I'll take it.

My dad's deep dislike for the female race, thanks in major part to my runaway mother, may not have come full circle yet, but he's working on it one day at a time.

The music picks back up again, pulling my attention to the end of the aisle, and in perfect timing too. I was starting to get worried that Angel was going to bail on me. Who could really blame her if she did? I treated Angel like crap for so damn long, it's a miracle she even wants to be in the same state as me, let alone marry me. I must've done something right in a past life to have the life I do now.

As I see my dad come around the last row of guests, and Angel steps into my view, I let out a deep breath I think I've been holding since the wedding planning started two months ago.

Angel is a vision in black. Leave it to my bride to go against the societal norms and wear a color that's the furthest from white that you can get. No matter what she would've chosen to wear, I know she would've been beautiful, but in this dress . . . this dress in particular . . . my Old Lady is stunning.

A sheer layer of black lace crosses Angel's chest, only showing her tan skin through the pattern, then it forms full sleeves ending at her wrists. From her chest down, the dress is solid black, as dark as a starless, midnight sky. It flows down her body, and as she walks, I see a flash of skin. Fuck me, her right leg is exposed because of a slit cut in the skirt all the way up to the middle of her thigh. The material trails behind her in what I think is called a train.

Fiery red hair, loose in its naturally wavy state, flows over Angel's left shoulder, and the right side is pinned back just behind her ear.

As she steps to my side, I see her eyes are sparkling with unshed tears, so the first thing I do is wipe the outer corners with my thumbs to pull them away. No crying on our wedding day, this is supposed to be a happy day. It is for me at least.

I'm very pleased to see her cheeks and nose are free from heavy makeup, allowing the beautiful freckles I love to kiss, trace, and make patterns with to stand out.

"Thanks, Dad." I thank him with a handshake before he takes a seat a few rows back, next to Tiny.

I take Angel's right hand into my left and turn so we're facing each other. Her eyes are still sparkling but only in happiness, and the corners of her mouth are upturned in a light, easy smile.

"You two love birds ready?" Bear asks.

"You got it, preacher man," My eyes never leave Angel's as I reply.

"Alright, then you go first, son."

So, I do.

"Temperance Ashley Hayes, I am in awe of you.

"You have dealt with so much shit because of me." I watch her lips twitch, fighting back a laugh, but I need to continue to get out everything I need to say to her.

"The way we started our journey, and everything I put you through to get us to this place right here, wasn't always the greatest. I kept you at arm's length for way too long, and I don't think any words I would say could ever repay you for that. Right now, all I can think to do is thank you for giving me another chance.

"Hell, you gave me way too many chances, way more than I deserved, but we still fought through everything pushing against us to get here. Somehow, through all the fighting and the hurtful words from me, and even after one nightmare-ish trip across the country, you ended up right where I always hoped you'd be. Right here by my side.

"In the back of my mind, I think I always knew you were the woman for me. I just had to get my head out of my ass and let you knock me off my high horse to see it. And because of that kick in the backside, we have so much to look forward to together.

"Because of you, we have our boys.

"Because of you, we have our home.

"Because of you, my beautiful, freckled, always looking at the glass half-full angel, we have each other.

"Because of you, I get to spend the rest of my life waking up every day, knowing you'll be right there beside me. I'm so undeserving of you, but I'll never let you go again.

"I wouldn't be a father if it weren't for you, and I'm not just referring to our two boys here today. I believe so deeply that our baby in heaven brought you home to me and is watching down on us and his brothers right now.

"It all circles back to you, Angel. Your sister is here because of you. We're all getting married today because of you and your crazy organizational tendencies and binders and notes and pictures. This is all because of you, and I couldn't be more honored to be called yours. Because that's what I am. I'm one hundred percent yours. I'm all yours, and you're all mine.

"As we celebrate this day with our family, I need you to know my promises to you.

"I vow to always provide you with a safe and happy home.

"I vow to love our boys unconditionally, and any more that you bless me with in the future. I hope they're all fierce yet gentle like you, strongminded yet kind just like you, and powerful yet humble just like you. Because, my love, you're all of those things and so much more.

"I vow to show you with my actions how much I love and need you every day. And yes, that means grabbing your ass as I walk behind you and kissing you very inappropriately whenever I damn well please." That gets me a few whistles and laughs and a few inappropriate for a wedding 'hell yeas' from my Brothers.

"I vow to always love you, cherish you, and forsake all others for you. Whether we're rich or poor, or in sickness or in health, I'll be right here by your side as long as we both shall live."

"Did you research wedding vows on the internet?" Angel asks, teasingly.

"Shh," I press a finger to my lips, but I can't hold back a smile of my own, "don't be tellin' everybody my secret."

"I won't," she says back with a silly grin of her own.

Bear nods to her. "Angel, my dear, it's your turn."

ANGEL

Dressed in his cut over a crisp white shirt, black suspenders, a long yellow tie, and black denim jeans that are tight as sin, my man is looking hot as fuck. Can someone say that about their soon-to-be-spouse at their wedding? I don't care if somewhere it says I can't, because this six-foot-six hunk of a man in front of me is looking mighty scrumptious.

As usual, Hammer has his beard brushed and oiled and looking perfect. I shaved the sides and back of his head a couple days ago, so he's good there, and someone, probably one of the other Old Ladies, twisted the long strip of hair on top of his head into a braid.

"Only my crazy man would copy his vows from the internet," I joke as I tug a little on Hammer's hands.

But, hey, what did I expect? Bikers and romantic words aren't two things you think of going together in a sentence. I've heard him say some very sweet things before, like the night he proposed, but if he felt better getting advice from who knows what or who out in the universe, more power to him. His vows were perfect.

"Before I start my turn, I have to admit I also had a hard time figuring out what to say today. I struggled because I knew no matter what I thought of, it never would seem like enough to describe how I'd be feeling.

"I thought I was going to be so nervous.

"I knew I'd be happy and excited to become your wife, but as the couple months of planning passed and the days started counting down, the more and more nervous I got. I had this fear that one day you'd wake up and realize this wasn't what you wanted after all."

"No, Angel." Hammer's plea is so soft, I barely hear his words. But his sad eyes give away everything he's feeling. He hates when I'm sad, and he always tells me never to be sad because he doesn't like my tears.

I hate him thinking I'm sad, but I need to get this all out.

"Everything has come together for us so fast, this little nagging voice in my head said it was all going to explode. And while that's all one hundred percent on me, I need you to know how much your words of encouragement and love have meant to me lately. You may not have been able to see the negative thoughts in my head, but it seemed like every time I was having one, you'd appear and say something to push the bad away.

"Whether it was with a kiss or asking me a question about the boys, or even a simple 'I love you', you knocked every one of those worries off the shelf and used the rubble to build me back up. You unintentionally knew what I needed without me having to ask you for it, and I'll never forget that.

"I'll never forget the love you show me every single day. I'll never forget the smiles on our boys' faces when they see you after a long day. I'll never forget the expression on your face the moment your dad walked me down this aisle, because even though we're sharing this day with so many of our friends, I'll always remember today as the day I was blessed to become your wife.

"I told you many months ago that this is what I wanted if we were going to give our relationship another chance, and you never faltered on your promise to make it happen. You made me your girlfriend, you made me your Old Lady, and today, you're making me your wife. But there's just one more surprise I need to tell you.

"There's one more thing you've unknowingly given to me, and I can't wait to start this new journey with you.

"It may have only been a few months since we brought our boys home, but I need you to know that you've blessed me with another bundle to come. Some might think of us as insane, but I wouldn't want to live this crazy life with anyone but you. Hammer, we're now going to be a family of five."

Pulling on his left hand, I take one step closer to him and place his palm flat on my stomach.

Hammer looks up and down between his hand and my eyes, and with each flutter, his eyes grow bigger and bigger. "Do you mean?"

"Yes," I whisper, nodding and smiling so big. "We're having another one."

"You're pregnant? Really?" He practically shouts in shock. His eyebrows lower and he growls out, "You're not shittin' me, are you?"

Not able to stop my laugh from coming out loud, my shoulders shake as I say, "Only you would say 'shit' at the altar."

"Holy goddamn Hades." Hammer places both of his hands at my waist, right above my hips, then drops to one knee and rests his forehead on my stomach. "Thank you, Angel. Thank you," I hear him repeating over and over.

I trace the zigzag of his French braid with my left pointer finger and rest my other hand on his shoulder. "I should be thanking you, Hammer. You gave me this gift."

Just as quick as he dropped to the floor, Hammer's back up on his feet, towering over me again. He gently takes my face in his hands, and before I know it, I'm swept into a deep kiss. I chase his tongue with mine as he takes every breath of my own for himself.

"It's not time for that, Brother," I hear Bear say with a chuckle just before I'm let up for air.

"Bear's right, mister." I wipe some of my smudged lip gloss off Hammer's lower lip. "We haven't exchanged the rings yet."

"Oh. Right. Let's do that." Hammer talks like he's getting his brain firing up again as he tugs his cut back straight. Both hands tugging on the seams of the leather, his shoulders set back and Hammer is at attention.

Jamie appears at my right with his ring bearer box, so Hammer and I grab our respective bands.

"Who goes first?" I ask Bear as I twist Hammer's ring around my thumb. Hammer slides mine halfway up his left pinkie.

"You do," he replies with a nod.

I take Hammer's ring off my finger, and after reaching for his left hand, I slide the wide, yellow gold band onto his finger. Looking into his eyes, the eyes I could look at every second for the rest of my days and never get lost, I give him my promise. "With this ring, I give you my life and my love forever."

I spent hours trying to find a ring I thought Hammer would like. I went to the jewelry store with Duchess, and as we browsed, the saleswoman approached to ask what I was looking for. I must've looked like a lost child at an amusement park because the lady swooped in and said she'd pick out a selection of bands in my price range for me, and then we could narrow it down from there. She was gone for no more than five minutes before she came back with a tray holding five different rings.

As she described the first four, I felt nothing, but as soon as she held this particular one up, it grabbed my attention right away. Then, as she started to describe it and said that the distressed surface on this one has what is called a hammered polish, I knew it was perfect. Who else has a wedding ring with his name in the description? No one I can think of.

Before Hammer takes my hand, I watch him fiddle with the back of the band with his thumb. He's staring down at his hand with a soft smile, and I know immediately I made the right choice.

Sliding the tiny band off his pinkie, he takes a half step forward and takes my left hand in his. With his eyes locked on mine, he slowly slides a row of tiny diamonds inlaid into a white gold band up against the three-stone engagement ring he gave me what seems like just yesterday.

"With this ring, I give you my life and my love forever."

Hammer lifts my rings to his lips, then threads his left hand into the back of my hair, tilts my head just a bit to the right, and closes in for a kiss. The last thing I see before I close my eyes are his deep caramel irises sparkling in the dim light from the lanterns around us. It's almost an ominous look of what's to come, but I crave whatever he has in store for me.

I hear words being spoken and cheers and claps all around us, but everything fades into the background as I kiss my husband for the first time.

Hammer . . . my husband.

If the me from three years ago could see this, she would call all of us batshit crazy. But then again, had she known then what I know now, I doubt she would've changed a thing.

CHAPTER THIRTY-TWO

BLUE

After Hammer finally let Angel breathe on her own again after the doozy of a kiss he planted on her, and Buzz and Star took their turns exchanging their vows, the ceremony part of the evening was done. All the couples took turns having their pictures taken under the wooden archway, and some with their families too, before it was moved to the side.

As the overhead lights were turned back up, the whole crowd pitched in to help turn the dark and eerily romantic wedding space back into a room where we can all sit around and eat the dinner we had catered together. The chairs were all moved out of their rows and rearranged around the dining tables, in addition to some extra ones we keep in storage for special occasions, though there's never been a wedding in the clubhouse until today. A space is left open at the far side of the room for the dancing that will happen a little later on.

We all eat and laugh and have a few too many drinks together. Everyone listens with wonder and amusement as four of the remaining original five Brothers reminisce about Brick, then go on to talk about the craziness and havoc they all went through turning an old, rundown, abandoned meat processing factory into the clubhouse we all love today.

The younger generation, meaning Whiskey, Hammer, Buzz, and a few of the others, tell stories of the shenanigans they got into when their fathers weren't around, making everyone laugh at their hijinks. Some of the things we 'older folks' already knew about, but there were a few new things I hear for the first time, and one of the adventures they describe answers some questions I've wondered about for a bunch of years.

Like, what happened to the assortment of pumpkins I had on my front porch as decoration one fall about fifteen years back?

As it turns out, our boys decided to sneak out of their rooms at three in the morning, load all of my pumpkins in the back of Whiskey's pickup, and joyride around town to steal as many other people's pumpkins that they could find. Then they decided to drive up to the top of a very steep hill in the middle of the next town over and dumped them all out. They proceeded to watch them roll down said hill until they crashed to the bottom in a million pieces. If I wasn't laughing so hard, half proud and half jealous of not getting to see something I would've loved to be a part of, I would be beating my nephew with a stick.

After dinner is done, and the lights go dim, this time to allow for the flashing colors from the accent lighting Cypher rigged up, the music is turned a little louder as to turn the room into a real party. Brothers and their families, sans kids who have been loaded up and sent back to Steel's moms' house for the night, are scattered all around the room in huddles, shooting the shit and enjoying their night.

I excuse myself from a circle of Belle, Angel, and Sara to powder my nose and use the ladies' room. Just as I raise my hand to push open the door, it swings in and I hurry to step aside as Jade, the newest club girl, rushes out and disappears into the crowd. Not needing to involve myself in whatever that was about, I make my way into the bathroom but quickly realize the back end of whatever I was trying to avoid is continuing right smack dab in front of me.

Toe to toe, Meredith and Brewer are in a standoff. They both have their arms crossed, and Meredith is tapping the top of her heel faster than a woodpecker. She looks pissed.

The door makes a thud as it closes behind me, causing both of them to swing around my way. Brewer looks at Meredith one more time, drops his chin to his chest, and lets out a sigh so hard, I can feel it in my bones. He mumbles a few choice curse words, then storms out of the bathroom.

Through the reflection in the mirror, I watch the patches on the back of his cut disappear and I see Meredith attempt to hide her face behind her hair as she wipes away a few tears.

Stepping forward, I set a hand on her shoulder and turn her to face me. There's no hiding her tears. She's got bloodshot eyes, red cheeks, and her eyeliner is a little smudged. "Silly question, I know, but are you okay, hun?"

Meredith's shoulders slump as she looks at me through the curtain of her dark hair. "I have to be."

"What do you mean?" I ask as I tuck her hair behind her ear.

"He's never gonna love me like I do him." She says the words to the floor and follows them with a tiny hiccup.

I remember young love, that feeling where you can't imagine your life without that one specific person, even though you look back on it years later and laugh at yourself because it was all so silly.

I don't know if that's what Meredith is feeling right now, but I do the only thing I can. I pull her in for a tight hug. "Oh, honey, I'm sorry."

"It's okay." As we back apart, she gathers a few pieces of paper towel to wipe under her eyes.

"Can I ask you a question? And feel free to tell me to take a flying leap if I step on your toes."

"Sure," Meredith says as she hops up on the counter and her cowboy boot covered feet start swaying. "Might as well get comfortable, these new boots aren't broken in yet and are killing my feet."

Totally agreeing about the uncomfortable shoes, I lean my hip against the counter beside her. "I don't exactly know what I just walked in on, but based on who I almost collided with when I did, then Brewer stomping off in a huff, I can take a guess. Are you okay? Do you want to talk about it? I can try and be a shoulder for you to cry on."

"I'd like that." Her attempt at a smile is only half successful, so she just shrugs it off. "I don't think I could face my mom with this."

Knowing she wants to talk to me makes me smile. Had I not lost my baby all those years ago, he or she would be Meredith's age, so being someone she feels comfortable enough to talk to is a good feeling. "That's what I'm here for."

"I really, really like him." Meredith clasps her hands in her lap almost like she's praying. "Is that wrong of me to feel this way about someone who's older than me?"

Oh boy, I had a feeling this was where this conversation was going. I may have seen a few of the longing looks she's given Brewer lately, but I didn't realize it was this serious for her.

"Let me start by asking this. Have you ever had a crush on anyone before Brewer?"

"I have," she replies with a nod. "A few times."

"Did any of those times, those boys, make you feel like you do right now?"

"No way." Meredith's head is shaking back and forth, her hair waving around her shoulders. "When I walked in here and saw them, I swear I felt my heart crack open."

"So, do you think what you're feeling is real," I ask, needing to know more, "or just another crush?"

"I know it's real. Ever since the day I almost ran him over, I've felt it in here." She points at her chest, right over her heart.

Shifting my feet a little, I kick off my shoes, then set them up on the counter. No more heels for this Old Lady. "And what about Brewer? Have you two talked at all? I mean before today."

"We've talked a few times about random stuff, but anytime I try and take the conversation deeper, he just keeps saying he can't be with me because of my brother. Steel this, Steel that, it's so annoying. What does my brother have to do with my love life?"

"You know the answer to that, Mer." I tilt my head and try to give her a sympathetic smile. "Your big brother is Brewer's club Brother. They have a whole different kind of relationship with each other that none of us will ever understand. That's part of them being in the club."

"I know. It's just that . . ." Her words trail off as she takes a deep breath. "We kissed once, but then he pushed me away and started going on and on about how I'm too young, that I need to find someone my own age. Yadda, yadda, yadda. It's bullshit."

"And what do you think? Is he right? Are you too young?"

"No. I don't think so." She hops off the counter and sets her hands on her hips. "I know I'm right for him. He shouldn't have been in here with her. It should've been me."

"Can I ask exactly what you walked in on?"

"He had *her* up on the counter, and they were so far down each other's throats, they didn't even hear me walk in." Meredith rolls her eyes and her lip curls up in a sneer. "His pants were unzipped, and they were sucking face, but that's all I saw before I yelled and they jumped apart."

I know the heartache she's feeling. I've seen this many times with women who've come around the club in the past, thinking they can find a Brother and make him commit and settle down. Those same women have left the clubhouse either in tears or cussing up a blue streak, because whoever they were 'in love with' was caught in a compromising situation with someone who wasn't them.

Now, I'm not saying Meredith doesn't have the gumption to make a Brother fall to his knees, because she's a tenacious one, I'd just hate to see her get hurt and then never want to be at the clubhouse even though she has family here.

"Can I be honest and say something you might not like?"

"I guess," she responds with a shrug.

"If Brewer doesn't want to be with you, for whatever reason, maybe you need to accept that."

"I know," and she sighs again, "but I don't want to. I know it makes me sound like the kid he seems to think I am, but I can't help what I feel."

"I'm sorry, honey." I hold a hand out to her, and she squeezes mine back. "Maybe you just need to give him time."

"Or maybe," Meredith's eyes get really big, and I know she's had a thought to do something crazy, "I just need to teach him a lesson." And I was right, her attitude suddenly does a complete one-eighty.

"I don't know. This doesn't sound good," I say hesitantly as I step back.

Her smile grows a bit wild as she begins pacing back and forth. "Maybe I do need to date someone my own age. That'll show him. I'll find someone else, and he'll realize he messed up and lost me for good and I can rub it in his face."

Yea, this doesn't sound like a good idea at all. I have to try and turn this around, to make her see this isn't the way to go about this. "What if you do go on a date and actually end up having feelings for someone else? Then what?"

"That'll never happen." She waves off what I think is a legitimate concern. "I just need to show him he's not my only option. Thanks, Blue." Then, she rushes out.

I try calling for her to come back, but the door closes, leaving me talking to myself. Shit.

Oh, fuck a duck, this could end very badly. I think I need to keep an eye out for that one, and if it weren't for the fact that Sunshine has two babies growing in her belly, I'd probably loop her in too on the trouble ahead, but this is more than she needs to stress about right now.

I have this feeling deep in my gut that Meredith is going to give Brewer a run for his money one day soon, and I hope he's ready. I don't think he knows what he's up against with that one.

Finally taking the time to do what I came in here to do, I take care of business, wash my hands, grab my shoes from the counter, then head back for the main room.

Coming out of the bathroom, I find Mountain leaning against the wall waiting for me. "Well, there you are, wife. I thought you got lost in there."

"Just a little girl talk emergency," I say as I lean up for a kiss.

"Everything okay?" he asks as he tucks me into his side.

"It will be, but thank you for asking." I wrap my arms around his waist and lean my chin on his chest. "What were you doing creeping around outside the ladies' bathroom anyhow?"

"I came lookin' for my wife to ask her if I could have this dance?" He starts swaying us side to side.

"I think I'd like that very much . . . husband."

CHAPTER THIRTY-THREE

MOUNTAIN

Not many things in the world make me wonder what heaven would be like, but this moment right here would definitely be close if I had to guess. My wife in my arms, dancing in the main room of our clubhouse, surrounded by our family, celebrating the multiple couples who just got married here today, is a pretty good way to picture the afterlife.

I feel Blue take a deep breath as she nuzzles her head against my chest, and I use this time of quiet amongst the noise around us to take everything in.

My son. Whiskey is currently forehead to forehead with his Old Lady and now wife, Duchess, as they sway back and forth a bit to my left. As they dance together, they're talking and smiling with each other, no care for anything around them.

I'm so fucking proud of my boy. I can't believe he's a few short months from turning thirty-two. He's the President of our club, has a wife, a son, and from the chatter I overheard earlier, maybe I'll have another grandbaby on the horizon soon. I don't know if Duchess is pregnant yet, but based on how fast Whiskey got her knocked up the first time, I wouldn't put it past him to do it again just as quick. Krew, their four-month-old son, is the cutest damn baby ever, and I hope I get blessed with many, many more grandkids very soon.

And speaking of which, I'm about to have two more grandsons coming very soon. Hearing that Sunshine is pregnant with identical twin boys is the second-best thing that happened to me today, next to my vow renewal to Blue, of course. The looks on both Steel and Ring's faces were priceless. Those two aren't ones to surprise easily, but Sunshine has knocked them out of their boots a few times recently, and seeing as she's my daughter, I couldn't be prouder.

Now that it's known that their twins are identical, it brings to light the fact that both babies obviously come from the same biological father, but for Ring and Steel, I know whoever it is won't matter to them one bit. In their little tribe, Steel may be Opal's daddy, but Ring is her Papa and he loves her just as much. It just goes to show that the Rebel Vipers are more than just friends and outlaws who ride around and do bad things. We're all family, whether related by blood or not, and we'd do anything for the people we love.

Sunshine is being passed from Steel to Ring, and she lets out a burst of laughter so infectious, I can't help but chuckle along myself.

Blue shifts in my arms and looks up at me with a smile so wide. "What's so funny?"

"Nothing really," I reply as I plant a kiss on her forehead. "Just happy is all."

"I like seeing you like this." Blue settles back in my arms, and we keep on swaying.

We slowly turn in circles, and from where I'm looking right now, I watch as Angel walks up to Hammer with something hidden behind her back. He turns from his conversation with a few other Brothers to give her his attention, only to be smashed in the face with a cupcake. Everyone around them bursts in laughter as Angel takes off running, Hammer right on her heels. She doesn't make it very far before he presses his frosting covered face into her cheek, making her scream out in objection.

One of the flavors on the ginormous tower of cupcakes that Duchess whipped up for today is red velvet. She has been giving all of the Brothers a cupcake flavor of their own as they claim an Old Lady, and it turns out that I now get my own flavor as well as a nod of acknowledgment for including Blue in today's festivities. Duchess somehow, probably from Whiskey, found out that my favorite cake flavor is red velvet and made them special for me.

Seeing the playfulness and easiness between Angel and Hammer reminds me a lot of Blue and myself back when we first got married. They love each other so much, and everyone around them can see it too.

Angel's antics with the cupcake also remind me of the morning after mine and Blue's first wedding. That day started out a bit different than I had planned, but as it went on, it only got better.

Stretching out my right hand, I expect to feel the warm, smooth skin of my wife but am only met with cold cotton sheets. I rub the fog from my eyes and blink to try and to see in the darkness of our bedroom. Sitting up, I notice the door is closed and I remember very specifically

last night having my hands full of Blue when we came to bed, so she must have shut it when she went wherever she is right now.

As I get out of bed, I hear the bass of some music through the walls and go to investigate. Hoping to lure Blue back to bed, I skip putting any clothes on and strut my naked self down the hall. When I reach the open living space of our cabin, my eyes find Blue right away, or should I say they find her ass covered in a pair of my boxer briefs.

Shaking away to the words of a kickass ZZ Top song, my wife has a bowl in one hand, and is mixing something in it with the other. Using the music as a distraction, and her belting along to the song, I sneak around the kitchen island and approach her from behind. I grab hold of her shaking hips and pull her ass tight against my very happy morning wood.

"AHHH!" Blue screams as she jumps in place, startled. She lets go of the bowl and it clatters to the counter, and the spatula she was using goes flying off to the side, somehow luckily landing in the sink. "What are you doing? Tryin' to kill me already?"

I reach for the radio sitting a bit to the right on the counter and turn the music down to a non-blaring level. Once my hands are back on Blue, I growl in her ear some of the lyrics from the song still playing. "You gonna give me all your lovin', baby?"

That makes her laugh, and I can't help but use her head thrown back as the perfect excuse to dive into her neck and trail kisses up into her hair. Her body shivers in my arms as she turns to face me. She loops her hands around my neck as she leans back against the counter behind her. Blue pulls me with her, so I lean the weight of my hips on hers.

"What will you give me if I do?" she purrs as she smiles up at me, one eyebrow raised suggestively.

"You already said 'I do' yesterday." I brace my hands on the counter on either side of her, and use the advantage of my height to

surround her with as much of myself as I can. "What else could I need?"

"Hmmm . . ." She pretends to ponder as her backside wiggles, rubbing her clothed front against my naked one. Her smile turns innocent and happy. "How about a cake?"

"A cake?" I can't help but pull back a bit in shock. Looking over at the clock above the sink, I see what time it is. "You're out here at seven a.m. baking a cake instead of in bed with your new husband?"

"I wanted to surprise you with breakfast, but then, when I realized we were out of bread, French toast wasn't an option." Blue slides her hands down my shoulders to rest flat on my chest. "So, I started digging in the pantry and found everything I needed for cake. Next thing I knew, I was mixing eggs and flour and now we get cake for breakfast."

"You want to spend the one morning we have free from my crazy, rotten son baking a cake? Did I not love on you enough last night that you don't want me more than cake?" My question is paired with a raised eyebrow and an over-exaggerated pout. I'm totally trying to milk this moment, because you only have one wedding morning after. Personally, I want to be spending it horizontal on the bedsheets, not vertical in the kitchen talking about cake.

"You loved on me very well last night, thank you." Blue presses up on her toes and pulls me down for a kiss. "I just wanted to have a wedding cake, is that okay?"

Well, when she puts it like that, how can I say no? We didn't have the most traditional wedding, and I barely gave her enough time to go buy a dress, so I guess the least I can do is let her have this.

But who could blame me for wanting to marry Blue like I did? After I popped the question three days after meeting, I waited the six months she asked for before getting married, so as soon as that date came around, I gave her one week to get all our affairs in order.

I told her we were getting hitched whether I had to drag her to the courthouse kicking and screaming, so one week later here we are. Blue kept her promise, and yesterday was our day.

"I guess we're having cake for breakfast," I say with a shrug. Looking around the kitchen but not seeing a cake, I ask where it is.

"It's still in the oven, but it's just about done." Blue presses on my chest, and I take a step back. She heads to the sink and rinses off the spatula that she threw earlier. When she turns back around, she waves it at me like a sword. "I was making the frosting when you decided to scare the bejesus out of me."

"But Blue—" I try to start, but she cuts me off.

She points the spatula at the entrance to the hall. "Go put some clothes on and check on Connor or something. I don't care what you do, just don't come back in this kitchen for another hour. By then, everything will be done and we can get back to spending the day together."

To give the newlyweds privacy 'to be gross', Connor spent the night two cabins down with his best friend, Adam, my Brother Butch's son. Those two are thick as thieves, and I have no doubt that when they grow up, they'll take this club and run it even better than I am right now.

One long, messy, aggressive kiss pressing Blue up against the cabinets later, I let her get back to her cake and march my still naked backside to the bedroom to get dressed. Though I plan on being naked again very soon, I decide to head out to the clubhouse and check on the damage from last night.

When I forced Blue to leave our impromptu celebration, the party was still going strong, and knowing my Brothers like I do, I have no doubt the clubhouse is a mess right now. Question is, how big of a mess, and what's it going to cost to repair it?

Oh, who really cares? Can you put a price on a kickass party? I think not.

When I came back to our cabin one hour later on the dot, my wife wasn't where I left her. I expected to walk in and see her in the kitchen, maybe the cake sitting on the counter, but I see neither her nor our unconventional breakfast anywhere.

Wanting to get back to being naked, I headed for our bedroom and found the best kind of surprise. Blue was sitting on our bed, legs crossed, buck naked, with a small round cake sitting on a plate in front of her. I stripped down to my birthday suit and crawled up to sit in front of her.

As it turns out, she baked us a red velvet cake with cream cheese frosting and I fell in love with her all over again. Not only did she make it just for me, which was special enough, it tasted so damn good. I'd never had that flavor cake before, but it became my favorite on the spot.

After feeding each other a few forkfuls of the fluffy red cake, frosted with the sweet *icing*, we spent the rest of our morning and well into the afternoon making love over and over again. But the extra bonus of that day was the little bits of frosting I got to lick off certain parts of my wife's body.

I think if people realized this is how the morning after weddings could go, everyone on this planet would be rushing to get hitched. Cake in bed may make a mess, but the clean-up in the shower is so fucking worth it.

Fuck, just thinking of that day, I decide it's time to take this party of two somewhere a little more private. Perhaps behind our bedroom door.

"It's time to go to bed," I whisper before tugging at Blue's earlobe with my teeth.

"But it's still early." Her words may be in protest of leaving, but her body is screaming yes. Her neck arches to the side, her back stretches to press her chest into mine, and I feel the bite of her fingernails as she claws at my back.

I reach behind my back, grab hold of her wrists from underneath my cut, and pull our now joined hands out to spin her around. I face us both in the direction of the hallway leading to our private room and whisper in her ear, "I need you. Now."

CHAPTER THIRTY-FOUR

BLUE

Much like our first wedding night, Mountain is insatiable. I barely get a word in as we make a beeline for our room, and as soon as the door is shut and locked behind us, I'm being pulled into the bedroom.

"How do I get you out of this thing?" I feel Mountain's fingers trail down the back of my dress, looking for the zipper, but by the time his hands land at my waist, still not finding the pull, he gives up. "Fuck it. I need you too much for this shit."

Next thing I know, I'm spun around and looking at myself in the mirror of my vanity-style dresser. Mountain is behind me, hunched over a bit, lifting the bottom of my dress with his hands on my legs. Once he's back at his full height, I can feel the cool air against my bare butt cheeks. It's then that the silence filling the room that makes my smile grow.

The shocked expression mixed with an evil grin reflecting back at me is exactly what I was hoping for when I got ready today. I'm not wearing any underwear.

"Like what you see back there?" I can't help but tease a little.

"Where are your panties, Blue?" Mountain asks as he grabs twin handfuls of my ass.

"In the drawer, where they belong." Shaking my hips a little, I get the reaction I was looking for.

Mountain pushes me forward, forcing me to brace myself by slamming my hands down on the wooden surface, then he presses his chest into my back. I watch as he nuzzles his face into my neck and then trails the tip of his tongue against my skin, making me break out in a full body shiver.

"Keep your hands right where they are . . . wife." His growled order is followed by a sharp bite to the top of my shoulder. "I'm gonna take you right here. I wanna watch your reflection as I give us both what we want. I need to see your face as I fuck you 'til you scream my name."

Just hearing his need for me gives me a rush of ecstasy. "Oh, please." I arch my back, pressing my ass into the denim rubbing against my skin.

"You gonna stay right there?" Mountain's voice sounds like a purr.

I nod, my eyes now closed. "Uh huh."

I hear rustling as he backs away just a bit. Fumbling to keep my dress up around my waist, I reach for the material with my right hand and hold it as I set my hand back on the dresser. Something clanks against the hardwood, presumably Mountain's belt and jeans, then I feel the warmth of his skin against mine.

One hand gripping my waist, I feel his other press his dick down into the valley of my legs, and with one thrust forward, I'm so full, I lose my breath. It takes two thrusts for my now even wetter passage to open completely to his forceful pounding, and I can do nothing but hold myself just as I am.

My body locks into a hold stronger than a soldier in formation, and my pussy takes the beating that it's been waiting for all day. In and out, over and over, skin slaps against skin as grunts and gasps and profanities are expelled with every breath.

There is nothing else I'd rather be doing right now. There is nowhere else I'd rather be. This is pure lust. This is fucking at its core. Mating with my husband is what I was put on this spinning rock to do, and I hope it never stops being like this.

"Yes. Yes. More. Please," I beg as I drop my chin to my chest. I feel my hair fall wild and loose around my shoulders, but I do nothing to stop it from swinging against my face.

"Like. This?" Mountain calls out, enunciating each word with not only a thrust forward but a jerk back on my hips, slamming me into him.

"Yes!" I shout before taking a big breath in. "I'm gonna . . ."

I can't even finish my own sentence, the sensations running through my body are too much. I feel a tightness growing in my stomach and know I'm about to fall over the edge. And Mountain must feel it too because he slides one hand around to my front before his fingers disappear into my folds and he pinches that magical bundle of nerves. And that's all she wrote.

Falling forward onto my forearms, I buck my hips back once as I come. I have no idea what word, or if it even is a word, that I scream, but it's done face down, eyes pinched closed tight. My center throbs again and again against the heat suddenly filling me.

"Oh, fuck. Oh, fuck. Ohhhhhh fuuuuuuck." The sound of Mountain's fall into nirvana fills the room around us. As I feel his chest shake, pressed against my back, he tries to catch his breath.

Nobody moves. No words are spoken. We just stand here, on very shaky legs, until the world begins its normal rotation, and only then do we adjust to standing up straight again.

Hands on my hips, Mountain takes a step back to free himself from my still twitching center. He bends down to pull his pants back up, then grabs my hand to lead me to the bathroom. We help each other to undress, and I watch as he sits on the chair in the corner to take his prosthesis off. Using his crutches, he leads me back to our room, where I pull down the comforter.

Settling into our respective sides, just like every night since or reconciliation, we gravitate toward each other in the center. Lying on our sides, both heads on one pillow in the middle, we lean in for a kiss. It's nothing heavy or forceful, more a meeting of gentle lips, a few slow battles of tongue against tongue, just pure bliss.

Mountain's left hand holds the side of my neck, angling me how he needs me. My right hand is pressed against his bare chest, feeling the steady heartbeat inside. Again, no rushing, no aggression, just love and need for each other taking priority.

My fingers trace up to Mountain's beard and I tug a little on the ends at his chin. His lips pull back, and a small smile twitches as he rests his head down on the pillow.

"You are the best Christmas gift I ever could've gotten," I whisper as I lean in for one more peck.

"Blue," he says so softly, tucking a strand of my hair back, "I know I don't deserve you, and I'll probably say this a million more times, but I'll never let you go."

"I never want to go anywhere without you," I tell him back.

"Good," he says with a playful harumph.

Still toying with the end of his short beard, I suddenly feel the need to ask him something.

"Can I ask you a question?"

"Lana Renee Hill," Mountain trails his finger down the bridge of my nose, "whatever you want in this world is yours."

"I know we talked about all this when we came back home last week, but I feel like I have more to say, and I need to tell you now."

"We promised that night that this bed would be our safe space, right?"

"Yea," I reply with a quick nod.

Mountains kisses our linked fingers. "Then tell me whatever is on your mind. I can handle it."

Taking a deep breath, I brace myself for whatever comes next. The two worst days of our married lives have always been a bone of contention, but something tells me I need to address them both right now.

"You know everything that's happened to us over the years wasn't your fault, right?" I beg with my eyes for him to know I'm for real. "Me losing the baby, you having your accident, none of that was your fault. Life just decided to throw us struggles, and we somehow came through on the other side."

"Yea, I know." He lets out a sigh that I feel in my bones. Rolling onto his back, Mountain pulls me with him, so I snuggle into his side and hook my right leg over his.

"I'd still love you even if you had no legs." I try to make a joke as I trace the lines of his chest tattoo.

His whole chest heaves with a single laugh. "Only you would stay by my side after all those days and weeks of me yelling at you during my physical therapy. Any other woman would've run for the hills."

"I don't need to run for the hills. I have my own hill. Right. Here." I look up to meet his eyes, then I wink as I tap his pectoral muscle with the tip of my finger.

All that gets me is Mountain rolling his eyes as I laugh. When I settle back down, I wait for whatever he has to say.

"Me and my leg is something I still struggle with every day." I feel him playing with my hair as he speaks. "But I'll try harder to talk to you if I'm having a rough day."

"I appreciate that."

"But I can't lie and say I never see a little hurt in your eyes when you hold one of our grandbabies. You sometimes wish we could've had more kids, don't you?"

I can't look at him without tearing up, so I keep my head down. "But I love them more than anything."

His hold on me gets a little tighter. "I know you do. I do too. It's just that every time I see you sad, I realize I failed at giving you a child of your own."

"I would've given anything to have had your baby," I whisper.

"How could you love a man like me? I feel like your miscarriage was my fault."

Now, that craziness has me sitting straight up. Looking down at where he's still laying, I press a little on his chest to try and shake some sense into him. "How could you think that?"

"You asked me to run errands with you that day, but I was too busy with club stuff. Had I been with you," Mountain shrugs his shoulders, "I could've gotten you to the hospital faster. Maybe—"

"No, Jethro, no." Shaking my head, I stick to my guns on this. Wherever he got that idea from, I need to nip it in the bud right now. "There was nothing you could've done that day that you didn't do. You came running the second I called you. You and I both know it was already too late by then. It was *my* body that had the problem."

"But had I been able to—"

I place my fingers over his lips, pinching them shut. "None of what happened that day was your fault, Mountain. Nothing. My body had issues we didn't know about until it was too late. That blood clot would've ruptured someday with or without a baby in my belly. I just happened to be unlucky that day."

Pulling me back down to lay with him, he asks, "If you could somehow have a baby now, would you want one?"

Thinking about it for a second, the answer is easy. "If I could go back like ten or fifteen years, I'd jump through any hoop, but not now. Hell, I'm fifty years old. I like my sleep too much to be waking up every few hours with a newborn."

We both laugh at that.

"Fuck," Mountain groans. "How did I get to be sixty-one? Where'd the time go?"

"I think we have exactly what we were meant to have," I answer.

"How so?"

"Well, we have a clubhouse full of grandbabies. We can dote on them all we want, fill them up with sugar, then send them home to their parents. And we don't have to go through the teenage years again like we did with Whiskey." I overexaggerate pretend shivers, allowing us to have a little silliness in our somewhat serious conversation. "I think we've both had enough sleepless nights to last us a whole other lifetime."

"I like the sound of that. That boy was a grouchy baby, then he put us through enough trouble sneaking out as a teenager." I watch the evil grin creep across his lips. Mountain's eyebrows wiggle as he says, "Now, it's his turn for a little payback for his younger daredevil days."

"Exactly." I press up for a kiss, then roll myself on top of his chest. I set my chin on the back of my hands, then remind him of one perk of being empty nesters. "And once the kiddos are shipped back home to their parents, you get to spend the rest of the night loving on your wife with no tiny person interruptions."

"Now, you're speakin' my language."

I can't help but let out a tiny squeak as I'm suddenly turned over onto my back before I'm loved only the way Mountain knows how until it's way past our bedtime.

CHAPTER THIRTY-FIVE

MOUNTAIN

It's Christmas morning in the Rebel Vipers clubhouse and it's a mixture of happiness, pure chaos, and outright pandemonium! There is wrapping paper flying everywhere, boxes being tossed across the room, and children of all ages yelling at the top of their lungs . . . and when I say all ages, I'm not kidding.

When Haze jumped over the back of the couch, swearing like a sailor in the middle of a hurricane because Smoke decided to get him a pretend spider as a gift, a riot ensued. I've never seen a grown man move so fast because of a stuffed toy, but apparently, he's scared shitless of the eight-legged creatures. I can't say I blame him because they are kind of gross, but his reaction was over the top. Granted, it was funnier than hell for the rest of us, but watching my nephew and his Old Man wrestling around, trying to get possession of said spider, was a sight to see.

Overall, the morning started out very lowkey. Everyone was told to be in the main room by nine o'clock for brunch, then we all settled to where we are now, lounging around in what Duchess told us had to be "child appropriate pajamas". Everyone is taking turns opening their presents, guzzling down insane amounts of coffee to try and stave the hangovers from too much beer last night, and munching on leftover pancakes and bacon.

The cutest moment of the morning was when Opal opened what her parents said was a gift from the babies. For a child who has been begging for a sibling, even threatening to move in with Duchess and Whiskey because she wanted Krew to be her baby brother, she's finally getting her wish.

We all watched with excitement as she pulled two tiny black t-shirts out of the box that said "little bro 1" and "little bro 2" on them. She held one in each hand and started jumping up and down. She practically threw herself at Sunshine to give her a hug, saying "thank you" over and over again. The box also contained a bigger shirt for her that says "best big sis" and Opal had to put it on right away overtop of her cute penguin jammies.

There was so much going on yesterday during all of the weddings, Opal didn't understand Sunshine's announcement about the twins being identical boys at the time, so in preparation of that possibly happening, she prepared a special gift to help Opal grasp the idea. While she knew there were two babies in her momma's belly, until the matching brother shirts came out, she didn't know the specifics.

I press a kiss to the top of Blue's head and give her a little nudge with my shoulder. "It's your turn to open your presents."

Blue sits up from where she's been resting her back against my chest. "What did you do?" Her question is filled with sass.

"Something I should've done a long time ago."

"What does that mean?"

I lift my chin, signaling that she should looks behind her. She turns to see Whiskey and Steel carrying two large boxes into the room and set them beside the couch we're on. I hid the boxes in the storage room until this morning so she wouldn't find them and get curious as to what I had up my sleeve. Blue slowly gets up to walk over to where the guys set them down.

Turning to face me as she starts ripping the wrapping paper, Blue's eyebrows are furrowed and she's mumbling to herself. Once the paper is tossed aside, she tugs on the flaps of the box so slowly, you'd think she thinks there's a bomb inside about to explode.

"Open it up, love," I call out. "I promise you'll like it."

Finally lifting the last edge, she stares down at what's inside. Her mouth opening and closing like a fish, Blue's eyes volley from the box to me and back at least a dozen times before she speaks.

"What are these for?" she asks.

"For us," I reply simply.

Whiskey steps back to her side and lifts one of the two sets of matching rolling luggage out of the first box as she continues to stare at me like she's never seen a suitcase before.

"Why do we need luggage?"

I get to my feet and make my way around the arm of the couch to stand in front of her. "Next year, the two of us are going on a vacation together. I never got to take you on a real honeymoon, so now is that time."

"Oh my gosh." Blue's fingers press to her cheeks. "Really?"

"You get to pick wherever you wanna go, and I'll take you there." I wrap her in my arms and pull her into my chest. "I promise."

After numerous 'is this for real' and 'am I dreaming' questions, to which I say 'yes it's real' over and over again, Blue tugs me down by the back of my neck for a not so child appropriate to view kiss. I then force myself not to escort her back to our room to continue such further adult activities, instead get us back on the couch to hang out with everyone . . . for now.

As the next few hours pass, I peek down over her shoulder to see what she's looking at on her phone. Currently, I see a picture of a couple walking hand in hand on a beach somewhere, crystal blue water at their feet and a few palm trees off in the distance. Something tells me Blue wants to go somewhere tropical, and as a man who was in the Navy, I can appreciate a good beach. So, if that's her idea of a honeymoon, sign me up.

Present time has turned into a movie marathon and everyone is glued to the big screen as a boy named Kevin runs around a park in New York City. The only action in the room is when either Teddy or Diva, our resident clubhouse dog and cat, decide to try and chase the other around. The two of them met and became fast friends, so if the worst they do is see who can run to their water bowls the fastest, I can't complain.

In fact, I have nothing to complain about at all. Everyone is happy, healthy, and full of cookies and coffee. The road to get here may have been riddled with potholes and cracks, but I think we all landed right where we're supposed to be.

This year, I got a giant serving of humble pie and had to face what my truest weaknesses are. But I dug down deep and fought to fix the problems that I had caused. I dug down deep to get my wife back and succeeded.

While gifts, toys, and trips are fun and all, the greatest gifts I've ever received are sitting all around me in this clubhouse. It's the people we choose to surround ourselves with who are the most important. Our friends, our family, they're what matter most. The life we've built for ourselves here, we really couldn't ask for more.

As we prepare to roll into the new year, I'm thankful that our club is bigger and stronger than ever, and I have no doubt we'll take on any challenge that comes our way and end up the victors. Because God, or Lucifer, or whoever you worship, forbid, the next person or persons who decide they want to cross us in any way, they better be prepared.

Because when you threaten a Rebel Viper enough to make him strike, there's no warning. The bite stings like a motherfucker and we've taken down many men for hurting what's ours. We don't back down until our enemies are defeated and turned to ash.

Thinking ahead, there's no doubt in my mind that Blue and I will be together until the day we cross over to whatever is waiting for us in the afterlife. I hope I go first, because life without her would be pure hell, but until then, I'll stand by her side every day, showing her how much she means to me.

Other than a few more grandkids, I have nothing left to accomplish. I've done so much in my sixty-one years, it feels like an eternity. My life has reached its pinnacle, and my greatest achievement is being the one who's able to hold Blue's hand as we watch our family grow.

What's that saying? Oh, that's right.

The best views come from the hardest climbs. And that's where I am—on top of the mountain.

THE END!

EPILOGUE

STAR

How I ended up here, I'm not quite sure. To be honest, the last year has passed like a blur, and I've found myself in a position I never intended to be in . . . but that's not to say I don't love it, because I truly do.

It's not a common occurrence for a club girl to end up as a Brother's Old Lady—in fact, it's only happened once before—but here I am. I'm married, have an Old Man, a baby on the way, and a whole new name.

How did I get here, you ask? Well, to figure that out, let me take you back to a little over four years ago, to the first night I walked into the Rebel Vipers MC clubhouse . . . back to when I saw Buzz for the first time. Because that was the night my life took an unexpected turn and really began.

I never would've expected to end up in a place like this, in a world I didn't even know existed until a few months prior. But even knowing now what I didn't know then, I wouldn't go back and change a single thing.

TO BE CONTINUED . . .

ACKNOWLEDGMENTS

Mr. J – I don't think I cooked one meal or washed one dish in the weeks it took me to write this book, but you stepped up to the plate and took care of everything so I could finish it on time. You are a rockstar when it comes to my deadlines, and I can't thank you enough! I promise to try and plan out my next few books a little better . . . and maybe make you the shepherd's pie you've been asking for. I love you to the moon and back!

Rebecca Vazquez – My book fairy godmother, well . . . we did it again. A few little bumps in the road with this one, all my fault of course, but after 24 days of you pushing me to write every day, I finally got it done. Thank you for your continued encouragement. I can't wait to see where this next steps in this journey take us.

#CoolKidsTable

Kay Marie – My Person! I'm so damn proud of you . . . and you know why! And I can't wait for all the signings we get to do together over the next year, it's gonna be a blast!

My KM Alpha friends – Kay, Becca, Heidi, and Olivia. – I owe you all sooo much! You've listened to lots of my crazy book related questions and given the best advice. Any person would be lucky to have friends like you, and I'm glad to be part of this crazy circle.

Charli Childs – Our rainbow continues. Thank you for dealing with my nit-picking over the tiniest of details. You always pull off the best covers, what we have coming up next is killer for sure!

And last, but definitely not least, YOU! THANK YOU, READERS! Mountain and Blue probably wouldn't have gotten another book if it weren't for you. Several of you messaged, commented, and asked for more about these two, and the ideas came flooding in. I hope this full-length book fills in some of the missing gaps of their story and that you love them as much this go around as you did in their prequel. They'll definitely be making more appearances in my future books, so their story isn't ending for a long while!

ABOUT THE AUTHOR

Jessa Aarons was born and raised in the frozen tundra of Wisconsin. She has had her nose buried in books for as long as she can remember. Her love of romance began when she "borrowed" her mom's paperback Harlequin novels.

After experiencing a life-changing health issue, she had to leave the working world and dove back into books to help heal her soul. She would read anything that told a love story but still had grit and drama. Then she became a beta reader and personal assistant to another author.

Jessa is the boss of her husband and their castle. He really is her prince. Thanks to his encouragement, Jessa started putting pen to paper and creating new imaginary worlds. She spends her free time reading, crafting, and cheering on her hometown football team.

SOCIAL MEDIA LINKS

Facebook Author Page

FB Reader's Group

Instagram

Twitter

Amazon

Goodreads

Bookbub

Pinterest

Spotify

TikTok

OTHER WORKS

<u>Rebel Vipers MC</u>
A Mountain to Climb
Whiskey on the Rocks
Ring of Steel
Hammer's Swing
A Smoke Filled Haze
Top of the Mountain

<u>Standalones</u>
Pure Luck – cowrite with Kay Marie

<u>Coming Soon</u>
Catching a Buzz – Rebel Vipers MC book 6 – previously part of the Twisted Steel 3 anthology
Master Brewer – Rebel Vipers MC book 7

Printed in Great Britain
by Amazon